"You buy whatever you need."

Asa cleared his throat. "Our fields will provide most of our food. I hunt in the fall. And in the winter, I work with leather. The blacksmith keeps it and sells it for me." He rose and went to the hearth. "Come here."

Judith obeyed him.

He showed her the loose stone that hid a cavity in the side of the fireplace and the small cloth sack of gold and silver coins stashed there. "We have plenty, Judith. Just tell Mr. Ashford to put everything on our tab. I pay him once a month."

"Thank you, Asa. I'm not an extravagant woman, but I do want to—" she waved a hand toward the room "—make everything more homey."

He returned to his place at the table, and she followed him.

"I want you to…do that, too," he said. *But you've done so much more.* The chain around his heart tightened. If only he had more than a house and sustenance to offer her. Judith deserved the best. But he would give her the best he could of the material world. The pity was that he could not give her more of his true self.

A *USA TODAY* bestselling author of over forty novels, **Lyn Cote** lives in the north woods of Wisconsin with her husband in a lakeside cottage. She knits, loves cats (and dogs), likes to cook (and eat), never misses *Wheel of Fortune* and enjoys hearing from her readers. Email her at l.cote@juno.com. And drop by her website, www.lyncote.com, to learn more about her books that feature "Strong Women, Brave Stories."

Books by Lyn Cote

Love Inspired Historical

Wilderness Brides

Their Frontier Family
The Baby Bequest
Heartland Courtship
Frontier Want Ad Bride

The Gabriel Sisters

Her Captain's Heart
Her Patchwork Family
Her Healing Ways

Visit the Author Profile page at Harlequin.com for more titles.

LYN COTE

Frontier Want Ad Bride

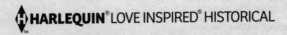
HARLEQUIN® LOVE INSPIRED® HISTORICAL

Recycling programs
for this product may
not exist in your area.

LOVE INSPIRED BOOKS

ISBN-13: 978-0-373-42535-8

Frontier Want Ad Bride

Copyright © 2017 by Lyn Cote

Printed in U.S.A.

Charity suffereth long, and is kind; charity envieth not; charity vaunteth not itself, is not puffed up. Doth not behave itself unseemly, seeketh not her own, is not easily provoked, thinketh no evil. Rejoiceth not in iniquity, but rejoiceth in the truth. Beareth all things, believeth all things, hopeth all things, endureth all things. Charity never faileth.
—*1 Corinthians* 13:4–8 (KJV)

To Laura Ingalls Wilder (born in Pepin, Wisconsin)
who left us such a clear and heartwarming account
of life on the frontier.

Chapter One

Wisconsin Frontier
March 1873

Standing beside her sister, Emma, on the deck of the steamboat, Judith Jones gazed out at the snowy, thickly wooded shore of the northern Mississippi River. The river ice had broken just last week.

"The porter said Pepin is coming up," Emma said, slipping her hand from her fur muff and through the crook of Judith's elbow.

Judith clenched her jaw to keep her teeth from chattering from the piercing wind. "I can't believe we've done this." Answering an ad to find husbands.

"Did we have a choice?" Emma challenged. "Our dear sister-in-law wanted our father's house to herself."

Leave it to Emma to speak the truth so…baldly. But her words brought to mind their brother's Kentucky wife's sour glare and her razor voice.

Emma jostled Judith's shoulder with hers. "We'll be

fine. We'll be together." Emma grinned and shivered. "Embrace the adventure."

At this bravado, Judith shook her head, glancing at her very pretty sister from the corner of her eye. Emma's cheeks were rosy from the brisk March wind, her big blue eyes were wide and she was dancing on her toes from either the cold or excitement. Judith guessed the latter, hoped the latter. But Judith knew her sister still mourned the fiancé she'd cruelly lost in the very last days of the awful war.

Neither of them had come here for happy reasons or without past loss. Still, Judith felt as if she was being squeezed between two unpleasant realities. Before her lay marrying a stranger. Would she and Asa Brant be a good match? No man had ever fallen in love with her. Was she a woman who could engender that kind of love? That doubt plagued her. Yet behind her lay an unhappy home. The memory brought the image of her sister-in-law, Mabel Joy, with hands on her hips, glaring at Judith. Staying in their family home had become impossible. She faced forward, refusing to open the deep well of rejection. Neither her brother nor father had stood up for Judith and Emma. There was no turning back.

"With that sour expression, you must be thinking of our dear sister-in-law," Emma teased.

Judith shook her head in reply, not taking the bait. But she tried to relax her tight face. She must not look peeved when meeting Asa Brant. She drew in a deep breath of cold air.

The steamboat horn blasted and as they chugged around the bend, a little town came into view. The porter appeared at Judith's side. "This is your stop, ladies. Pepin, Wisconsin." Behind him another two porters stood beside the twins' two trunks and various baggage.

"Wonderful!" Emma said, slipping her arm from Judith's.

Judith checked her coat pocket to make sure she still had the gratuity to give the porters. And then they were on the shore and faced with a crowd of people pouring out of every building. Judith took a step backward.

Emma tugged her forward. "Oh, look, everyone's waving."

Judith allowed Emma to drag her. What choice did she have? They'd reached their destination. Nerves appeared to affect Judith's sight. She saw the people but had trouble focusing on any faces. In this crowd was the man she'd come to meet and marry sometime soon. He'd promised to make all the arrangements.

At the last moment, Judith remembered herself and turned to give the porters the money from her pocket. "Thank you."

They accepted it and, after bowing, hurried back on board, holding on to their hats against the wind.

"Welcome to Pepin!" a middle-aged lady with silver in her hair said, reaching them first. A man and a young girl, probably her husband and daughter, hurried just behind her.

Judith looked past them, trying to spot a boarding-house where she and Emma would stay, but saw none.

"We're the Ashfords. We own the general store here. You must be the Jones sisters. But I thought you were supposed to be twins."

Emma eagerly shook the woman's hand. "We're fraternal. That means we're just sisters who were born at the same time. I'm Emma Jones, and this is my sister, Judith."

Judith curtseyed, a custom almost out of style.

Mr. Ashford beamed at her approvingly as he introduced himself and his daughter and shook her hand. "But you aren't interested in meeting us." He looked around in the crowd of people. "Come on, Asa. Meet your bride."

Judith's gaze flew upward, seeking her first look at Asa Brant.

A tall man approached her. He'd bundled up against the cold. For a moment he looked familiar but, of course, they'd never met. "Miss Judith Jones?"

She offered him her hand. "Yes." Her voice came out as a squeak compared to his deep, rich voice that seemed to warm the air around her.

"I'm Asa Brant. So happy you came." He looked down at her, holding her hand in both of his as if frozen at the sight of her.

Blushing warmth enveloped Judith as she gripped his gloved hand. "Asa." That's all she could say, her voice failing her.

"All the arrangements are made as promised," Asa said, sounding strained. He edged back slightly as if not knowing how to behave.

Judith felt the same awkwardness. They'd corresponded over the past few months, so they were strangers but not complete strangers. What a confusing feeling.

"Yes," Mrs. Ashford agreed. "Now, you two ladies come with me. I have everything ready for the bride in our quarters above the store. Is your wedding dress in your trunk?"

Judith stared at the woman, unable to reply. Why was the woman asking for her wedding dress? She glanced up at Asa and found him staring at her as if he wasn't quite sure she was real.

"Where's my intended?" Emma spoke up in the gap. "Where's Mason Chandler?"

Everyone fell silent. The crowd all looked away as if embarrassed.

"He hasn't jilted me, has he?" Emma asked in her usual frank way.

"No, no, nothing like that," Mrs. Ashford assured her. "Come now, ladies. It's freezing out here. Everyone, you know the plan. We'll see you all at the schoolhouse as soon as the bride is ready."

Judith tried to make sense of what was happening. She still clung to Asa's hand. What plan was Mrs. Ashford talking about?

"Don't worry," Asa assured her. "Just go with Mrs. Ashford." He squeezed her hand and turned away.

The men in the crowd gathered up the sisters' belongings and departed as Mrs. Ashford drew them out of the wind through the general store, then up the back stairs to the living quarters. Judith felt as if she were an oarless boat being swept along helplessly in a strong current.

"Now come stand by the fire," Mrs. Ashford instructed, "while we unpack your wedding dress and press it." The woman glanced at Emma and worried her lower lip. "I'm afraid Mason Chandler couldn't be here." With her daughter standing just behind her, the woman drew a letter from the mantel above the roaring fire and handed it and a slender opener to Emma. "Things happen," the woman said sympathetically.

This forced Judith out of her daze. She moved beside Emma, who had navigated through all the furniture to stand closer to the window for more light. Judith slid her arm around Emma's narrow waist. Emma stared at the letter and then slit it open. She held it so Judith could read it with her.

February 28, 1873
My dear Emma,
It grieves me that I will not be in Pepin to meet you as arranged. I have received a letter from my father and have gone to be with him in his final days. The Ashfords have promised to make sure you have a place to stay until I can return. I am so sorry, but this could not have been foreseen when we made our plans to marry. I will stay as long as I must to be with my father at this sad time and settle up matters of business here.
Your obedient servant,
Mason Chandler

Judith read the letter twice before it made sense. She tugged Emma closer still, uncertain what to say.

"Well, that came out of the blue," Emma said.

Judith thought she might have heard a trace of relief

in her daring sister's voice. Had Emma been granted a grace period, whereas Judith must marry today?

"Don't you worry," Mrs. Ashford said. "We have a guest room for you, and you can help out in the store till he comes home."

Emma folded the letter and slipped it back into its envelope. "Thank you."

"Now that's taken care of," Mrs. Ashford said, "let's unpack the wedding dress and get it pressed. Everyone's waiting at the schoolhouse—it doubles as our community church—to see Judith and Asa marry."

Judith's mouth opened and closed, but no words came out. Marry? Today? But she and Asa had just met. Again she felt the sensation of being swept along.

"Come. Come." Mrs. Ashford waved at them. "Where's the wedding dress?"

Emma moved forward. "In Judith's trunk, wrapped in tissue paper." Emma went to the right trunk and undid the clasp. Soon the two women hovered over the trunk while Judith stood by the window, frozen. She'd never thought they'd marry the day she arrived. A sinking feeling gripped her.

Mrs. Ashford rose, holding the full dress over both her arms. "The perfect shade of blue. A good choice. You'll look lovely, and it will serve as your best dress for years to come."

Judith shook herself and came toward the woman as if wading through cold water. When Asa had assured her in his last letter that he would take care of all arrangements, she'd assumed he'd meant finding her a place to stay and something to do while they got to know each other. She ruefully thought that she'd just learned the first lesson of marriage—not to take for granted that what she assumed he meant was what he actually meant.

She gazed at Mrs. Ashford, seeking some kind of reassurance.

And the lady read her expression aright. "Asa Brant has lived here almost two years. He is an honest man, always pays his bills. He attends church regularly, and whenever the community needs to do something as a whole, he always pitches in. He is well respected and well liked, though he usually keeps to himself." The woman frowned on this last bit of information. But no doubt to a woman such as Mrs. Ashford, a desire for privacy and quiet might be seen as unusual.

Judith digested this and drew in a deep breath. "Thank you."

Mrs. Ashford came nearer. "Miss Jones, you'll find that no woman really knows what kind of husband a man will make until they are married. You are pledged to an honest, well-respected man. That's a good place to start."

Judith nodded, mentally clinging to the final phrase, *a good place to start.*

"Now, let's get this dress pressed. Everyone's waiting!" Mrs. Ashford carried the dress into the kitchen to the ironing board. "Amanda, take the ladies into Miss Jones's room so they can freshen up."

The young girl moved out of her mother's shadow and showed them to a cheery but small room with a comfortable-looking bed that took up most of the space.

Amanda pointed out the pitcher and copper bowl filled with warm water. Then she left them.

Judith and Emma exchanged glances. Emma held up a hand. "We'll discuss my odd turn of events later. Let's wash up and get our hair back into order. That dress will be ready before we know it."

Judith let Emma pull her along, preparing for this unexpectedly immediate wedding. But doubts still swirled in her stomach. The one man she'd loved had spurned her. Now she, who'd previously given up on marriage, was going to marry a man she knew only through letters exchanged over the fall and winter. The nuptials would happen today, within the hour. *I'm going to be married today*, she repeated to herself, trying to believe it.

In the schoolhouse cloakroom, Asa shed his winter coat and muffler, still stunned by seeing Judith Jones. For a moment, he saw her again stepping off the boat and then looking up at him. He had not expected to recognize his bride, but he had—from a tintype he'd seen long ago. The tintype had belonged to her brother, his comrade in arms. But she hadn't recognized him, which was a relief.

Surely she would never realize that she'd seen him twice before, never learn of their connection. The shock of recognizing her equaled the shock of seeing that his bride was not what he'd expected. He hadn't anticipated the wave of instant attraction to her. He'd had trouble saying the few words to her that he'd managed to voice.

"Well, you have a neat-looking bride," said the town blacksmith, Levi Comstock, slapping Asa on the back.

Asa nodded. Judith was a lot more than neat. She was trim and pretty with thick dark hair and deep brown eyes. He'd expected a woman who couldn't attract a man and had prepared himself for someone plain. He shook his head as if trying to clear his mind of his pre-conception. He'd wanted someone plain, a woman who would fill the lonely hours and demand nothing from him deeper than kindness and respect. Judith Jones was not that sort of woman, commonplace, unremarkable. She was the complete opposite of those terms. His pulse sped up. He clamped down his reactions.

"Miss Jones appeared to be a pleasant and mod-est young woman," said Noah Whitmore, the town preacher, leading them through the schoolhouse, where people were already gathering. The three of them went into the teacher's quarters in the rear. The teacher had invited them to use it as a place for them to await the bride, out of the public eye.

"I don't know how I'd handle marrying a woman I'd just met," Levi said, buttoning himself into his suit coat.

Asa fully agreed with this. But he'd had no choice. No young women flocked to this frontier town. Out of desperate loneliness, he'd offered marriage to this woman. He could not face another winter with hours of remembering the past he yearned to erase from his mind. Women talked, and he planned for Judith's voice to fill up the long, empty, silent days. But Judith's large, honest eyes warned him that this woman was more than he'd bargained for.

"Sunny and I didn't know each other very well when we wed," Noah said, checking his reflection in the small shaving mirror on the wall and smoothing back his hair. "Being married is a special relationship. It might help to know a woman well before one weds, but many other couples have met on their wedding day."

Asa appreciated Noah's calm voice. He also knew that Noah was a Union veteran like himself. Asa's deep-down worry thrust up into his throat, preventing him from speaking. He'd spent four long years during the war killing men, destroying everything in his path. He'd seen things no man should see. How did a soldier put that behind him and become a husband and maybe a father? He felt himself seize up inside as battle memories surged through his mind and his arteries pumped his blood hard. He wished he could ask Noah how he'd come to a place of peace. But men didn't ask other men those kind of questions.

He drew in a deep breath. He'd come this far and he couldn't back out, couldn't jilt a sweet-looking, scared-looking woman like Judith. This was harder for her. She was putting her life in his hands, trusting him to be her provider and protector. He could do that, offer her that. But he had nothing more to offer. Did she sense that?

"The ladies are busy in my upstairs," Ashford, the storekeeper, came in, rubbing his hands together. "Wish we had nicer weather for the wedding. But we'll manage. We'll manage."

And that was what Asa must do—manage. He had gone along with Mason Chandler's suggestion that they advertise for wives. No one had forced him. He'd done it of his own free will. He recalled Judith's hesitant, shy letters and how he'd come to look forward to them, how he'd read and reread them. Straightening his back, he faced life. He would marry Judith today. He just wished that he was a better man for her and that his heart would stop pounding as if scolding him for not telling her what a poor husband he would make her.

Soon Mrs. Ashford knocked on the guest bedroom door and reentered. She and Emma helped Judith into the royal-blue dress with tiny mother-of-pearl buttons and hand-tatted lace at the high collar. Judith had labored over it for several weeks. She'd decided on a classic style, which, though it followed the new fashion of a slimmer profile, would indeed last her many years.

"Such fine stitching," Mrs. Ashford remarked. "You are quite a seamstress."

Judith managed a smile. Finally dressed, she was led to the hallway to a full-length wall mirror.

"You look beautiful," exclaimed the young daughter, Amanda, and Emma echoed the sentiment.

Judith could only hope Asa Brant thought so. She'd never been deemed pretty, as Emma was, something people had found necessary to point out all through her childhood and teens.

"Every bride is beautiful, but Miss Jones, you do look lovely," Mrs. Ashford agreed.

Judith finally let herself examine her reflection. She did indeed look well in her dress, but also stunned. Didn't anybody notice that?

Soon they were layering up coats, gloves, shawls to meet the winter cold that still lingered and then walking out to the church-schoolhouse combination.

There the women paused just inside the cloakroom and shed their outerwear. After handing both twins bouquets of dried flowers that had been waiting on the shelf, Mrs. Ashford and Amanda hurried on inside to take seats, while Mr. Ashford offered to walk Judith down the aisle to her groom. He told them there would be no "Wedding March" since there was no organ or piano.

The urge to bolt shot through Judith like lightning. But she could not go back home, so she had to go forward. She mastered herself and took the man's arm.

Emma slipped in front of them. "Ready, sister?"

Judith nodded, unable to speak.

Emma stepped into the open doorway to the large classroom, lifting her shoulders, and then she began to walk sedately down the aisle toward the front.

Mr. Ashford paused with Judith and then started after her sister.

From nerves, Judith's vision wavered, but she was able to see the preacher holding an open book in front of the room, flanked by Asa Brant, obviously in his Sunday best. Another man stood beside him, no doubt the best man.

Emma arrived at the front and moved to one side to leave room for Judith next to Asa. Mr. Ashford squeezed her arm, released her and moved to sit with his family in the front row.

Judith's heart was leaping beneath her breastbone. She felt a bit light-headed.

"Please join hands," the pastor said. "Miss Jones, I

am Noah Whitmore, and it's my honor to join you in holy matrimony to Asa Brant."

The man's calm voice soothed her. She managed a smile but could not bring herself to look up into her groom's face. If she did, then she might panic, so she concentrated on Noah Whitmore's voice and Asa Brant's firm grip on her icy kid-gloved hand.

Asa held on to his bride's hand like a lifeline. His mind brought up the face of a woman whom he'd courted before the war and who'd sent him a letter in 1862 telling him she'd married another and was bound for California to leave the dreadful war behind. She'd wished him well. He'd been sitting in an army tent buffeted with cold wind and rain, exhausted from burying dead comrades.

He shoved this memory out of his mind. He barely remembered her except for that moment when she'd cut their connection. That day he'd been hoping for a consoling letter. He'd burned hers.

He forced himself back to this important occasion. The wedding ceremony proceeded along the usual lines. He faced his bride, determined.

Noah's words penetrated. "Asa, repeat after me, please."

Asa swallowed to clear his throat and voiced this pledge. "I, Asa, take thee, Judith, to be my wedded wife, to have and to hold from this day forward, for better, for worse, for richer, for poorer, in sickness and in health, to love, honor and cherish till death do us part." He felt guilty promising things he might not be able to do. But he'd do his best.

In a voice that trembled on some words, his bride voiced her vows to him. And she accepted the simple gold band he slipped on her finger.

"Those whom God hath joined together, let no man put asunder," the pastor intoned.

Behind him, Asa felt a relaxation of tension. Had the assembly expected his bride to flee? He couldn't blame them. The pastor continued, "Forasmuch as Judith and Asa have consented together in holy wedlock, and have witnessed the same before God and this company of witnesses, and thereto have given their pledge, each to the other, and have declared the same by giving and receiving a ring, and by joining hands, I now pronounce you husband and wife." The pastor beamed. "You many now kiss your bride, Asa."

Asa leaned down slowly, self-consciously. He hadn't kissed a woman in so long. His bride gazed up at him as if stunned. He pressed his lips to hers lightly. The unexpected shock of the contact whipped through him. He ended the kiss and tightened his hold on her hand. He couldn't stop himself from whispering, "I'll do right by you, Judith."

His bride barely nodded in reply.

The pastor brought him back with "Ladies and gentlemen, I now present to you Mr. and Mrs. Asa Brant."

There was loud applause and some foot-stomping, and a few children shouted, "Hurray!"

Asa couldn't help himself. In the face of everyone's

obvious enthusiasm, he smiled though his lips felt tight, unused to the expression.

The next few hours passed in a blur of a festive meal; a special and delicious cake provided by the local baker, Mrs. Rachel Merriday; and many well wishes and gifts. Finally, just as darkness was stealing over the sky, Asa brought the wagon to take his bride home.

He halted the team just outside the door and got down.

Judith's sister, Emma, stood by her side. "I wish all the best to the best sister," Emma said. The two sisters clung to each other for a moment. Then Emma stepped away.

Asa helped Judith up onto his wagon. Someone had already loaded on her baggage and all the presents. The schoolhouse emptied, and people shouted congratulations to them as Asa drove up the uneven trail through the town and forest, very aware of his bride on the bench near him.

She shivered.

"My...our place is a little over a mile from town," Asa said as they left everyone behind. "Won't be long and I'll have you by the fire. Warm enough under the lap rug?"

Judith nodded. "It all happened so fast."

"Soon as I talked to Noah Whitmore, the women just took over. I tried to rein them in but got nowhere. I decided just to stand back, sure they'd do a better job of planning a wedding than I would." He couldn't believe how he was babbling. He shut his mouth. What might come out if he kept this up? He needed to guard his tongue. He couldn't let her connect him to her brother. Doing so might bring up matters he didn't want to discuss, didn't want known here.

"After meeting Mrs. Ashford, I understand. And it was really a lovely wedding."

Asa nodded but concentrated on navigating the narrow trail through the snow. He felt a shiver shudder through her. "You're cold," Asa said. "Move closer."

She scooted over the few inches separating them, shutting out an avenue of the cold wind. "That's better," she murmured.

He tried not to stiffen. Having her this close awoke his senses in an unexpected way. Why couldn't she have been a plain, unexciting woman? In the scant light left by the fading sun, Asa held himself back. "Not far now," he said.

Judith found she couldn't speak, her throat frozen. Grateful for the low light, she nodded against his shoulder. Then, up the trail in a clearing, she saw the roof of a large log cabin and barn facing it. Asa drove up to the door of the cabin. Within minutes he had her inside. "Stand by the fireplace." He knelt and stirred up the banked fire. "I need to get your things and put the horses away."

A little disappointed he hadn't carried her over the threshold, she quelled any complaint. He'd wanted her in by the fire. That showed concern. Men didn't often feel the same way about customs as women did. "Can I help?"

"Just keep warm." He hurried outside. Soon he carried in her trunk and then her hatbox and valise. "Won't be long." He went outside again, shutting out the chill of early March. She stood in place like one of the surrounding forest trees, unable to speak for fear she'd burst into tears. This was hard.

The fire began to throw out some heat, and she fed it more kindling and wood. Before long, she began to feel the warmth, though inside she still felt chilled.

The door opened again and Asa walked in. She turned to him, her pulse thrumming in her ears. In the low light, she gazed at this man, now her husband. She wasn't afraid of him, but what would be expected of her tonight? She'd had no mother to explain the workings of marriage to her. She'd never been allowed alone with a man in his home before. And now she stood here with a stranger. Her throat tightened and she felt a bit faint. What would happen next?

Asa went to the table opposite the hearth. She heard him strike a match. Even this tiny sound caused her to flinch. She watched him light an oil lamp.

He straightened and turned to her. "Warmer?"

She nodded, frozen in place.

He passed her and held his ungloved hands toward the fire. "Winter can linger this far north."

Once again she was struck by his rich voice, and her stomach was doing little hops and skips now.

He faced her and rested his hands on her shoulders. "We're strangers, and here we are, married." His voice curled around her nape, making her shiver with awareness. "Don't worry."

She didn't really know how to take what he was saying.

"You'll sleep there." He pointed to a curtained doorway. "I'll sleep in the loft till we get...more acquainted."

His words finally made sense to her jumbled mind. "Thank...you. This all happened so fast."

"For me, too." He looked uncertain. "I have something for you," he said, motioning toward the other side of the cabin.

Judith turned and gasped. The lamplight glinted off the gold paint on what looked like a brand-new Singer sewing machine. Unable to stop herself, she moved toward it. When she reached it, she almost feared to touch it. "For me?"

"Don't do much sewing myself," he said, again sounding uneasy.

Then she did touch its smooth metal and wood. "I can see you're going to be an indulgent husband."

"No," he replied with something like a grin in his tone. "Arbitrary and overbearing to the end."

His unexpected but almost teasing reply eased her tension. "No one has ever given me such a lovely gift." Impulsively she whirled to him and, standing on tiptoe, kissed his cheek. Shocking herself.

He looked abashed. "I wanted to give you something special but useful."

"I love it. So thoughtful." She felt herself blushing.

He stepped away from her, acting uncomfortable. "I'm going to feed the fire, bank it down for the night."

She watched him, not knowing what else to do.

Then he escorted her to the bedroom curtain. "Night… Judith," he said formally.

"Good night, Asa," she replied, her throat thick with gratitude for his understanding. It felt strange to call a stranger by his given name and to hear him address her in the same way.

She entered the room and sat down on the bed, suddenly spent. For a moment she just sat there, gazing around in the scant light, listening to Asa moving about the cabin, barring the door and then extinguishing the lamp. She heard the ladder rungs creak as he mounted them to sleep in the loft.

Finally she let out a sigh. Sights, sounds jumbled in her mind. She swept them away by rising and preparing herself for sleep. Light from the fire around the curtain provided just enough for her to do what she needed, and soon she snuggled into the chilly bed, shivering slightly.

Her deep fatigue and rampant confusion fought it out, but fatigue won and her eyes closed just as she finished her nightly prayer. It included concern for her sister, whose day had not gone as expected, either.

At the last moment, she recalled that upon meeting Asa, she'd thought she'd seen him somewhere before. But that was ridiculous, probably just nerves. She'd given her promises to Asa, and even if she wasn't the pretty sister, the one men always paid attention to, she would do her best to be a good wife.

Asa soon wrapped himself in his quilts on the pallet he'd made up in the loft. The knowledge that someone else was sleeping here leaked through him, easing a tightness in his chest. A woman was here, and he wouldn't face another long winter alone in his cabin.

Yet after the war, he'd come to the cabin wanting to be alone.

Army camps had been crowded, teeming with thousands of men. He'd never been able to get away, by himself. And when he'd returned home, people had sought him out and brought up the war every time they met him. He'd finally left home to come here to homestead, find peace. Put the past behind him…if he ever could. But he found that silence only caused him to remember sights he longed to forget.

He tried to relax and stretch out, forcing himself not to dwell on how pretty his bride was and how sweet. He began to tell himself that everything was going to turn out right. He had a place of his own and now a wife.

After they got used to each other, life would smooth out. His past, his secret guilt, would remain secret. She had not said a word about recognizing him. After all, she would have seen him only at a distance, and he'd been in uniform and bearded both times. He would be able to keep the past and the present separate.

He continued to reassure himself. He'd made a wise decision to go along with Mason Chandler and put that ad in the Dubuque paper. Everything was going to turn out fine. He'd survived a war. He could survive adjusting to marriage. Though the war had burned away all his tender feelings, he would be a good provider and try to think of his wife's needs before his own. That's the best he could do.

Chapter Two

The next morning, Judith dressed and walked out through the curtain. She'd heard Asa, who had already built up the fire before he left, telling her he was going to milk the cows. She approached the area near the hearth that appeared to be the kitchen, preparing herself to make her first meal in her new home for her new husband.

She'd never cooked over an open fire before. Her home had always had a wood stove, but cooking was cooking, right? And she definitely didn't want to make a mess of her first meal for Asa. On a wooden counter she found a bowl of brown eggs. Nearby in a barrel were a sack of flour and some other necessaries, and she began to mix up pancakes.

Outside she heard someone stomping his boots and then, with a gust of cold wind, Asa hurried inside. "Got a dusting of snow last night." He hung his coat and muffler on pegs by the door.

"Well, that's not surprising for March," she replied, trying to sound natural, though her stomach was doing some kind of nervous jig.

"What're you mixing up?"

"I thought pancakes for breakfast?"

He nodded. "Soon I'll be tapping trees." He set a jug of milk on the counter.

"Tapping trees?" She glanced over her shoulder at him.

"To make maple syrup."

She sent him an approving glance. "You are an enterprising man, Asa Brant."

He grunted in reply and walked over to warm his hands by the fire.

She was curious about this man. Now they could get to know each other better. "Did your father teach you how to tap trees?"

"Noah Whitmore taught me."

"Noah?" She mixed in some of the milk he'd brought.

"Man who married us."

"Oh." The scene yesterday in the schoolhouse where they'd exchanged vows flooded her. She shook it off. "I've never cooked over an open fire before," she admitted. "I take it I pour the batter into the skillet and then hold it over the fire?"

He moved to her side. "Right. Always warm the skillet over the fire first, melting the fat." He opened a crock that obviously had fresh rendered tallow in it. "Here are a couple of trivets so you don't have to hold the heavy pan and try to flip at the same time." He pointed to the trivets stacked under the counter. Both wrought iron, one with shorter legs and one with longer.

"Thank you," she said. "I'll become accustomed."

"Should have got you a wood stove. It might have been more practical than a sewing machine—"

Judith halted in midstep. "Asa, you chose the perfect

wedding gift. I love to sew, and I've wanted a sewing machine…forever." Their gazes locked. The air between them seemed to thicken, and she felt herself blush.

"Glad you like it," he said finally.

"I do." She looked down, and her stomach growled embarrassingly. "I better get these pancakes done."

He stepped back.

She moved toward the fire and the trivet he'd positioned for her.

He suddenly gripped her arm. "Be mindful of your skirt near the fire. A woman was burned just this winter from not being careful."

She halted with a gasp. "I'll be careful." She looked down to her skirt and where the fire was on the hearth. She set the cast iron skillet on the trivet, poured in batter and reached for the spatula. "I'll be careful," she repeated.

Asa grasped the coffeepot bubbling on a hook over the fire, moving to sit at the table. "Coffee?"

"Thank you, Asa." She concentrated on the batter bubbling in the pan, then on flipping the first pancake and keeping her skirt back from the fire. Soon she carried a platter of pancakes to the table, where Asa had poured cups of coffee and set out a cruet of maple syrup and a jug of cream.

She bowed her head, waiting for Asa to offer grace. So far the morning was going well. Her husband was not talkative, but after all, they were strangers. And he had showed concern for her safety. That loosed the tightness within her.

She wanted him to pray? After a hesitation, Asa said simply the prayer his father had always prayed, "Thanks for the food and for the hands that prepared it. Amen."

She looked up, shyly smiling.

Asa nodded and helped himself to the top two large golden pancakes. His mouth watered.

Judith waited for his first bite before she forked one onto her plate.

"Mmm-mmm." He could not stop the sound of pleasure. "Made a nice big stack, too."

"I guess I'm used to cooking for more than two," she admitted. "My brother brought home a wife from Kentucky, but I still did the majority of the cooking." She looked to him. "Do you have brothers and sisters?"

"Some of each." Asa took another bite and chewed. A personal question—just what he wanted to avoid.

Judith was staring at him. The silence between them grew.

He couldn't think of a safe subject, nothing too personal, to talk about. He'd forgotten how to make conversation.

Finally she broke the silence. "What kind of man is Mason Chandler?"

"Honest. Hardworking. I'm taking care of his cow and we hope a new calf soon," he continued in between bites, "till he gets back."

Another silence hung over them. He would have been happy just to eat with someone else at the table. But he could tell she wanted to find out more about him. How could he steer the conversation away from personal questions? He combed his mind for a topic.

"We have a cow, and I think I heard chickens outside?" she asked finally.

"Two cows of our own and about a dozen chickens."

He took another bite of pancake dripping with butter and syrup. They were so tasty and light, he felt like... doing something to thank this woman. She was watching him, so he continued the conversation as best he could. "I plan on buying a couple of shoats this spring to fatten through the summer. Make pork sausage this fall and cure some bacon."

She nodded and continued eating. In between bites— and to his relief—she chattered about her home farm and family.

He got the distinct feeling that she didn't like her sister-in-law. Soon breakfast ended and he rose from the table. And before he knew it, he said, "Fine meal, ma'am." These were the words his father had said at the end of each meal. Asa hadn't seen his family since he moved here and barely wrote. Having this woman here was stirring him up, making him remember what family was.

"You're welcome," she said. "What are you up to today?"

"Have some work in the barn, and I'll bring more wood in, too." He motioned toward the nearly empty wood box near the door.

"I'll wash up," she said, "and then I need to get more acquainted with my kitchen."

"Make a list of supplies, whatever you need." And then, pulling on his jacket, he shut the door behind himself.

Taken aback by his abrupt departure, Judith stood and carried the dishes to the counter, where a dishpan sat. Well, dirty dishes constituted a common and inevitable part of her life. She wondered for a moment if Mabel Joy, her brother's Kentucky wife, was enjoying being on her own without help from Emma and her. Mabel Joy had wanted them gone, and they were.

Her husband's use of the married title, *ma'am*, had startled her. She'd been a *miss* for so long, thought she'd always be. Mabel Joy had taunted her, telling her it was too bad she was plain and no man would ever marry her. Well, someone had married her. *I am married.*

Judith tried not to let the newness, the strangeness of this cabin, of having a husband she never expected to have, unsettle her. "I'll become accustomed soon and then this will feel like home." Tears rushed into her eyes. Was this mere homesickness? Or regret? Or fear? But of what? Everything had gone well.

Except that Asa's reply to her one personal question had gone unanswered. Why hadn't he just told her how many brothers and sisters he had? It had been a commonplace question. Had he been teasing her? He hadn't sounded so. A feeling of unease flickered inside her. She shook herself and began cleaning up breakfast. The large midday meal would come soon enough. *I'm being foolish to fret. My husband is just not a talker by nature, that's all. He will come to know me and then he will speak more.*

On the wagon bench two mornings after their wedding day, Asa and Judith set out for town to do a few errands. Normally they would have walked into town, but he needed the blacksmith to check one horse's shoe, and the metal rim of one of his wagon wheels needed fixing. And he didn't know how much Judith would be buying at the store.

He felt his wife warm at his side. *I'm not alone anymore.* A blessing. And a worry. So far he thought he'd done a pretty good job of keeping up the pretense of a good husband. After all, she couldn't see inside him, inside where he was a hollowed-out shell. He'd drawn on memories of how his mother and father had behaved together. If he could just keep that up, all would be well. Under a clear blue sky, he drew in a deep draft of the sharp early March air.

Though the sun shone bright and warmed his face, the horses' hooves still threw up snow on their way into town. He and Judith had navigated through two days of marriage. He'd successfully avoided any and all personal questions. She'd asked him what his hometown was; he mentioned visiting Chicago. She'd asked if he'd served in the Union Army and he'd nodded and then asked about her family. He thought he'd done pretty well under the circumstances. He understood his wife's wanting to ask him things. Women did that.

But soon she'd be more used to him and then there would be no more personal questions. And also no more temptation for him to answer them. Somehow his new wife caused him to want to open up, tell her about himself. But if he started, couldn't that go too far? Reveal everything? He mentally shook himself. Enough thinking.

"Wish the thaw would begin in earnest," he said to break the silence. "These bright sunny days make me want to get out and begin tilling my fields. Yet it's way too early."

She turned to him and looked pleased that he'd spoken. "Yes, I understand. It would be good to open the cabin and let the fresh air inside."

And he thought that their relative idleness might be another reason for her asking questions. Once they were busy with the productive part of the year, farming, gardening and such, they'd settle into an easy pattern of being busy, too busy for personal questions and they'd just make do with idle conversation. He wanted to hear her fill up the silence but not ask him to join in. Even he noted the inconsistency in this. But it was the truth.

"And I'm looking forward to seeing my sister, Emma."

To this, he nodded. He'd almost forgotten her sister would be there.

As soon as they reached town, Asa pulled up in front of Ashford's. He guided Judith inside and breathed in the scents of the tidy general store—primarily dried apples and cinnamon. He felt relieved. He could leave her here for a while and not have to watch every word he said or she said.

"Mr. and Mrs. Brant! I saw you from my window." Mrs. Ashford hurried into the store from the rear. "How are the newlyweds?"

Asa nodded politely. "Doing fine, ma'am." He touched Judith's elbow and then turned and left. Saved by the storekeeper's wife. She'd talk Judith's ear off, and perhaps that would satisfy his wife's desire for ready conversation.

* * *

Bolstered by his touch and being greeted as a wife, not a pitied spinster, Judith smiled at Mrs. Ashford. "I'm here to buy some spices. I guess bachelors use only salt and pepper."

"You give Ned your list, then come on up," the woman instructed. "Your sister and I are just finishing up a few chores and have time for a chat."

Judith watched the woman head up the back stairs. She went to the counter and handed the storekeeper her list. After discussing the items as to quantities and specifics, she followed Mrs. Ashford.

How was spontaneous and lively Emma faring living with these strangers, and was she upset her intended had not been here to meet her? Judith also craved a private chat with Emma about her puzzlement over Asa. She hoped that Mrs. Ashford would grant her and Emma a few moments alone to talk.

Judith found that a vain hope.

Mrs. Ashford poured them all fresh, steaming coffee and then sat at the head of the dining table. Judith had been given the seat with the view out the windows toward the river. She watched a steamboat heading toward the Pepin pier. "I love your view."

"Yes, I told Mr. Ashford to build on this side of Main Street. I wanted a good view. The forest can be so forbidding. Plus if the river ever floods, we'll be on higher ground. The shops across the street are much too close to the river."

Judith glimpsed the blacksmith's sign across and to her right. That's where Asa was. Her heart tightened.

Something was trapped within Asa and she didn't know what. He was like a parcel glued and tied shut. Was this just due to their being strangers to one another? Yes, that must be it, she hoped.

"Now, how is it going with you and Mr. Brant?" the storekeeper's wife asked the very question Judith could not quite figure out herself.

And what did the woman expect her to say? *"He won't talk to me and I can't figure out why"*? "We're doing fine. Just getting to know each other. Asa is so considerate." But secretive. Or maybe not. Maybe men just didn't talk much about themselves. *But why can't he even tell me how many brothers and sisters he has or the name of his hometown?* Judith pushed this out of her mind and hoped her expression revealed nothing.

Mrs. Ashford was staring at her, obviously wanting more details about the newlyweds.

Casting around for a safe subject, Judith lifted her cup in front of her face. "Mr. Brant—Asa—presented me with a sewing machine for a wedding gift."

"I know!" Mrs. Ashford crowed. "I helped him choose it from the catalogue for you. Such a thoughtful gift, and so useful."

Judith agreed, interrupting the flow of the woman's conversation.

"It's too bad the weather has been so cold. We usually have a lovely spring here in Pepin." Their hostess kept up a steady stream of chatter, to which she and Emma merely had to agree.

Judith was aware that her sister was trying to hide mirth at Mrs. Ashford's curiosity and constant chattering. Emma possessed a ready and sometimes inappropriate sense of humor. Judith sent her a reproving glance.

Emma bit her lower lip.

Judith thought, *Please, can't I have a moment alone with my sister?*

As if Mrs. Ashford heard Judith's thought, she rose from the table. "I need to brown the beef for lunch and start it cooking. Please excuse me."

Judith drew in a relieved but silent breath.

Emma muffled a giggle behind her hand.

Judith scolded and quizzed her sister with a glance.

"She never stops talking," Emma whispered, "unless she's eating or sleeping."

Judith lifted her hands in a gesture that said *What can I do about that?*

"She's really nice and kind, but I have trouble not teasing her. I don't think she'd appreciate it." Emma's expression became serious. "How are you doing? What's worrying you?"

Though she and Emma weren't identical twins, they had always been attuned to each other. "It's nothing, really." Judith spoke in a low tone. "It's just that Asa…avoids everyday questions. I asked him if he had brothers and sisters and he said, 'Some of each.'"

Emma laughed.

Judith glared at her. "It's not funny. We get along very well unless I ask him a personal question."

"Perhaps he's just a very private person," Emma suggested.

"Even with his wife?"

"His very new wife. Just give it time, Judith." Emma pressed a hand over Judith's, which clutched her coffee cup.

Judith nodded. Her sister had given her good advice. She relaxed her hands. "What are you keeping busy doing?"

"I help with some chores, and yesterday I helped in the store. Mr. Ashford did it out of kindness, I think, to give me a chance to talk to someone besides his wife and daughter. The people here are really—"

They heard the sound of rapid footsteps and then Mr. Ashford called from the back door, "Katherine! You'll never believe this!"

Both Judith and Emma turned to see the storekeeper hurry into the room and over to the front window. Mrs. Ashford bustled out of the kitchen, wiping her hands on her apron. "What is it?"

Mr. Ashford waved a paper. "This is his letter of resignation, and there he goes. He's getting on the boat! I can't believe it!"

"Who?" Mrs. Ashford said, joining her husband at the window. "That's Mr. Thompson, the schoolmaster!"

"Yes! He just resigned!"

"What?" Mrs. Ashford squawked. "He can't leave in the middle of the school year!"

"Well, there he goes," Emma said. She'd moved to stand beside the Ashfords at the window.

"What got into him?" the storekeeper's wife asked.

Mr. Ashford frowned down at the letter. "It just says he must go home because of a personal crisis."

"What will we do come Monday? Who will teach?" Mrs. Ashford wailed.

"We can't ask Mrs. Lang. She's busy with her little ones." The storekeeper stared out the window. Then he swung to Emma. "Miss Jones, will you please take over downstairs? I need to go to Noah Whitmore and Martin Steward, the other school board members, right away."

"Of course," Emma agreed. "I can handle matters."

"Thank you." Mr. Ashford was taking off his long store apron and hurrying toward the rear entrance. "I'll be back as soon as I can, Katherine. Just keep a plate warm for me." And then he was jogging down the steps, pulling on his jacket and hat.

"Well, I never," Mrs. Ashford said. "What is the world coming to?"

"I don't know," Emma replied. "I'll head downstairs."

"Thank you," Mrs. Ashford said. "Call me if you need any help."

"I will." Emma snagged a shawl and headed down the back steps. "Sorry, Judith!"

Judith rose. "I don't know what to say. May I help you in the kitchen? Or go help my sister?"

Mrs. Ashford pulled herself together. "Why don't you go down and help your sister finish your shopping? I'm making plenty of lunch. When your husband comes back, you two are more than welcome to stay and eat with us."

The woman was indeed kind and hospitable. "Thank you. But I think he'll want to go home as soon as we're done."

"I understand." The woman beamed at her. "Newly-weds." And then she returned to the kitchen.

Blushing, Judith donned her shawl and carried the rest of her warm wraps outside and into the store. The thought occurred to her that people here might look to her sister to fill in at the school, but that wouldn't work. Emma had applied to teach in their home district and had been turned down as "not having the serious temperament necessary in an educator of children." Nonjudgmental Emma had been surprised, but Judith hadn't.

Very smart and good at all subjects, Emma would have made a lovely teacher, but all through school she'd been scolded for her humor and sudden outbursts of excited interest. Emma would never be the strict spinster teacher that school boards preferred. Emma was too pretty and jolly for them.

Carrying a sack of spices, Judith hurried inside, chilled from the short ride home. Asa came in after her and set several bags on the table. He went immediately to the banked fire and stirred it back to life.

"That woman can sure talk," he said, rising. Asa had surprised her by accepting Mrs. Ashford's lunch invitation.

Judith chuckled. "Yes, but her Salisbury steak and potatoes did not disappoint."

"Can't argue that. You need me right now? I have to take care of the horses."

"No."

He headed toward the door.

"But," she said, halting him, "it occurred to Emma and me that we haven't written home to our father. He isn't in good health, and I want him to know Emma and I arrived safely and are doing well."

"A good idea. We can give it to Ashford tomorrow at church. Mr. Ashford's the local postmaster." He opened the door.

"Asa, wait. I'd like you to write a line to my father. I think that would reassure him." Her father had been very concerned about his twin daughters going away to marry strangers.

Asa paused, his expression froze into vertical lines. "I'll see about that later." He escaped out the door.

Escaped exactly described his exit.

Judith stood by the dry sink, unable to move for a moment. Then she walked to the chair by the table and sat. Why would writing a line to her father flummox her husband? What could be more natural or simple? Something more than natural reticence was at work here. She thought over the many letters he'd written her. It wasn't that he couldn't write a few lines. He didn't want to. Why? Why did he avoid any mention of anything personal? What was wrong with her simple request? What was going on within her husband?

Feeling confused, she bowed her head and whispered, "Heavenly Father, something is not right. What is it? What should I do? Say? Should I confront Asa plainly?"

At the word *confront*, panic swept over her. The old pang twisted around her heart. She pictured again that day in 1861. Tom Southby had been going off to war, and she'd decided she couldn't let him go without telling him how she felt. With a red face, Tom had thanked her for caring for him but said he couldn't return the same to her. Once again she flushed with the heated humiliation over those horrible moments. He'd said they'd always been the best of friends and he wanted to leave it at that. Best of friends. She'd been in love with him since sixth grade. Yet it wasn't Tom's fault that she wasn't pretty enough.

With effort, she mastered the old hurt and shame. Praying for guidance and peace, she sat for several minutes, hoping for something to occur to her. Then she recalled her late mother's favorite verse, Isaiah 26:3. "You keep him in perfect peace whose mind is steadfast because he trusts in You."

One thing came clear. She was allowing Asa's hesitance to reveal anything about himself to disturb her peace. And that was what she'd really come here to find—a husband and a peaceful life with him. She went over the past two days and the innocent questions she'd asked her new husband and his avoidance of replying to each one.

She recalled Mrs. Ashford's favorable assessment of Asa's character. "Lord, I feel I've married a good-intentioned man," she murmured. "I sense nothing false about him. He doesn't make up answers to suit my questions. That's what a dishonest man would do. But why is talking about himself an issue for him?"

No answer came, but her tension eased. Heartened just a little, she straightened and slowly rose. She had chores to do and a life to live. "I'm not alone, Father.

You are here with me, and I trust You. I would not have come here just to escape my contentious sister-in-law. You opened this door, and Emma and I walked through it. We both had peace about this decision. And now I've given my sacred pledge to Asa. No turning back."

She picked up the sack of spices and looked for a place to store them. She continued her audible prayer. "And, Lord, help Emma find a place and a new beginning here. It's too bad she's not suited to teach."

She drew herself up and began humming her mother's favorite hymn, drawing strength from its words and hearing her mother's voice in her memory. "Come thou fount of every blessing." Judith had much to sing about—a husband and home of her own along with a beloved sister nearby and, as always, a faithful God—and finally work to do, a kitchen to organize.

Maybe she wasn't a woman that a man would fall in love with, but she could take care of a house and be a helpmeet. She could hold up her end of the bargain she'd made with Asa. She could be a good wife. Experience had taught her that love was for pretty girls like Emma and even unlikable Mabel Joy, but not her.

Chapter Three

On the way to church on Sunday morning, Asa thought over the few days he'd been married. When he had rejoined her yesterday, Judith had not repeated her request that he write a note to her father. In the end he'd decided he must write a line in that letter or cause more questions. What were the odds that the woman he married would be someone he recognized? The memory of when they had seen each other in person over a decade ago came flooding back to him. He'd been elected captain of the Rock River Illinois Militia, and all the volunteers had gathered at the train station in Rockford to set off for war. Remembering how callow and naive he and the other militia volunteers had been expanded through him like hot grapeshot. They'd thought the war would end in weeks, not years.

As Asa drove down Main Street past all the shops closed for the Sabbath, his thoughts filled with the past.

That day in 1861, all the militia families had come to see their men off. Judith and Emma had been there in the crowd. Of course he hadn't been introduced to Judith individually but to all the families of the Illinois militia. Later, however, her brother Gil had often showed him the tintype of his pretty twin sisters, a connection to home.

But obviously Judith didn't remember seeing him that day, or the day when what was left of the militia had returned in '65. Relief whistled through him once more.

Bringing him back to the present, the schoolhouse door came into view. Soon he halted his team and went around to Judith. She braced herself on his arms as he helped her down.

The soft expression on her face worked on him. He resisted the urge to pull her close. Instead he handed her the cloth-covered cake she'd baked for the after-church social. "I'll take the horses to their area and then join you inside," he said.

"Thank you, Asa." Judith paused. "Where do you usually sit?"

Asa grinned, understanding that even in church, people claimed their places. "Near the back on the right."

She smiled in return and walked over the packed snow to the school entrance. The door opened and a man's voice called, "Welcome. Come in from the cold."

Asa steered his team to the long hitching shelter. He had already blanketed his team before leaving home and had slipped on their blinders to block their interacting with the other teams of horses also tied under the roof.

He'd helped build this shelter himself last fall and had suggested the windbreaks on three sides. His team would be fine under cover and out of direct wind. He turned and walked resolutely toward the schoolhouse. He noted his wife had dressed with care for the Sunday service. Of course everyone would be watching them.

Getting married had disturbed his ordinary life, during which he'd kept everyone at arm's length. It was all so confusing. And he must keep this new inner confusion over his unexpected attraction to his bride—to her thick, dark hair, pert nose and warm brown eyes—concealed behind an untroubled face.

Tense, Judith stepped inside the school, carrying her cake plate. Asa had told her that in the winter, everyone who wanted to brought a covered dish and stayed after services to eat and talk. So she'd baked a brown butter cake yesterday. Today would be the first time since their wedding that she and Asa had appeared together before the whole community. Though Emma liked attention, Judith did not. But now it would be unavoidable. She crafted a smile and put it in place. No one must see any division between Asa and her. Or it would invite speculation.

The worship service went smoothly, and then it was time for the potluck dinner. Within a very few moments, the men had set up folding tables and positioned the school benches around them. And after the deacon, Gordy Osbourne, said grace, the potluck began. Everyone filled their plates from a variety of fragrant bowls and platters.

Judith didn't want to slight anybody, so she took a spoonful or piece of everything. With her plate full, she found herself and Asa sitting with the couple who had welcomed her at the door and another young couple, the blacksmith and his wife, Levi and Posey Comstock. Judith had hoped to sit near Emma, but her sister had stayed near the Ashfords.

Judith waved to her and Emma waved back, her expression one of suppressed excitement. What had happened to cause that? Had she gotten word that her intended husband, Mason Chandler, was returning?

Judith ate and replied to those who spoke to her, but primarily she listened in order to learn more about her new neighbors. Then, near the end of the meal, Mr. Ashford rose. "May I have your attention, please?"

Everyone fell silent and turned to look at the storekeeper.

"Many of you know but others may not be aware that we lost our teacher yesterday."

A few startled gasps, and then the room swelled with upset murmuring.

Mr. Ashford held up his hand. "The school board has already met and has found a replacement so that school will go on."

Judith then glimpsed her sister's face. And she thought, *Oh, no.*

"Miss Emma Jones has consented to finish out the school year as interim teacher."

Judith felt her jaw drop and quickly shut her mouth so no one would detect her hesitation over this development. Would Emma be able to curb her naturally lively personality enough to please the town?

"Miss Jones," Ashford continued, "completed eleventh grade with honors and is of impeccable reputation.

And we have stressed to her the importance of preparing our students to compete in the upcoming Third Annual Pepin Regional Spelling Bee in April."

The murmurs switched from surprised dismay to approval, many heads were nodding and everyone was smiling at her sister. Judith forced herself to look pleased and approving. But the phrase from years ago played in her mind: *"not having the serious temperament necessary in an educator of children."*

Had Emma forgotten? That didn't seem likely. Judith tried to remember how Emma had reacted to that rejection. But it had happened in the midst of the war, and that conflagration had overshadowed everything else.

Should she say something to Emma? No. The matter had gone too far. And since the school year would no doubt end in May, perhaps all would be well. And after all, Emma was nearly a decade older than she'd been during her first attempt at becoming a teacher. She might not upset the school board with her liveliness.

Then Judith recalled Emma's advice to her as they chugged into sight of Pepin a week ago: *"embrace the adventure."* Well, Judith only hoped Emma's latest adventure would turn out for the best. She didn't want her sister's feelings to be hurt.

Asa leaned close to her ear. "Something wrong?"

She turned to him and whispered, "No. I just wasn't expecting this." She would tell him what she really felt when they were alone.

He nodded and rested his hand over hers.

For that moment she forgot how to breathe. She tried to dismiss this and behave as though his touch had not affected her so. She looked to the front of this room where they had pledged themselves to each other. She recalled his gentle, chaste kiss and Asa's whisper, "I'll do right by you, Judith." She trusted Asa, but the worry lingered. What wasn't he trusting her with?

Late on the next day, Asa finished washing up at the dry sink and then took his seat at the table. Judith had prepared another deliciously fragrant meal for him. She was using up the last of the venison from the smokehouse in a stew. She set the pot in the center of the table. And then sat down across from him. The pleasure of the moment of having a pretty, cheerful woman here and the scent of well-prepared food flooded him. Caution leaped up inside him like a wall, a fortress around his feelings. He couldn't afford this softening. He couldn't let down his guard or all the regret might unman him. He didn't want anyone to know about his war record. If he did, the talk would begin. And no one would let him live in peace.

She bowed her head, waiting for him to say grace. Then, with effort, he voiced his usual grace without betraying his anxiety and looked up to watch her dish up his plate first.

Judith paused and pursed her lips. "Emma is very bright and very good. But sometimes her high spirits can carry her away."

He wondered what she was leading up to.

She sighed and then looked across at him. "I hope her high spirits don't upset the school board."

Hearing the concern in her voice and not knowing

what he could do, he shrugged. Then a thought came. "What everyone is really most concerned about is that she prepare the students for the big spelling bee in April. If she does that right, I don't think they'll care about her high spirits."

Judith gazed at him. Then, reaching across the table, she touched his hand. "Thank you. I know I'm only four minutes older than her, but in temperament, I am the older sister. And I worry about her sometimes."

She glanced downward. "Asa, I'd like to invite the Ashfords and Emma for dinner someday. But there are a few things that I'd need to buy for the house before we have company." Still not meeting his gaze, she raised a hand. "Nothing extravagant. I need fabric to make window curtains and dishcloths. I'd like to buy a set of dishes, not china, just sturdy everyday dishes." She glanced up then, looking uncertain.

He looked down at the dented tin plates and mugs he'd always used. Of course a woman would want better than this. "Sorry," he said, his voice coming back. "I should have discussed our finances with you. You buy whatever you need."

He cleared his throat. "Our fields will provide most of our food. I hunt in the fall. And in the winter, I work with leather. The blacksmith keeps those belts and harnesses and sells them for me." He rose and went to the hearth. "Come here."

She obeyed him.

He showed her the loose stone that hid a cavity in the side of the fireplace and the small cloth sack of gold and silver coins stashed there. "We have plenty, Judith.

Just tell Mr. Ashford to put everything on our tab. I pay him once a month."

"Thank you, Asa. I'm not an extravagant woman, but I do want to—" she waved a hand toward the room "—make everything more homey."

He returned to his place at the table, and she followed him.

"I want you to…do that, too," he said. *But you've done so much more.* The chain around his heart tightened. If only he had more than a house and sustenance to offer her. Judith deserved the best. But he would give her the best he could of the material world. The pity was that he could not give her more of his true self, his empty heart.

The thaw had started. All around, Judith heard the sound of water trickling and dripping from the roof and the rivulets that ran down the trail toward town. She hummed as she finished setting the table for six. Her first dinner party would be today. The Ashfords and Emma were coming for supper. The cabin door and both windows stood open to let in the breath of spring. This would be her debut as the mistress of her own home, inviting others to a meal.

She'd planned the supper carefully. Fried chicken, mashed potatoes, tender dandelion greens salad, her mother's cloverleaf rolls and cherry pie for dessert. She glanced toward the window, where the two dishcloth-covered pies were cooling on the sill.

Then, glancing at the clock, she took the last of the chicken out of the skillet, spitting hot and golden. She set it on the pan in the warming oven. Then she went out to the springhouse to get the cream to whip up for the pie.

She heard the voices of people walking up the trail. She quickly retrieved the cream from this morning's milking and hurried toward the house.

"Judith!" Her sister's happy voice carried to her.

"Emma!" Judith replied and then hurried inside to change into her clean apron for the final preparations.

As she walked in, Asa stepped out of the bedroom, where he dressed. He looked very handsome in a blue-and-white-striped shirt she'd pressed this morning. He was freshly shaved and his hair was neat. She stood rooted to the spot. She had married a handsome man. Once again the sensation of recognition trickled through her and then vanished.

Emma reached the door first. "Sister!"

Setting down the pot of cream, Judith swung around and welcomed her sister with a quick hug for her first visit there. "I'm so glad you're here."

"Me, too," Emma replied, sniffing the air. "Your fried chicken?"

Judith nodded, looking past her sister and welcoming the Ashfords inside. A happy hubbub of welcomes and greetings filled the next few minutes. Then everyone had entered and their guests had sat down on the benches by the table—all except Mrs. Ashford, who was walking around as if on an inspection tour.

She paused at Judith's grandmother's sampler. "This is very fine handwork. And is it on silk?"

"Yes," Emma spoke up and explained the history of the piece.

Judith listened as she mashed the potatoes, mixing in butter, salt and pepper with warm milk.

Mrs. Ashford pronounced her verdict. "That's an heirloom." Then she beamed at Judith. "You have a very cozy home here."

Pleased, Judith finished the potatoes and set them on a trivet near the fire. "I just need to whip up the cream for our dessert and then we can eat."

"Is there anything I can do to help?" Amanda Ashford asked.

"No, I think everything is in hand." Judith walked to the window, holding the bowl of cream in the crook of one arm and whipping the cream with a wire whisk. Then she gasped. One of her pies was missing.

"What is it, Judith?" Emma asked.

Judith turned. "I baked two pies, but one is gone."

Everyone rose from the table to look at the window-sill, where one pie still sat under a dishcloth. The two men hurried outside to see if the pie had somehow fallen off the sill.

Asa looked at Judith through the open window. "No sign of it."

Her husband appeared as puzzled as she felt.

"What could have happened to it?" Amanda asked.

"An animal?" Mrs. Ashford suggested.

"That would have left a mess here." Outside, Mr. Ashford pointed toward the ground.

"Yes," Emma agreed, "and an animal would not have any use for the pan."

"A tramp," Mrs. Ashford pronounced, frowning. "Must have snuck up, snatched it and run. We get them this close to the river. Drifters following it north or south."

"I wish he'd just asked," Judith said. "I'd never let anyone go away hungry."

"Well, one pie's gone, but we still have one," Asa said. "When do we eat, ma'am?"

Judith shook her head at him but smiled at his teasing tone.

"Yes, let's not spoil our meal," Emma said.

The men came back into the cabin and settled around the table. Judith soon set out the dishes family-style. The dinner guests ate with gusto and offered many compliments. Judith ate and replied, but she still wondered. Who had taken the pie?

Two mornings later, Judith awakened with a plan. Yesterday, which was laundry day and the day after the pie had gone missing, someone had taken one of Asa's shirts drying on her clothesline. Someone was not only hungry but also needed clothing. She thought of the verses in Matthew 25.

"Come, ye blessed of my Father, inherit the kingdom prepared for you from the foundation of the world: For I was hungered, and ye gave me meat: I was thirsty, and ye gave me drink: I was a stranger, and ye took me in: Naked, and ye clothed me."

But how to do that? At home in Illinois, usually tramps had stopped at the door to ask. She didn't think this person was going to do that. Then the plan had come to her. She needed to bait the hook and see who nabbed it. After breakfast, Asa had reminded her that he was helping out a neighbor with clearing more land and would be gone till lunch.

Perfect. She didn't want Asa to know what she was doing. Her plan sounded…childish, but it might work. She bid Asa goodbye and then baked two cinnamon cakes, set one on the windowsill where the pie had been and then slipped inside the springhouse, which gave her an excellent view of the window. The scent of cinnamon from the cake floated on the wind.

At first, anticipation and a bit of apprehension kept Judith alert, but an hour passed with only squirrels on tree branches eyeing the prize on the sill. She began daydreaming, thinking of fabric she'd seen at the Ashfords' store.

Then she heard it—soft padding of feet and the brushing back of branches. She peered out the cracked-open springhouse door and saw them. She nearly gasped aloud.

She glimpsed two children, a boy of around nine and a younger girl, who was wearing Asa's shirt as a dress. The boy left the girl in the cover of the evergreens and approached the house with stealth.

Judith sat very still, watching the boy reach up and take the cake and stuff it into a small cloth bag. Then he hurried back to the girl.

Judith nearly leaped from her seat, but she counted to ten, then slipped outside, going after the children. She needed to find out where they were coming from. Did they have family? Fortunately, as a child, she and

Emma had played Cowboys and Indians with their older brother, so she knew how to creep behind someone. The trees and wild shrubs concealed her. She followed the two more by sound than by sight.

Finally the two stopped muting their voices and halted.

Judith peered through the evergreen boughs and observed them devouring her cake. Behind them, the opening to what must be a cave explained where they lived.

Two children living alone in a cave? Why? Where were their parents? Family?

She sat very still, watching them as they sat on the bare ground, eating and then drinking from a natural spring that ran from the rock near the cave opening. They needed her assistance but they were hiding, not coming to her door to ask. Why not?

Well, right now she must attempt to help them, regardless. She rose and stepped out of the cover of the forest. "Good day, children."

The two of them leaped up. The boy shoved the girl behind his back and picked up a large rock. "Don't you come any closer!"

She opened her hands and showed that she held no weapon. "I'm Mrs. Brant. What are your names?"

"I'm Lily," the girl said.

"Nice to meet you, Lily." Judith smiled but stayed where she was, letting them get used to her.

"This is Colton—" Lily began.

"Hush," Colton said. "Lady, you go on home. Lily and I are doin' fine."

She surveyed their matted hair, grimy hands and faces, clothes caked with mud, and thin arms and legs. Though unhappy at their plight, she still smiled and kept her voice gentle. "I've come to invite you to eat lunch with my husband and me."

"Lunch!" Lily jumped with obvious excitement. She hurried toward Judith.

Colton tried to stop her, but the girl skirted him, went to Judith and took the hand she offered. "Do you cook good?"

Judith was caught between amusement and sadness. Lily must have been only around six, so she still had a child's trust, but Colton had lost his. Who had driven these children into the forest to fend for themselves like Hansel and Gretel?

"Colton, I know you don't know me well. But I am offering you a free meal. You can leave afterward. And I promise not to tell anybody but my husband about this place." She didn't want Colton to leave for fear of her.

Colton studied her for a long time.

She waited.

Finally the boy put down the rock and walked toward her. "Okay. We'll come, but we ain't stayin'."

"I only invited you for lunch," she replied. "I mean you no harm."

He snorted.

Her heart ached for a boy trying to care for himself and a little sister. She longed to rattle off questions, but pressed her lips together. The two were like wild deer. She didn't want to spook them. Then Asa came to mind.

What would he say when he came home for lunch

and, without warning, found two tattered urchins at his table? Now she realized that she should have discussed this with her husband. Would he object? With a deep sigh, she began praying for wisdom, for guidance, not only for her but also for Asa.

Would he be displeased with her for acting on her own, for not minding her own business? The fact that her husband was still somewhat a stranger to her— and that he held her at arm's length—kept her feeling insecure. Surely he wouldn't send the children away, would he?

Chapter Four

Out of the forest, swishing through the ankle-deep just-greening wild grass, Judith led the children the last few feet into her clearing, praying that Asa, taken by surprise, would not say or do anything that would frighten them away. With regret, she again scolded herself that he wouldn't if she'd prepared him for what she had planned. She prayed for Asa's underlying goodness to shine out and be sensed by these children.

Lily skipped along beside her, chattering away about Clara, her soiled, limp rag doll lying over her arm. "That's my favorite name, Clara," the little girl said.

"That is a very pretty name, but so is Lily. I love lilies, especially tiger lilies." Judith sensed Colton lagging behind. Glancing over her shoulder, she observed him studying the area as if looking for any possible danger. Or perhaps an escape route.

"What's a tiger lily?" the little girl asked.

"It's a yellow or orange lily that blooms in the summer. We may have some growing around here." Judith sent the girl a happy smile that masked her growing misgivings. Mimicking in sound her tightening tension, a chickadee in a nearby tree called out, "Chickadee-deedee. Chickadee-dee-dee."

What would Asa say when he saw whom she'd invited for lunch? Her lungs tightened.

As if he heard her thought, Asa stepped out of the barn and, when he saw them, halted.

Colton halted.

Lily halted.

Judith clung to Lily's hand and drew her forward. "I'm so happy you accepted my invitation to have lunch," she said a bit louder than usual. "Hello, Asa! This is Lily and her brother, Colton. Children, this is my husband, Asa Brant."

Asa sized up their guests, his expression unreadable. "Hello, children."

He studied Judith as if asking a question and awaiting the answer. And she mouthed, "Pie. Shirt."

After studying the little girl's makeshift dress, his shirt, he nodded slowly. He inhaled. "What's for lunch?"

Judith thanked him with a smile. He was going along with her plan without asking questions. "I made salt pork and beans and some brown bread. And—" she hoped this would help lagging Colton come the last few feet to their door "—I baked cinnamon—"

"Cake!" Lily crowed. "It's good." With these words she revealed that they'd already sampled one.

"Better wash up," Asa said. He walked over to the outdoor pitcher and basin and began to soap his hands.

Lily let go of Judith's hand and ran to stand beside Asa. "I know how to wash my hands all by myself."

"Good." Asa handed her the bar of soap. He glanced over his shoulder. "Boy?"

Colton caught up with Judith but did not approach Asa. He waited till he and Lily were done. When Asa stepped away from the basin and went to pump more water into the pitcher, Colton washed his hands, but stuck close to Judith, still watchful of his sister. That told Judith much. They did not deem her a threat, but the man of the house might be.

Soon the four of them with clean hands sat at the table, the children side by side on a bench, which was usually tucked away against the wall. Asa offered his customary brief grace, and then Judith began to dish up bowls of the beans, fragrant with molasses, and thick slices of bread. The contrast between the children's clean hands and their grimy faces and matted hair caused Judith to itch to give both children a good scrubbing, brushing and combing.

"Can I have butter on my bread?" Lily asked.

"You may if you say please," Judith replied automatically.

"Please, can I have butter on my bread?" Lily asked.

Judith buttered a slice thickly and set it on the girl's plate.

"What do you say?" Asa prompted, sounding stern.

"Thank you," Lily said, then bit into her bread. "Mmm."

Grateful for the way Asa had gone along with this unexpected turn of events, Judith still worried. How could they keep the children here? Would Asa want that? What did the town do with orphans here? But were they orphans or runaways? How had these two little ones ended up on their own in a cave?

She chewed mechanically, trying to come up with what to do. The children ate as if starved. The pork and beans disappeared. Soon she was setting a second cake on the table, the first having served as successful bait.

Asa ate his portion and then looked at Colton. "Think you know something about a pie that disappeared from our windowsill?"

Colton jerked up from the bench.

Why had Asa said this? Not knowing and not wanting to contradict him, Judith held her breath. Would the children bolt?

"Sit back down," Asa said. "I'm not going to turn you over to the sheriff."

Judith stilled. She did not know what Asa was doing so she had no way of countering it, softening it.

Colton stayed standing, wary.

"We took the pie," Lily said. "We were really hungry, and Colton's trap didn't catch anything. Sorry." The girl bowed her head and set a forkful of cake back on her plate.

Asa looked to the brother. "That what happened, boy?"

"Yes, sir," Colton said, facing Asa squarely.

"Then I have a few chores you can do to work off what you owe me…us."

At first Judith had to swallow a protest, and then she saw the wisdom of this. Or thought she did.

"What kind of chores?" Colton asked.

"I'm sharpening the blade of my plow. You could oil my plow harness." Asa glanced toward Judith. "You have something Lily can help with?"

"Yes. She can dry the dishes and help me dust," Judith improvised.

"I can do that," Lily said, sounding happy that the chores were not beyond her abilities.

Asa looked to Judith, communicating something she couldn't decipher. "Then we have a deal." He rose from the table. "Children, thank Mrs. Brant for lunch. Good meal, ma'am," he said, which was his usual end-of-meal phrase.

The little girl consumed the rest of her cake in two bites. "Good meal, ma'am," Lily parroted.

Colton sat back down, finished drinking his glass of milk and ate the last bit of cake. "Thank you for the good lunch, Mrs. Brant." He stood again. "Where's that harness?"

"Where is that harness, *sir*?" Asa prompted.

Colton glared, his lower lip protruding. But he repeated the sentence, though with a surly edge.

Judith held her breath. Had Asa gone too far? Would he push the children to run?

Instead, Colton followed Asa outside. Lily drained her glass and popped up. "I can help."

Judith rose and carried most of the dishes to the dry sink and counter. Lily followed her like a shadow and watched her intently. "I like your house," the little girl said.

"Thank you. I do, too."

The two of them chatted. Lily seemed happy to contribute her part, but she avoided all questions about her family. Once the little girl looked about to cry, so Judith returned the conversation to something light and easy.

The afternoon was far along when Colton appeared at the open cabin door. "You done with your chores, Lily?"

Lily looked up at Judith, her expression begging her to say no.

But the chores were done. "Yes, but won't you stay—"

"We gotta go," Colton insisted. He waved insistently at his little sister. "Come on."

Lily left Judith's side and went to her brother. Just before they left, she turned. "Thanks…thanks."

Colton took his sister's hand, and the two of them headed back to the forest.

Judith stepped outside and watched them go. Would they return to the cave or would they move on, afraid of…what? Who had made them afraid? Her heart hurt for them.

Asa remained in the barn.

Judith rarely ventured there, sensing that her new husband liked his privacy. Being married to a stranger who wouldn't reveal anything about his past or thoughts often became awkward. The barn was his haven, hers the kitchen. But now she entered the barn, her emotions a storm.

Asa stood near his upturned plow in the shadowy interior that smelled like a clean barn should, earthy with the distinctive scent of horses and cows. Everything in the barn reflected Asa's desire for neatness and order. The walls were adorned with pegs that sported all manner of tools and horse paraphernalia. She paused in the doorway, looking at him. She tried to come up with a way to introduce the subject of the children and what to do about them. Two children that young would not thrive living in a cave. And though spring and summer were ahead, winter would come again. Her husband did not like to talk, but they must discuss this. The children had come to their window. God had brought Colton and Lily to them. She cleared her throat and prayed for inspiration.

Hearing her come in, Asa, sitting at his small, slender work table, gazed at Judith, seeing her silhouette outlined in sunshine. Already knowing her tender heart, he shouldn't have been surprised at her showing up with two ragamuffins. "Where'd you find them?" he asked.

She filled him in on the cake trap she'd set to catch the pie-and-shirt thief.

Fear for her, and anger, ricocheted through him. He stood. "You did that without telling me?" he snapped. "What if it hadn't been children but a man…a tramp? Someone who might have hurt you." He closed the distance between them.

"I don't know why I didn't tell you." She lifted her hands in a helpless motion. "I guess I'm used to taking care of things myself. Father hasn't been strong for a long time. My brother was gone to war. I'm the oldest."

He drew a few deep breaths, calming himself.

"If a man had come, I would have stayed in the springhouse." She looked up at him—and burst into tears.

He didn't know what to do. "I didn't mean to make you cry—"

"You didn't." She wept on, waving her hand toward the open door. "They are living in a cave. What are we going to do? Colton can't be even ten. He can't take care of Lily all by himself." She covered her face with both hands. Her weeping intensified.

Her freely expressed emotions pointed out his own hollowed-out aching within. No doubt she'd never before seen ragged, grimy children begging. But he had. Urchins—both white and black—had come into camp begging even for hardtack, the worst food ever.

He closed his eyes, trying to block out the memories. Then he looked at his wife. What did one do with a weeping woman? He recalled the few times he'd seen his mother cry and how his father had handled it.

Uncertain, he put an arm around her and patted her back, mimicking his father's words. "There, there."

It worked.

She stepped closer and rested her head against his chest, quieting. The fragrance she always wore, which reminded him of lilacs, floated up from her hair. He nearly bent and kissed the top of her head. But he held himself in check. His father had never kissed his mother when comforting her. And Asa and Judith were married but not close…his fault.

"Asa, what are we going to do? We can't let two little children continue to live in a cave in the woods."

She spoke the truth. In the past he could give only what he had in his knapsack to the orphans of the war, but now he had a house and food to share. Yet he didn't know what to say, so he patted her shoulder some more.

"You were very wise about the pie and chores," she said, glancing up.

I was? he thought.

"I could see Colton understood that. When I invited them to lunch, he didn't want to come, but Lily came right along. Someone, some man, has mistreated him. You noticed that, too?"

Asa considered this. "You're right. He came with me but kept his distance, always out of arm's reach. And we're assuming that they are orphans, but they might have run away."

Judith pressed her face into his shirt again. Then straightened. "I hate to think that, but yes, some parents or guardians can be ill-tempered."

Asa almost lost himself looking into her eyes, which shone with tears of concern.

"I think the offer of payment by chores reassured him that you—we—weren't trying to pull something over on him." She looked at Asa, obviously asking for a reply.

"It worked." Those were the only words that came to him.

She nodded. And then sighed and wiped her cheeks with her handkerchief. "I'm sorry to break down like that. I just was so shocked to see children living there. And on top of that, I'm worried that I still haven't heard from home. We sent that letter weeks ago."

Judith began twisting the hankie in both hands. "Emma wrote Father, too. No reply."

Asa shifted from foot to foot. He didn't like talking

about family. "What do you think is keeping him from answering?"

She mangled the lacy scrap of linen some more.

"You can tell me, Judith." His words mocked him. He expected her to trust him, but he didn't want to trust her. Bile rose in his throat.

She moved to sit at Asa's work table. "My brother returned from the war with a bride from Kentucky." She pursed her lips as if hesitant to say more.

Asa said nothing. He couldn't coax her to talk. It felt dishonest of him.

"My sister-in-law, Mabel Joy, is a contentious woman. That's all I'll say."

"Maybe your father can't write…" As soon as the words left his mouth, and he saw her stricken look, he knew he'd said exactly the wrong thing. Contrite, he patted her back again. "Might just be that men aren't good at writing letters."

Again his own words slapped him. He had yet to write his own parents to tell them he'd married Judith. Guilt froze him in place. What kind of son didn't even write his parents when he got married? Had his bride noticed that?

Judith touched his sleeve. "You are probably right. Father was never one to write letters. And if Mabel Joy were a kind woman, she'd have written back or coaxed him into doing so." She sighed.

"Is there a neighbor you could write, or a relative?" Asa suggested.

Judith's eyes brightened. "Of course. Why didn't I think of that?" She squeezed his hand. "Thank you,

Asa. I'll write to our neighbor, and I know she'll write back and give me all the news." She sent him a trembly smile. "So, what should we do about these children?"

He could do nothing but say the truth. "Let's both think on it."

She nodded. "A good idea." She surprised him by standing on tiptoe and kissing his cheek. "Thank you, Asa." Then, as if embarrassed, she hurried out with a wave of one hand.

He stood still, savoring the quick peck on his cheek. With tiny hitching breaths, he was able to relax. It was good to have Judith here. Yet troubling. She caused him to feel his inner lack, his inability to react like a normal man. But so far he'd evidently not revealed his deficiency, his emptiness to her. So far, so good.

In the back of his mind, Asa recalled that he'd heard a husband and wife in the area had died over the winter and there had been children. So after listening to Judith repeat her worries about the children the previous evening, Asa decided he needed more reconnaissance before he took action. He'd go to the fount of all local news and information, Ned Ashford.

So this morning after breakfast and chores, he entered the shadowy store. A few remaining strings of dried apples hung from the rafters and still faintly scented the air. Two women were just finishing up their purchases. He waited, looking over Ashford's supply of ammunition.

When the ladies left, jingling the bell on the door, Asa approached the storekeeper. "Morning."

"Morning. What can I do for you?"

"Could use some more buckshot." Asa knew he must not appear that he came just for information. He didn't want Ashford too interested. These two waifs, proba- bly orphans, had come to Asa's door, and Judith would want to have a hand in deciding what should be done for them. So did he, for that matter. He'd been unable to help orphans in the war-ravaged South, but he could help two here.

As the transaction proceeded, Asa asked in a non- chalant voice, "Didn't I hear that a couple farther out died over winter?"

Ashford looked up, alert. "Yes. Why do you ask?"

Asa had come prepared. "My wife was wondering if anybody needed help with anything. She likes to be a good neighbor."

"You got yourself a good wife there," Ashford said. "Everybody thinks so."

Asa did not like how this comment revealed that he and Judith were the topic of discussion locally, but he ignored this for now. "Do you know what happened to the couple?" Asa prompted Ashford.

"Well, they were nice young people, name of Far- rier, homesteading like you and your wife. We think it might have been pneumonia. Their neighbors, the Smiths, came to church—something they didn't do often." Ashford paused to frown at this. "Anyway, the Smiths said that their neighbors had died and before the ground froze deep, they'd buried them.

"The Smiths asked Noah to come do a graveside ser- vice. He did. A few of us went along, a sad task. Noah

looked at the Farriers' family Bible and some letters
from the Farriers' place to find out if any kin wanted
the children. He wrote. But he never heard back. And
the Smiths had already taken in the two children, a
boy and a girl."

A boy and a girl. Asa concealed his reaction to the
news. This might explain two children without parents.
He wished he'd taken more notice at the time. But the
Farriers had been near strangers to him. "Smiths took
them in?"

"Yes, said that the Farriers and they were distant
cousins, but—" Ashford paused "—if I recall correctly,
the Farriers didn't cotton to their neighbors and never
said anything about being related."

"So the Smiths took in the children." Asa repeated
the information, mentally examining it.

"Yes. Noah Whitmore visited again when the
weather permitted. But the children had been taken in
and were being cared for, so he merely discussed the
matter and offered help. The Smiths turned him down.
And that was that."

Asa nodded, paid for the buckshot. "Sad story."

"It's a hard life on the frontier. You take care of that
sweet wife of yours."

"Will do." Nobody and nothing were going to get
past him to Judith. And now he knew that Judith would
make sure these children were taken care of for her
peace of mind. And his own peace of mind, for that
matter. The wary look in the boy's eyes wouldn't leave
him alone, either. And hands down, he couldn't ignore
two children living in the wild alone.

Out in the sunshine, Asa wandered over to the blacksmith. He waited till Levi, in his leather apron, finished
the horseshoe he was pounding on the anvil, making
sparks fly. The heat from his fire warmed Asa's face
uncomfortably.

"Hello." Levi swiped a grimy cloth over his sweaty
face.

Asa returned the greeting. "Need to know if you ever
heard of the Farriers or the Smiths."

Levi looked thoughtful. "The Farriers died last winter. Sad. The Smiths were their neighbors. Why do you
ask?"

"Tell you later. Need to know where the Smiths'
place is."

Levi motioned toward the trail that followed the river
north. "Head up to the Chippewa River. Follow it west
about four miles. That's where they live."

"Thanks." Asa turned to leave.

Levi said, "Let me know if you need any help."

Asa thanked him again. Levi reminded Asa of what
he had once been, a young man who had not been
drained and polluted by the war. He liked to talk to
Levi and enjoy the easy friendship they shared. But
now he had to go home and discuss the children with
Judith. He thought he knew what to do, but he wanted
to hear what she had to say. His wife had a good grasp
about people.

And she had more than that. Judith's open-hearted
ways were a temptation to him, and her soft voice had
a way of swirling inside him, rustling the dry leaves
of his heart. He stopped his thoughts there. The two of

them were working out a way to live together just as he wanted, respecting each other's privacy. His mind tried to bring up the sensation of her lips on his cheek. He shoved it away. Or at least, he tried to.

That evening at supper, Asa cleared his throat. "I went to town and talked to Ashford."

Judith looked into his eyes. "Oh?"

He didn't want to talk, but he needed to get her ideas, see if she'd come to the same conclusion he had. "I found out that a couple named Farrier did die this winter." He filled her in on the details, scant as they were. "The Smiths probably wanted the children for work on the farm." Done, he waited for her to comment.

She worried her lower lip. "I don't think the children would have left the Smiths'—was it...?"

He nodded.

"...without good cause. They are too young to be rebellious, like children somewhat older than they are can be. It sounds like something bad happened at the Smiths'."

"That's what I thought, too."

"I will pray about it. God brought them to us. They need us but are afraid. I don't know how to overcome that."

"Right." Asa had exhausted what he wanted to bring up, and she had reinforced what he thought of the situation. Judith would pray and he would come up with a plan. In his experience, prayer didn't always help. It hadn't in the war. Images of starving children buffeted him. He closed his eyes, wishing he could banish the cruel memories.

* * *

A cloudless sky overhead, Asa rode his chestnut horse. He'd already reached the Chippewa River and was heading east, nearing the Smiths'. Two days had passed since the children had sat at his table. Yesterday his wife carried food to the children at their cave. He'd stayed away, concerned that he might spook them and cause them to bolt if he came too near.

Of course, he had work to do today, but planting time hadn't come yet, so he could look for the Smiths. Ever since finding the children, his wife had not been her usual cheerful self. The plight of Lily and Colton was weighing on her. He'd heard her crying last night. The sound had motivated him to venture out today.

Overhead, crows swooped, and then a falcon screeched. The frontier had a special peace, one undisturbed by train whistles, steam engines, gunfire, hoarse shouts, the chaos of battle. He shook his head, trying to shake away the sudden fire of many cannons blasting in his memory. Smoke. The stench of death and screams of wounded men and animals.

He stopped his horse and drew in deep breaths, letting the calm of the forest wrap around him, the truth of his current situation settle in his heart. It was very unlikely that anyone here was lying in wait for him, aiming a rifle at him. He closed his eyes. Then opened them and urged his horse forward, following a track through the trees, the river rushing nearby.

He came around another river bend and happened onto a clearing with a cabin and barn. Asa sized up the homestead. And decided Mr. Smith didn't know what he was doing. The man had built too close to the river, which had been steadily rising with the snowmelt. He'd be flooded out if spring brought heavy rains.

Asa called the common frontier greeting when approaching a dwelling. "Hello the house!"

A woman opened the door and looked out. A man came out of the barn, carrying a rifle. He barked, "Get inside, woman."

The woman obeyed, shutting the door.

"What do you want?" the man called out. He kept the rifle down but held it in both hands, ready to raise it.

Asa didn't want to make hasty assumptions. He himself was cautious with strangers. He'd come armed with a pistol at his belt and a rifle where he could reach it. He realized that he'd not thought up a plausible reason for coming. He didn't want to let on about the children if they'd run away from here. He racked his brain for a good excuse.

He saw a gray-and-white kitten peeping out of the barn door. "I'm Brant. Live near town."

"Yeah?"

"Yes. Heard that you might have some kittens for sale. I need barn cats."

The man eyed him. "Who told you that?"

"Storekeeper."

"That old woman in pants." The man snorted.

Asa bridled at the insult to Ashford. Yes, the storekeeper liked to talk, but it was no reason to speak that way about him. Asa nodded toward the kitten and another that had wandered outside. "Well, do you have an extra pair I could have?"

The man rubbed his stubbled face and squinted up at Asa. Then he dropped one hand from his rifle. "Sure. Cat had a litter of six this time."

"I'd like to take two off your hands. Once I plant corn, the mice will come running."

The man chuckled at this.

"Your cat a good mouser?"

"If she wasn't, I wouldn't keep her."

"So let's do business." Asa slid from his horse.

The haggling over the price of two barn kittens allowed Asa more time to size up the homestead and the man. The man was rough and his place disorganized, sloppy. Asa didn't respect a man who didn't know how to take care of what he owned.

When he finally paid a price he deemed exorbitant for the cats, he was ready to leave this man. He scooped up the kittens and stuck them, heads out, one in each deep chest pocket of his jacket and buttoned them in. They were tiny, probably just old enough to leave their mom. Mewing, they dug their little claws into him, holding on for dear life.

Asa mounted, tipped his hat toward the woman staring out the window at him. He felt Smith's gaze on his back as he rode away. Around the bend he was happy to be within his sight no longer. Something about Smith just didn't feel right. Asa pushed this thought aside. The kittens were mewing and trying to climb out of his pockets, their little noses peeping out. He began murmuring to them about his house, his cow and its good milk, and his wife Judith.

Thinking of her caused him to urge his horse to pick

up a little more speed. He wanted to be home—home where a neat, pretty woman would no doubt be making something good to eat. He glanced up at the calm blue sky, wishing he could be more for her. She deserved the best. A man who still had feelings to share.

"Judith!"

She heard Asa's voice, interrupting the cooing mourning dove. The bird had been sounding its lonely call as she waited for Asa to return. She stepped outside. Where had he been gone all these hours? He'd eaten breakfast and the next thing she knew, he was riding away. She pressed her lips together, holding back a scolding. She didn't know Asa well enough for that. "Yes?"

Then she glimpsed two little furry gray-and-white heads peeping out of his jacket pockets. "Kittens! Wherever did you get them?" She hurried forward.

He slid from the saddle, lifted out one kitten and handed it to her.

She accepted the ball of fur. "Oh, so tiny." She petted its head with one finger. "So soft." She glanced up, smiling. "Where did you get them?" she repeated.

"A homestead north of here."

"I've missed our cats and dog." She reached out and touched the other one. Then she looked up, wondering at this development. What was going on in her husband's head?

"We need to talk." Asa lifted out the other kitten for her. "I'll unsaddle." He turned, leading his horse, and she followed him. She didn't enter the barn but paused at the door.

His comment was unexpected and somewhat cryptic. Talk about what? She knew what she wanted to bring up again, the plight of the cave children, but instead she cuddled the kittens near her cheeks, luxuriating in the soft, silken fur. And waited, hoping Asa would explain. Then she'd made up her mind whether to ask him if they could somehow persuade the children to come for a visit. Someone needed to decide what to do about those poor waifs. She would gladly take on the responsibility, but Asa was the husband, the man of the house, the head of their new family. He must lead. And she must follow.

Asa lifted off the saddle and proceeded to put away his tack. "Talked to Ashford, you know."

"Yes." She waited.

He began currying his horse. "Decided to find the people who I think took in Colton and Lily after their parents died. Went to see them today."

It hurt that he hadn't discussed this with her before he'd gone, but whining about it wouldn't help her cause, which was to get those children out of that cold cave. She quelled her reaction. "I'm glad. What did you find?"

"Wouldn't leave a dog in their care," Asa said, sounding angry. "The man was a rough sort, and his wife looked cowed. Got a bad feeling just being there."

"Oh, dear." Judith's ready sympathy was stirred. The kittens strained to get down, but she held on to them.

"I bought the kittens so he wouldn't wonder why I'd just popped up out of the blue." He began brushing the horse's mane. The animal leaned into his hand as if enjoying the attention.

"Good thinking." She crooned to the two little ones, trying to think up names for them.

He chuckled. "I'm a silver dollar shorter than when I left."

"A silver dollar for two kittens?" The price shocked her.

"Yes, I got him down from a dollar apiece." He finished dealing with the horse and led the animal outside, heading to their pasture, where it could graze under the trees with their tiny leaves.

Judith kept up with him.

"Need to get those children out of that cave," Asa said. "Orphans that young won't make it."

Judith couldn't hold back her relief at his words. "Oh, Asa, I've been so worried for them."

His horse nudged him as if asking for a treat. Asa stroked his nose. "Stayed on my mind, too." Then, on the flat of his hand, he held out a sugar cube from his pocket, and the horse took it. "Invite them to another meal and afterward, ask them to stay. They need someone to look after them. And they came to our door."

Judith hurried forward and touched Asa's arm. "Thank you. I didn't know what to do."

He turned to her. "Well, I don't know, either, except that we can't do nothing."

Judith nearly kissed his cheek again.

But her husband, as skittish as a colt, shied away slightly.

Smiling in spite of this, she carried the kittens inside, praying for the children, praying that God would enable the youngsters to trust them. She worried that when she went back to the cave again, Colton and Lily might be gone. She rubbed the kittens' furry heads under her chin as she had as a child. She remembered her first kitten, and that brought her father to mind.

Why hadn't she heard from him yet? And it would be a while before she heard from the neighbor she'd written to. Then she stopped to give thanks for her husband going to find out about the children. *He is a good man.* She knew this, but when it came to their marriage, something tightly bound him, holding him back from her. *Dear Father, give me wisdom. And please let us help the children. Show me how. Show us how.*

Chapter Five

A clap of thunder. Judith jerked awake. Sudden rain pounded on the roof, making it hard for her to hear anything but the steady beating. Remembering the roof at home, she looked up, not surprised to see no leaks. Asa Brant was not the kind of man to allow his roof to leak.

"Judith," Asa said loudly just outside the bedroom curtain-door, "It's after dawn. I'm going to the barn—"

Lightning streaked outside the window, and almost immediately, thunder shook their cabin. Judith leaped out of bed and hurried to the curtain. "Asa! That's very close. Should you go out?"

Another lightning strike. Boom! A tree nearby sounded as if it had exploded.

Judith plunged through the curtain and clung to Asa. Like a boxer, the thunder pounded the cabin. The window panes rattled. Rain mixed with sleet sluiced down the windows, running, rushing away. She wrapped her arms around her husband's chest, feeling the strength of him, breathing in his distinctive scent, her cheek against the soft flannel of his shirt. Asa's arms encircled her, protecting her. She shivered with each blast of thunder throughout the violent assault overhead and all around.

Then the unusually violent storm moved on, not lessening, just no longer overhead.

She realized she'd been holding her breath and released it. "That was...frightening." Then she remembered that she was in Asa's arms and still wore only her nightgown. "Oh." She retreated swiftly to the bedroom. She babbled, "I'll be out right away and get busy with breakfast."

"No hurry."

She heard the door open, the insistent rain louder. Then the door shut, the rain hushed and she was alone again. She shook herself. She shouldn't feel abashed. The storm had shocked her out of her reticence. And into her husband's protection.

After all, Asa was her husband, and her full, heavy flannel nightgown revealed only her hands, head and stocking feet. She sat down for a moment. The new kittens scampered into the room and leaped onto her bed. That jogged her mind.

All thought about herself vanished—and she remembered the children. Alone in this storm. Would they come when invited? What would she and Asa do if they didn't?

At the breakfast table, Judith waited till Asa finished saying his brief grace. "I'm worried about the children weathering this storm."

Chewing, Asa considered her.

She waited.

"Is their cave deep enough to provide cover?" he asked.

Judith consciously relaxed herself, taking her cue from his calm question. Asa was right. She needed to think, not just worry. Glancing at the kittens asleep by the fire, she picked up her fork. "It had a rock projecting over the entrance. I don't know how deep it was, though. I just glanced at it."

Asa gazed at a point over her right ear. "I reckon they must have left the Smiths only when the snow melted. Not easy to be tracked then. Boy's pretty smart."

That might have been true, but he was still just a child. "It would have been a few days before the Ashfords and Emma came, and the pie disappeared."

"So they've been on their own a little over a week." Asa folded his hands above his plate. His strong, capable hands always reassured her. "They should be coming to the conclusion that they need help."

"But you saw how skittish Colton acted, and you met Mr. Smith. The children are afraid of getting back into a bad situation. That makes sense, but how do we show them they can trust us?"

Asa gazed at her then, seeming to weigh her words.

She waited, resisting the urge to prompt him to speak. *How can we help them, Asa?*

"When this rain has passed," he said finally, "go invite them for a visit. Just a visit. Don't want to spook them. Make them run again."

She tried to figure out his final words. Ah, so Asa thought if they feared that she and Asa would force

them, they might run from the relative safety of the
cave. Her tension eased. "I will, Asa." And though she
had no appetite, she began eating the warm, honeyed
oatmeal, wishing she could share some with the children. She almost felt guilty as she ate.

"Take them nothing but food."

His flat statement gave her pause. She tilted her head
in question.

"Can't stay on their own. A blanket or anything will
just keep them out there longer. They must feel their
need is greater than their fear."

How had he known she'd just thought of taking them
a blanket? Bowing her head, she nodded. "I will do as
you say. It makes good sense." She rested one hand on
the table very near his, wishing he might reach for hers.

For a moment, she recalled him holding her through
the intense storm. Yes, Asa would always protect her,
and he cared about these poor orphans. He'd gone to
the Smiths'.

Once again she wondered what he guarded so closely
inside himself. Wondered about what kept him bound
up, trapped, which bound her and their relationship up,
too. But he had told her to take food to the children and
she would, with gratitude.

After washing up, Judith packed a few butter-and-
jelly sandwiches, a half-dozen oatmeal raisin cookies
and a jar of fresh milk. The storm had moved far east
of them, but outside everything dripped, and downed
branches littered the clearing around their cabin. In the
shade, some hail still lay white and frigid.

She stopped at the barn door. She hadn't appreciated Asa not telling her where he was going when he'd
found the Smiths. But she had done the same to him,
not telling him when she'd set the cake trap.

She hoped that they could start working together,
more as they had in discussing the children, not just living almost in parallel. "I'm going now, Asa. I shut the
kittens in the cabin so they wouldn't try to follow me."

"Good."

She bid him goodbye, and off she went in her rubber boots, into the trees. From the tall, tall pines, an
occasional rain drop plunked onto the top of her bonnet. By the time she reached the cave, her boots were
liberally coated with mud. And she shivered from the
damp chill in the air.

"Children!" she called out, approaching the cave.
"It's me. Mrs. Brant!"

Looking damp, Colton was tending a small fire at
the opening of the cave. A welcome sight. At least they
had some warmth. The boy rose and gazed at her. His
expression mixed wariness and relief.

"I brought food." She stooped down near the fire and
drew out what she had. She glanced around. "Where's
Lily?"

"She's sleeping," he said, unwrapping a sandwich.
He nearly shoved it whole into his mouth.

"Sleeping? This late?"

He chewed and swallowed. "The storm woke her.
She fell asleep again after it passed."

Judith tried to decide whether she should worry about
this. She wanted to crawl into the cave to see Lily for

herself, but Colton and the fire blocked the entrance. "Colton, Mr. Brant has told me to invite you and Lily to come for a visit."

The boy stopped eating and stared at her. "We're fine. My traps work most every day, and soon there'll be stuff to pick. My pa taught me. Lily and me'll do fine."

"But we'd love to have you—"

"Thanks, ma'am, but I'm taking care of Lily. We'll be fine."

She studied Colton's face. She read there—in equal parts—determination and resistance. Judith swallowed words of opposition. Two children alone in a cave. Maybe they could make it through the summer, but again, what of the coming winter? "Very well, but the invitation will remain open. And if you need anything, you can come to us." Asa hadn't told her to add that, but she couldn't help herself.

"Ma'am, thanks for the food. I'll make sure Lily eats."

She found herself holding back offers of a blanket, soap, a comb. These two needed her for much more than food. Instead she straightened. "Well, then, I'll head back home."

"Thanks again!" the boy called after her as she forced herself to walk away.

She waved, afraid if she turned back, she'd grab both children and try to drag them home.

When she reached her clearing, she went straight to the barn. Asa stood in the doorway, working beside the sawhorse table on his leather goods. "Colton said Lily was sleeping. He had a fire going at the opening of their cave, so I couldn't go in and check on her. He refused our invitation."

Asa looked up. "Probably been picking up downed wood and storing it inside. Smart boy."

She worried her lower lip. "Everything is still soaked, the spring dampness is coming up from the thawing ground and it's chilly."

He plainly considered this, gazing down and working at the leather with both hands. "The boy must figure it out. He can't take care of his sister, do it all by himself."

She knew he was right, but that didn't make it any more palatable. She turned to go in the house to begin her chores.

"No more food," Asa said to her.

She swung back, startled. "What?"

"That's hard. But the quickest way. They get hungry enough, they'll come."

Judith didn't want to agree, but how could she disagree with his common sense? Still, worry churned in her midsection. "Very well, Asa." She proceeded into the house, where she pulled off her muddy boots and damp jacket.

She began praying as she moved to the kitchen counter to check on lunch, which was simmering over the fire. For a moment she paused, gripping the edge of the counter, drawing the strength to face this and follow Asa's sensible advice. *Father, bring the children home, here.*

The next day came. Though she didn't want to leave home, hoping that the children might come at any time, Judith walked to town to join the quilting circle. A sharp west wind whipped at the trees. She pined over the children. She'd so hoped that the chilly, damp night would have brought them to their door for breakfast. But no. Worry for them plagued her like a stitch in the side, a physical ache.

Asa had been more somber than usual at the breakfast table. She had gotten maybe ten words from him. Did that mean he was worrying, too?

At the top of the stairs behind the general store, she shed her muddy rubber boots and shook off a sudden tightening of her nerves. This would be her first social occasion alone with women of the town. She wanted to make a good impression. She knocked.

Mrs. Ashford called, "The door's open! Come in!"

Judith stepped inside and shivered once from the difference from the damp cold outside and the warmth inside. And she smelled fresh coffee as she hung her shawl and bonnet on the pegs by the door. She followed the sound of voices to the front room, where ladies were gathered around the dining table. "Hello."

A chorus of women's voices greeted her. Mrs. Ashford sprang up from her place at the head of the table and urged Judith to take the seat next to her sister. Judith sank into the proffered seat and shyly looked around at the faces turned to her.

Most of which by now looked familiar. Mrs. Ashford repeated the names for her: Sunny, the preacher's wife; Lavina, the woman who led the singing on Sundays; Ophelia, a school board member's wife; and of course, Amanda needed no introduction.

"A few are missing. Mrs. Lang, Ellen Lang," Mrs.

Ashford said, "Pepin's first schoolteacher, couldn't come out today. Sick baby."

"And Nan Osbourne," Sunny added. "She wasn't up to coming, so she said she'd watch our children."

Judith smiled at everyone and said all that was polite. Outside the large front windows, she saw the same thick layer of clouds that had hung over them since the hard rain. She tried not to think of the children in the cave. A day had passed since she last took them food. *Father, please don't let Colton wait too long.*

Worry acid bubbled low in her stomach. She brought up another polite smile. "What are we working on?"

"We're making another quilt to send to those Indians up north," Mrs. Ashford said, sounding somehow disapproving and gracious at the same time.

"My son Isaiah is helping an elderly missionary to the far northern tribe," Lavina said, "mostly Chippewa, or some say Ojibwa. There is such want there."

"Yes," Sunny agreed. "We are all working on quilt top squares, and then Mrs. Ashford and Amanda sew them together into a patchwork quilt top on her sewing machine. Then we put the quilt together."

Nodding, Judith drew out her needle, thread and fabric pieces she'd brought north with her with the purpose of beginning a quilt for her own home. Soon she was sewing her square, thinking of the cave children who needed much more than a quilt.

"And how are the newlyweds?" Mrs. Ashford broke the companionable silence.

Judith looked up, her face warming. "We're fine. Just fine." She hoped she sounded convincing. Her husband continued to hold her at arm's length. *Asa just needs to trust me with whatever he is holding back.* The twin worries clutched her heart.

Then they heard rapid footsteps coming upstairs and soon the greeting, "Hello!"

The women all replied, "Rachel!"

A petite woman with light brown hair entered, carrying a pan covered with a cloth. "I tried a new recipe." She whipped off the cloth with a flourish. "Shortbread!"

In all the gaiety of the ladies admiring the square golden cookies and tasting them, Emma leaned close to Judith. "Have you heard from Father? I sent him a letter and haven't heard back. Do you think Mabel Joy would keep our letters from him?"

The thought had not occurred to Judith. "Surely not," she whispered in return.

Then the two sisters were caught up listening to the conversation around them. Judith sampled a sweet, buttery shortbread. "Delicious."

"Rachel is married to the new county sheriff," Mrs. Ashford told Judith and Emma with pride.

"And his son, Jacque, is in my school," Emma added. "He's quite good at spelling."

This launched a full discussion of the upcoming spelling bee. The people here certainly deemed it serious. Judith's mind drifted away to Asa at home and two children huddled in a cold cave.

Asa heard him before he saw him. Stepping to the open barn door, Asa saw Colton running through the brush toward their clearing. The boy's haste alarmed

Asa. He put down the tool he held and stepped outside. "What is it?"

"Where's the lady?" The boy bent over, panting. "We need her."

"She's in town." Asa hesitated, then moved forward. "Where's your sister?"

After staring at him as if coming to a decision, the boy turned and, waving to Asa to follow, began running back the way he'd come.

Asa tried not to think through all the things that could go wrong with two little children alone in a cave. He caught up with the boy, running, hoping Colton hadn't waited too long to admit he needed help. "What's the matter?"

The boy ignored him and ran faster.

Worrying, Asa followed Colton as he burst into the small clearing. He saw the cave opening. "What's wrong?" he repeated. He'd barely said the two words when he heard what was wrong. From inside the cave, a hacking cough, one filled with congestion. He'd heard that in the war, men dying of disease, their lungs filling up. No, not here. "Fever?"

"Yes." The boy stared at him, his hands gripped together, white-knuckled.

Asa bent and crawled into the cave. The little girl lay wrapped in a soiled quilt. "Lily, I'm here."

The little girl's eyelashes fluttered. She looked shrunken and white like a crumpled piece of paper. He'd seen this before in the camp hospitals. She was dehydrated, and that was bad. No. He wouldn't let death have her. Judith would know what to do.

Quickly he tugged her to him and crawled backward out of the cave. When he could, he stood and lifted her into his arms.

"What're you doing?" Colton shrilled.

"Taking her home to my wife." Asa was already running through the woods, his heart racing. The child in his arms was burning with fever. *I should just have come and carried them out of here two days ago.*

Over an hour later, Judith glanced out the window and was shocked to see the west sky had turned a darker, more ominous slate gray. "Looks like another storm moving in."

Heavy boot steps shook the back stairs, and then the door rattled as someone pounded on it.

Mrs. Ashford went toward the sound. "Who is it?"

"Asa Brant! I've come for my wife."

His tone alarmed her. Something was wrong. Quickly stuffing her sewing materials into her bag, she hurried after Mrs. Ashford, who opened the door and let Asa in. Judith began donning her shawl and bonnet. "I was just getting ready to leave, Asa."

"Good." He handed in her boots to her. "Another storm's coming."

Leaning on his arm, Judith put them on quickly. "Thank you, Mrs. Ashford. Goodbye, everyone!"

And then Asa was leading her down the stairs in the stiff wind. To keep up with him, she clung to his arm as they walked swiftly up the trail. The towering pines' tops swayed around them. Something more than this storm had brought him. "What is it?"

Asa leaned close. "Colton came. Lily's sick. I brought her home."

"Sick?"

"High fever. Bad cough."

"Oh!"

"You know what to do?"

"Yes, I do. I just hope—" Lightning crackled, interrupting her.

As they left the town behind, Asa slipped his arm around her waist, half lifting her, helping her to quicken her step.

Her pulse quickening with her pace, she finished silently, "I just hope I know enough to help her." *We should just have brought them home sooner*, she thought.

Soon Judith burst through the cabin door and found Colton sitting beside his sister, who was lying in a soiled quilt before the fire. The sight increased her concern from a simmer to a boil.

She turned to Asa, whose expression begged her to take charge. "Asa, bring down the spare pallet. I'll get the kettle filled with water and start it warming. We need the steam. Colton, stand up and wipe those tears off your face. I'm going to take care of your sister, set her right." Her brave words were for the child and for her. *God, help.*

Asa sprang up the ladder to the loft and hurried down with a bedroll. "Keep her by the fire?"

"Yes. Unroll that pallet and we'll lay her on it."

The little girl moaned as Asa gently moved her onto the pallet.

"What can I do?" Colton asked, wringing his hands.

"Pray," Judith commanded. "Asa, get him some food and milk. I don't want two sick children. One is enough." She ran into her room and brought out a chemise. Soon she had the child out of Asa's sweat-soaked and probably rain-soaked shirt dress and into the fresh, much-too-big but dry chemise. She went to a shelf and brought down her mother's medicine chest.

Returning to the fireside, she paused to examine the little girl more completely. Flushed face. High fever. Coughing. She listened—was it croup? No, but definitely congested.

"Is she going to die?" Colton asked, his voice shaking. He sat in the corner by the stone fireplace.

"I don't think so…"

The boy burst into tears. "I shoulda come when you asked us."

"Boy, you aren't old enough to have to care for yourself and Lily," Asa said.

Judith wished he'd softened the rebuke, but it was the truth.

"But I'm all she's got," the boy wailed and turned away.

Judith knelt by Lily and applied camphor to the girl's neck and chest. Then she began bathing the little girl's face with alcohol to lower her fever. "You've got us." She hazarded a glance at Asa. Would he repudiate her words? No. And in his usually closed face, she glimpsed a flash of stark worry.

The next dawn glimmered at the windows. Stiff, Judith sat in the rocker where she'd spent the night. She had prayed all night and ached from sitting. A few times over the long hours, Lily had surfaced from her fevered delirium and had been able to sip broth and willow bark tea. Yet her fever still raged. Colton slept in the corner by the fireplace, wrapped in a blanket. The scent of camphor hung in the air.

Asa climbed quietly down the loft ladder. "Is she better?" he whispered.

Touched by his concern, Judith couldn't help herself. She held out her hand to him.

Though ignoring her hand, he went to the chair near her and sat down. He repeated his question.

She drew her hand back, trying not to show disappointment. "I think it's influenza. I can tell her body aches from the way she moans whenever she moves. I'm doing my best for her. But it's bad. Yet it should run its course, and then I just need to make certain that in her weakened state, nothing else gets the best of her."

"Lily's gonna be all right?" Colton sat up, rubbing the sleep from his eyes.

"Mrs. Brant is doing her best," Asa replied. "Judith, I'll start the coffee. You sit."

"Please, Asa. I'm tired of sitting. I'll make the breakfast. But we need more wood, please."

Asa motioned to Colton. "Come on."

Judith's hand still longed for Asa's reassuring touch. When would she learn not to reach for him? He was a caring man—or the children wouldn't be here. Why hadn't she been born prettier? She blinked away tears. She had no time for them. She must be thankful for what she had.

* * *

The boy followed Asa out into the chilly morning and over to the woodshed. Asa loaded the boy's arms with short quartered logs and then did the same for himself. Seeing the girl sick had stirred past scenes in his mind, ones he had tried to forget. Even in the midst of a war, the death of a child had moved all his men to pity. He blinked rapidly as if he could banish the image of standing mute at a graveside, a very small grave.

"Colton," he said, his voice coming out harsh, "you two will not be going back to that cave. You can't take care of Lily all by yourself. Not even for the summer. And in the winter?" Asa shook his head no.

Colton took a step back, his expression fierce.

"Storekeeper told me what happened to your family. I went to the Smiths'."

Colton jerked backward as if Asa had shoved him. His face twisted with a combination of fear and anger.

"Don't worry. I wouldn't leave a dog with that man." Again he couldn't stop the harshness in his voice.

Colton just stared at him. "Is that where you got the kittens?"

Asa gazed at the child. "Yes."

Colton nodded. "I thought they looked like our cat, Sadie. You won't send us back to him?"

"No." Asa led the boy the short distance to the cabin. He wouldn't take him back to the Smiths. The children had to be taken care of, but was he the man to do it? "I will not let Smith or anyone else who…shouldn't have children take you. Trust me?"

Colton looked up at him just as they reached the door. And paused just a moment. "Yes, sir."

Asa pushed open the door and let the boy go in first. Asa felt the weight of this new responsibility settle over him. But what choice did he have? He was an empty shell. He was not fatherly in any sense, but he could protect and support these children just as he did Judith. These children wouldn't suffer more. Might even be a family close to town that would be better for them anyway. A family with two loving parents.

For the third night in a row, Judith sat in the rocker, wrapped in a blanket. Lily remained delirious with fever and moaning.

"Mama," Lily muttered. "Mama."

The simple word ignited inside Judith, and the same words echoed in her heart. Weren't there times when they all wanted their mothers? Somehow one's mother was the person who could set everything right.

Judith unwrapped herself and slid off the rocker, onto the wood floor. Feeling the warmth emanating from the child, she began to bathe Lily's face again, trying to evaporate the heat from her skin. Afraid of pneumonia, Judith had elevated Lily's head and shoulders with a bolster.

"Mama, Mama," the little girl moaned.

Tears, held back for weeks, flowed down Judith's face. *Mama, I need you. I've married a man who doesn't love me and probably never will.*

She swallowed down the tears, drawing on her well of faith in God's strength. *Dear Father, I'm doing all I can.*

Please let this child live. Her brother will feel so guilty if she dies. He did his best to protect and provide for her. Forgive me for not overriding Colton and just having Asa bring them here. I didn't know what to do. And Father, teach me how to be the wife Asa needs. He's caught in some trap I don't understand. Give me Your compassion.

Then the little girl began to jerk, thrash, her eyes open, unseeing. Judith pressed her hand to her heart. Convulsions. *What to do?* She repeated the phrase over and over.

Then, frantic, she got up and carried Lily outside into the chill air, the girl jerking in her arms. In the moonlight she ran to the pump and, laying the child down, began to pump water.

It worked. The cold water shocked the child's body. Lily stopped convulsing. Judith pumped a few more times and then heard the cabin door open.

A tall form, Asa, moved toward her. "What is it?" He nudged her away from the pump.

She held up a hand. "That's enough water. Carry her inside. Take her back near the fire, but not on the pallet."

He obeyed without question.

She ran into her room and grabbed another clean, dry chemise. Back in the main room, Asa retreated into the darkness.

Judith stripped off the sopping chemise and tossed it behind her. She heard Asa lift it and hurry outside. She quickly dried the now shivering girl and slipped on the fresh chemise. The cold water had shocked the girl out of convulsions. But would this help her or make her sicker?

Chapter Six

"Ma'am...ma'am?"

In the dim morning light, Judith sat up, alert, and looked down.

Lily was gazing up at her and appeared to be in her right senses.

"Lily." She dropped to her knees on the pine floor and felt the girl's now cool forehead. Relief sighed through her. "Your fever's broken."

"Thirsty," the little girl whispered hoarsely.

Judith immediately rose and fetched the water dipper. She supported Lily's small shoulders and helped her sip the water.

Lily drank it all and then collapsed against Judith. "My back hurts."

From all the lying. Judith set down the dipper and helped Lily sit up. "Do you think you can stand?"

The girl tried and was able to pull herself up with Judith's help.

Colton stirred from his place by the fire. He sat up and rubbed the sleep from his eyes. "Lily?"

"Col…ton."

The boy shot to his feet and scrambled to his sister. "You've been sick."

"Yes, but her fever's broken at last," Judith said. "I'm going to help her sit in my rocker so she can watch me make oatmeal for breakfast. You'll like oatmeal, won't you, Lily?"

"Yes," she said, and the girl's stomach rumbled.

The two kittens pranced over to see what was happening. "Oh, kitties," Lily cooed.

Each moment that showed Lily's recovery set Judith's spirit soaring. *Thank You, God. Thank You.* She helped Lily onto her rocking chair, draped the blanket over her lap and then turned to Colton. "Sit and talk to your sister."

"He'll come with me. We got to bring in wood," Asa said as he came down the ladder from the loft.

Colton left his sister and went to the door. The eager-to-play kittens leaped into Lily's lap.

Asa paused by Judith. "Her fever broke?"

"Yes." Resisting the urge to draw nearer him, Judith lowered her voice and continued, "But she'll need careful tending to recover fully."

Asa nodded and then led Colton outside.

"Ma'am, I'm hungry," Lily said.

Judith rejoiced. "I'll have breakfast done right away." She hurried to the kitchen and began the routine of preparing the morning meal.

Feeling battered by the past few days, Judith had

nearly reached for Asa again. She stood a moment to steady herself, regain her bearings. Her gruff husband had gone to that wretched cave and brought the children here. He'd gone to the Smiths and returned with two kittens. Actions spoke louder than words, she reminded herself, and forced herself to begin humming to cheer Lily, to cheer herself.

Only a little over a week had passed, but Lily, getting stronger day by day, was standing beside Judith, who had measured her for a new dress. One kitten played around the little girl's feet, rolling on its back and batting at the frayed strings that hung down from the girl's ragged chemise hem. This little girl and her brother were becoming dear to Judith. Was that a mistake? Her husband gave her no indication of what he wanted in this situation.

"I haven't had a new dress since…" The child's voice trailed off.

A pang around her heart, Judith silently filled in the blank—*"since my mother died."* "Well, we'll be going to church this Sunday, and you both need Sunday clothes." She and Asa had missed last week because they hadn't wanted to leave the children, and Lily had not been well enough yet to go to town.

"Church?"

"Yes. You remember church, don't you?" Judith asked, feeding the rosy pink fabric under the bobbing needle, listening to its metallic rhythm.

"Is it like everybody in the schoolhouse? And people singing?"

"Yes." Judith paused in pressing down the foot treadle. She heard hoofbeats and looked out the window. "We have company." Noah Whitmore had come. Why? Was it about the children? Or something completely separate? Well, either way, the children would be discussed. Feeling herself frown, she smoothed her forehead.

Lily sidled closer to Judith.

"Don't worry. I see that the preacher is come to call." Judith touched the thin little shoulder. "And Mr. Brant is here. He won't let anyone hurt you."

"He's strong and big, but he doesn't hit me."

The comment squeezed Judith's heart tighter. She had a thing or two or three she'd like to say to Mr. Smith. Instead, she rested an arm around Lily. "Let's open the door and greet the preacher." *And hope he's not here to suggest you go elsewhere.*

The weather, now nearing May, had warmed, but intermittent April showers had kept them inside while Lily recuperated. She was still too thin and pale, and she tired easily. Judith opened the door in time to see Noah Whitmore slip from his saddle and meet Asa and Colton in the shadow at the barn door.

She wondered if perhaps Asa had sent word to Noah concerning the children. Asa had been to the store a few days ago. Again her husband might have done something without talking it over with her. Was that the way of most men? Her father and mother had always discussed matters at the table over coffee. But perhaps that wasn't common. She clamped down her displeasure at not being consulted—if this was to do with the children.

"I'll put a fresh pot of coffee on!" Judith called out,

hoping that would bring the men inside so she could hear the purpose of the visit. She sweetened the offer. "And I have cinnamon cake."

"Be right in, Judith," Asa replied.

Soon the two men and Colton were washing their hands outside the door.

After setting the coffeepot to boil, Judith had hurriedly brought out a carefully folded, starched tablecloth and napkins for their guest. A visit from the preacher was a special occasion. The kittens sat on the floor at the end of the table, watching all this with eager anticipation, in contrast to Judith's apprehension.

By the time Noah entered, doffed his hat and hung it on a peg by the door, the fragrances of coffee and cinnamon filled the air. "Morning, Mrs. Brant."

She observed his concern at seeing children here with them. Of course he had known the Farriers and recognized the children. The normal courtesies of a call were observed, and soon the three adults sat at the table with cups of steaming coffee and the cinnamon cake on plates. Grim-faced, Colton sat next to Asa, while Lily huddled close to Judith.

Noah finally nodded toward the children. "I see you have taken in the Farrier children."

"Ned Ashford filled me in about their parents. That you left these two with the Smiths," Asa said, going straight to the point. His tone and expression announced he wasn't happy that this man had left defenseless children with Smith.

Noah sipped his coffee, obviously waiting for Asa to proceed.

"Visited the Smiths." Disapproval flowed into Asa's tone. "Won't take the children back there." His face set in grim lines. Then he told of the cave and Lily's illness. Lily rested her head in Judith's lap.

Asa's concern for the children touched Judith, but she tightened herself against reading more into this than she should. Asa consistently put himself beyond her reach, but that had nothing to do with his good character. She stroked Lily's silken blond hair, trying to reassure her silently.

Obviously troubled, Noah appeared to weigh his words. "I, too, had reservations about leaving the children in their care. But it was deep winter, hard travel out so far, and I thought they could stay there until we located family for the children to go to."

Asa's expression did not lighten.

"Did you find any family?" Judith asked, trying to offset Asa's disapproval. She should have been happy if family had been found for the children. She should have been.

"The letter I sent was returned to me with a notation that the person no longer lived in the town. So I sent a letter to the Illinois postmaster of the town explaining the situation and asking about the Farrier family."

"What did you hear?" Judith asked, wishing Asa would join the exchange again, not sit there, frowning.

"I haven't heard back," Noah replied.

"Where is the town in Illinois?" she asked, trying to come up with another solution.

"Sterling. A small town near Rockford."

Judith worried her lower lip. "That might be a half-day's ride from my home, my brother's home." If she'd heard from her family, she could ask her brother to ride over there and see what he could find. But neither she nor Emma had heard from their father or neighbor.

"It's hard with so many people moving around," Noah said. "I will write again to the postmaster. The first letter might not have reached him." He looked to Colton. "I was going to check on how you children were faring."

Colton didn't reply in words, but his expression spoke of distrust and resentment. Then, as he watched Asa, Colton asked, "What if Mr. Smith tries to take us back?"

"I said I won't let you children go back there," Asa spoke up.

"And the community will back this decision," Noah said.

Lily relaxed against Judith with a sigh.

"I think God brought you to the right door, children," Noah said. "For now. Still, your extended family might be wondering about why they haven't heard from…your parents."

"I like it here," Lily said, snuggling closer to Judith.

But Judith didn't know whether Asa wanted to keep the children or meant to keep them only till other arrangements could be made. Taking on the responsibility of two children when they'd been married a tad over a month might not be wise. She still didn't understand her husband enough to know what had caused him to take these children in other than their dire necessity and his Christian duty.

Once again she recalled him riding to the Smiths' and bringing home kittens. Would she ever understand the silent man she'd married who usually did the right thing but remained a closed book to her?

On Sunday morning, Asa sat in church, feeling the attention of everyone present on him. His collar tightened from their scrutiny. He'd felt the same scrutiny on the first Sunday after he'd wed Judith and now again with the two Farrier children and his wife beside him. How had this happened? He'd been alone for so long.

"As you have noticed," Noah said from the front at the teacher's lectern, "the Brants have taken in the Farrier children." At this, every gaze would have turned to them—if everyone hadn't already been staring or trying not to.

Asa sat straight and focused on Noah. How had he gotten himself into this position? He felt aggrieved, but at himself.

"The Brants found the children living in a cave," Noah continued.

A horrified gasp swept through the church.

Noah continued the story of the missing pie and onward.

From the corner of his eye, Asa glimpsed Lily burying her face in Judith's arm. So he wasn't the only one who didn't like being on display. He glanced down at Colton, who sat straight just like Asa and was staring darts at Noah. Plainly Colton did not forgive easily.

For two years, Asa had lived here alone, kept to himself, minded his own business. Then, when the solitude had become unbearable, he'd married Judith, and now these two children had come. One thing led to another.

Where would this take him? He collected himself, making sure nothing of his inner turmoil showed outwardly.

But he couldn't quell the shifting emotions within. Faces from that day at Gettysburg flashed through his mind. His heartbeat pounded as if he were running. He gripped his self-control tighter.

"Peace. Be still." The words Noah had just spoken startled Asa from his inner turmoil. They were words he'd heard many times in the past and now they whispered through him. He looked forward, realizing that Noah had begun reading from the Gospel of Mark, the story of Jesus sleeping through the storm on the Sea of Galilee.

"'And he was in the hinder part of the ship, asleep on a pillow: and they awake him, and say unto him, Master, carest thou not that we perish?

"'And he arose, and rebuked the wind, and said unto the sea, Peace, be still. And the wind ceased, and there was a great calm.

"'And he said unto them, Why are ye so fearful? How is it that ye have no faith? And they feared exceedingly, and said one to another, What manner of man is this, that even the wind and the sea obey him?'"

Asa had heard this passage spoken aloud before and had read it many times himself. But today he found himself longing for this peace with a physical yearning. The war had been over for eight years, and he still had no peace. He still hadn't truly come home. He resisted the urge to rest his head in his hands, but holding up his head had become hard labor.

Noah's voice repeated in his mind. *"'Why are ye so fearful? How is it that ye have no faith?'"*

Fear. He'd never known real fear—teeth-chattering and nauseating fear—till he'd faced his first battle. He glanced around the schoolroom, picking out others like Noah who truly understood fear. Yet the fear in battle was nothing like the horror afterward.

Again, black powder–darkened faces of men who died that day at Gettysburg streamed in his mind, and he watched them die again. Battle sounds—gunfire, cannons, the Rebel yells, screams—bombarded him. So many had died, yet he'd lived.

Noah's firm voice continued. The word *peace* penetrated the din within Asa's mind.

Still, he sat without moving as guilt rolled over him like a river at flood, drowning him, burying him alive. He tried to breathe normally, calm his heart.

Lord, I want to be free of it. I want peace. Please.

He'd never prayed that before. He panted silently, secretly. Then he felt it—Judith's hand on his arm. Just a touch. So light. Gentle. Caring. She deserved him to be free of it. Could he finally shed the past and be the man he wanted to be again?

After the service ended, people crowded around them, offering sympathy to the children, offering help.

Colton shoved his way outside.

People looked shocked and affronted.

"Colton has been through a lot," Judith murmured with Lily huddled close to her side.

Asa headed out after Colton. He saw that the boy was hot-footing it to their wagon. Through the people milling around outside, Asa hurried after him. He caught up with him at the wagon. "Colton?"

The boy turned to him, his expression fierce, angry.

Asa tried to come up with words, but instead he just rested a hand on the boy's shoulder.

"He left us with Smith," Colton said, resentment in each syllable.

"I did, too," Asa said. "Didn't think about you till you came to our door."

Colton looked up, arrested. "He's the preacher."

Asa let this wash over him. Noah was the leader here, and Colton held him responsible. In the war, Asa had been the one in charge, the one in command, too. He looked heavenward as if he could find the answer in the sky, the rain sky, thick with gray clouds. "No one makes the right choice every time, boy. Not even preachers." Not even captains.

Judith and Lily reached them. "Shall we try to get home before the rain starts?" Judith suggested.

"Yes." Asa helped her up onto the wagon bench. Then he lifted Lily to sit between them.

Colton hurried to the rear and climbed up into the wagon bed.

Asa walked around, and as he passed the boy, he touched his shoulder, but said nothing. Colton would have to work this out for himself. *Peace. Be still.* The words were what Colton needed. But since Asa had not been able to heed them before, how could he offer them?

"Asa, we need to make one stop on the way home. My sister has received a letter from the neighbor I wrote back home." Judith's voice was low and unhappy. "We need to stop at the Ashfords' so I can read it with her. She hasn't opened it."

Asa just wanted to get home, but he had no choice. He drove the team the short distance toward the store. Now he'd have to face Mrs. Ashford's constant barrage of words, and behind him Colton, stony-faced, sat bubbling like a closed pot about to burst. What next?

Throughout the worship service, Judith had sensed Asa's struggle with something. She knew that after the service, he'd want to go directly home. But how could she wait till tomorrow to read the letter from home? It had been a month since she'd first written her father and then, at Asa's suggestion, a close neighbor.

The Ashfords had walked to church, and Emma was leading them toward Judith and her family. That term startled Judith. A *family*? Were they a family? She didn't know if Asa would let the four of them become a family.

I can't think of that right now. "I'm sorry, Asa. I know you don't want to stop," she murmured.

"I understand." He halted the team and immediately, without grumbling, left his seat and walked around to help her down as usual. His constant courtesy spoke to her. He'd been raised to be thoughtful, but something—probably the war—had closed him up, robbed him of… She tried to come up with the word. The closest she came was *ease*. Asa was never at ease somehow.

"Judith!" Emma called. "The letter's in my bedroom!"

Her thoughts switched to her sister. Asa's strong hands clasped her waist and swung her down. "Sorry," she whispered again.

"Go on—"

"I want to come," Lily said, rising, holding out her arms to Asa. "Please."

Asa lifted her down, too.

"I'm staying here," Colton announced with obvious rancor.

"You two go on in," Asa said, waving them on. "The boy and I will stay with the horses." He looked up at the rain clouds as if silently urging her not to tarry too long.

Judith ran after her sister up the stairs and into the Ashfords' quarters. Then down the narrow hall to Emma's small bedroom, Lily right behind her.

Emma tossed her bonnet on the bed and lifted the letter from her bedside table. "It has nearly killed me not to open it, but I couldn't do that without you."

"Why did she write to you and not me?" Judith asked, sitting down beside Emma on the coverlet. "I was the one who wrote her." Lily climbed up beside her.

"I don't know." Without waiting another moment, Emma slit open the diamond-shaped paper protecting the letter and unfolded the one page.

Dear Emma and Judith,
I lost Judith's letter, so am sending this to the general store at Pepin since that's where Judith said Emma was living for now. You asked me how matters are at your house. All I can say is that sister-in-law of yours doesn't know how to get along with people. Who raised her? Such dreadful manners, and that awful Southern twang. I've

seen your father at church, but your brother is not in attendance regularly.

I'm afraid people are talking. I'm not adding to the gossip but I don't know why Mabel Joy married your brother if she didn't want to live with us Yankees. And she is no joy to anybody that I can see. Again, this is just for your ears. I know why you two left. And that has not gone over well here, either. A Southerner forcing two lovely girls out of their own home—dreadful. I have braved her "Southern hospitality" to visit your father. He is not better than he was. He spends most days sitting on your porch. No doubt to escape that woman. Well, I wish I had better news for you. But my husband and I are watching matters over there, and if your father needs a place to go, we'll let him come here. Such doings.

Your friend always,

Anne Forthright

"What does it say?" Lily asked, leaning over Judith.

Judith exchanged a look with Emma. Judith was certain that Emma, like she, had heard Anne's familiar voice coming through clearly in this letter. She was a good woman but very direct.

Lily tugged on Judith's sleeve. "Please?"

"Everything's fine," Judith fibbed. "Our father is fine."

Emma rose abruptly and walked to the small window, her back to Judith.

Judith followed and hugged her from behind. "I can't stay longer. Asa is waiting, and it looks like rain."

Emma turned and hugged her in return. "You take the letter or I'll have to read it to Mrs. Ashford." She smiled ruefully.

Judith nodded and tucked the letter into her pocket. She kissed her sister's cheek and hurried out to the parlor. Mrs. Ashford tried to waylay her, but she was saved.

"Rain's starting," Mr. Ashford said, nodding toward the window.

"We must go! Thanks!" Judith led Lily down the stairs in the moist air. Rain sprinkled down on them. They ran to the wagon. Asa lifted both of them onto the wagon bench, and then he was urging the team to take them home.

Judith tucked Lily underneath her arm, protecting her from the rain. The urge to weep over her father's predicament choked her. She raised her face to heaven and let the rain weep for her.

After letting the females off at the door, Asa and Colton drove the wagon into the barn and unhitched the horses, listening to the rain on the roof. Asa glanced around at his haven, the neat, snug barn with the stock, his faithful but silent companions of two years. The kittens came to him, mewing from their favorite spots in the hayloft. Then he turned toward the open doors and the cabin across the yard. The thought of Judith inside laying the table for Sunday dinner pulled at him like a fishing line. But even he could see that she'd gotten bad news in that letter. *I'm no good to her in a time like this.*

But he was her husband.

"We going in?" Colton asked petulantly.

Asa inhaled, patted the rump of the horse nearest him and then led the boy to the barn door and outside. He stowed the kittens into his pockets so they wouldn't get wet feet. Under cover of an oilcloth Asa kept hanging by the barn door, he and Colton ran across the yard.

Stepping inside, Asa turned, shook the oilcloth outside and then hung it to drip-dry on a peg by the door, along with their coats and hats. Colton lifted the kittens out of Asa's pockets and set them on the floor. They leaped around each other happily. Delicious smells drew him toward the table. Soon the four of them sat around the table to a dinner of baked chicken, seasoned with dried sage, and potatoes that had simmered over the fire all morning.

"You cook good," Colton said.

"Thank you," Judith said.

Asa seconded it, observing her downcast face. The news from home must have been really bad. He ate, savoring each bite for its flavor but also because he knew that after dinner, Colton would go back to the barn and convalescing Lily would lie down for a nap, leaving him and his wife alone. This was the calm before the storm of female emotions. He would have to face whatever news had come in that letter.

And his prediction proved accurate.

Soon just the two of them sat alone by the fire. He wanted to join Colton in the barn, but women liked to talk over things—that much he knew. He could at least listen.

"I'm not going to make a fuss," Judith said, glancing at him sideways. She closed her eyes as if drawing up her composure. "The neighbor you suggested I write to—" She paused to touch his sleeve for only a moment.

The touch ignited a spark of warmth within him. It flickered and died. But he'd felt it.

"She wrote to us that our sister-in-law is not…not being kind to my father."

"You said she was a contentious woman."

Judith nodded, as if holding herself in. "There is little I can do. I don't understand my brother. He is a good man. But…after the war—" she frowned "—he has not been himself."

Asa wondered if any of them had come back "themselves." He tried to think of something comforting to say and failed.

Judith sat with her head bowed. "I am going to pray and write back to the neighbor. Asa?" She looked up hesitantly. "I was wondering if I could invite my father to visit us this summer. I think he's well enough, especially since the riverboat is such a comfortable way to travel."

He tried to reply and found his throat dry. He cleared it. "Course. Your father's welcome." He did not want to say the words, but they came anyway. Surely if Judith hadn't recognized his connection to her brother, her father wouldn't, either. But the worry hitched his breath. Nonetheless, he couldn't take the invitation back now.

"You're so good to me." She gazed at him.

He did not believe what she said. She deserved better. And was he supposed to do something else? Say more?

A shriek rent the quiet cabin.

Judith jumped up. "Lily!"

Asa sprang up, too. What would make the child safe in their bedroom cry out?

Chapter Seven

Judith flew through the curtain into the bedroom, leaving Asa standing at the parted curtain.

On the bed, Lily thrashed, clearly in the grips of a nightmare. "Mama! Papa!"

Judith sat on the bed and drew the little girl into her arms. Lily struggled, but Judith held her tightly, murmuring, "You're safe. You're here with me and Mr. Brant. You're safe." She repeated this chant over and over. Her own dear mother's face, undiminished by time, flickered in her mind.

Judith recalled how heartbroken and lost she'd felt the day her mother had been carried away by death. But they'd still had their father. Lily had lost both parents. A ball of emotion lodged in Judith's throat. She refused, *refused*, to give in to tears for the orphans or for herself or for her father's sad situation. Lily didn't need to see her in tears. Judith tightened her face and held the struggling child close, stroking the soft cotton back of her dress.

With a start, Lily woke and blinked. She sobbed a few more times, rubbed her eyes and then gained control. "I had…a bad dream."

"I know. We all have bad dreams sometimes." Judith smoothed the little girl's hair away from her face and wiped her tears with her hankie. "But I'm here. You're safe here."

Swallowing a final sob, Lily nodded and pressed closer to Judith. "You won't let anybody take us away?"

Poor child. Judith allowed herself to glance toward her husband. His face turned down in grim lines. What was he thinking? When he said nothing, she said, "The preacher is trying to find your family. But Mr. Brant has said that he will not let anybody—not even kin—that should not have charge of children take you and your brother. He is a man who keeps his promises." This final phrase, meant to comfort Lily, both comforted and pained Judith.

Her husband had proved to be a trustworthy man. Mrs. Ashford had been right about that. Yet though Judith could count on him, could she ever penetrate the fortress he'd constructed around his thoughts and heart?

She clasped Lily close, giving her one more encouraging embrace. One of the kittens hopped up onto the quilt, and Judith called to it to come closer, another comfort for the child.

Asa let the curtain fall, and she heard him heading to the door, escaping to the barn again, though Colton would be there with him.

Judith sighed silently. God had given her both a wounded husband and these orphans. He must think she measured up to these twin challenges, but right now she did not feel adequate to meet them. God would have to provide what she lacked.

Under a fiercely slate-gray overcast sky, Asa once again found himself in town in the midst of everyone waiting for the big Regional Spelling Bee. Of course, since his wife's sister, Emma, was the schoolteacher, he and Judith and the children could not miss it. And people from the surrounding counties had flocked by water and by boat to see their students compete.

In fact, another school had joined the contest this year. He estimated around fifty people had gathered in the street in front of Ashford's General Store. Thunder rumbled in the distance. Would the spelling bee finish before the next storm arrived?

A platform had been built, and the children took turns mounting it to spell the words that the solemn and bespectacled judges who sat in a row to the side of the platform tested them with. In the surrounding audience, the women sat on benches brought out from the school, and the men stood around in the rear, watching. Everyone took this annual event very seriously. But even during the tense concentration on the words and spellers, people kept casting their gazes skyward. Because another storm was definitely approaching.

Asa noticed then that Colton, who was standing beside him, was silently spelling along with the children. So the boy had some learning, and he should have been in school over the winter. Didn't matter that the Smiths lived farther out. Children should be sent to school.

So far Asa had seen nothing of the Smiths. But it was only a matter of time before the Smiths would find out that the Farrier children had come to them. That didn't bother him. He could handle Smith. Would handle Smith.

And he knew the community would back him and Judith to keep the children till they heard some news from Illinois. Surely there was some decent Farrier left who would want these children. Thunder rumbled again— closer. He glanced skyward. When would this end so he could get his family—that word felt odd, but it was true—safely inside?

In her blue wedding dress with mother-of-pearl buttons, Judith sat on the bench with Lily beside her. Emma perched among the other teachers opposite the judges. For a moment, Judith let the pride over Emma's new position expand within her, feeling the corners of her mouth curve slowly with satisfaction.

In contrast, Emma sat very straight and proper in a subdued but well-cut lavender dress with hand-tatted lace at the high neck and cuff. Nonetheless, it was plain for everyone to see that she was the prettiest schoolmarm here.

And so far, the Pepin students were holding their own in the competition. So even if they lost, no one would be able to say that a poor showing was due to the new schoolteacher. Judith hoped she'd find a moment to tell her sister that Asa had agreed to let her invite their father for a visit.

Worrying lightning flashed over the Mississippi off

to her left, and after several seconds, thunder boomed in the distance, drawing closer. Another storm was advancing.

Judith found herself glancing again toward Asa and Colton. She felt another ripple of pride in her two "men." She'd cut Asa's and Colton's hair for this event, and both looked good in their Sunday best. Her gaze connected with Asa's, and he almost smiled. How could the lifting of one side of his mouth cause her pulse to flutter? She gave him the slightest smile in response and then turned back to the platform, where the sheriff's son, Jacque, a boy with black hair and a thick Southern accent, was spelling *archer*.

The round for the younger students finished. Then the older students stepped forward, the pace quickened and the words became more difficult. The tension in the moist air heightened.

As she mentally spelled the words along with the children, Judith let Lily in her ruffled pink Sunday dress lean against her. Another student from the Pepin school was eliminated for misspelling *mendacious*. But three Pepin students were still in the bee.

Lightning split the sky overhead. Thunder boomed almost immediately. The judges sprang to their feet. "We must finish at the schoolhouse!" said school board member Martin Steward. "Men, pick up the benches and head to the school! Ladies, please take your children directly there!"

The crowd obeyed. Lightning crackled all around them, and thunder exploded over the river and town. As sudden rain pelted, Judith ran with Lily's hand in hers.

The women and children arrived at the schoolhouse, damp and breathless.

Soon the men hustled through the door. In the middle of the milling crowd, they went about setting the benches and platform in place. It was a tight squeeze, which was the reason the spelling bee always took place outside. To ease the crowding, the men opened the connecting door to the unused teacher's quarters so some people could stand or sit there to listen.

Everyone settled in as best they could, crowded together on the benches and against the wall. And though the thunder and crack of lightning periodically interrupted the spellers, the excitement continued unabated.

Judith held her breath as the final Pepin student, a boy named Johan Lang, spelled the word *accommodate* correctly—and won the gold ribbon. The applause echoed in the schoolhouse, rivaling the cascade of thunder that rolled over them.

The ribbons were awarded with much ado, and after one more round of applause for all the spellers, Martin Steward announced that refreshments, cake and fruit punch, would be brought out from the teacher's quarters as soon as possible.

Judith fought her way through the crowd to hug her sister. "Well done, Emma! Well done! Father…" Her voice caught on the word. "Father would be so proud."

"I keep telling everyone that it wasn't due to me. My students were so eager to learn. A pleasure to teach such." Then she leaned forward and whispered, "I received a letter from Mason Chandler yesterday."

Judith felt her eyes open wide. "What did he say?"

"I'll tell you later," Emma whispered before turning to receive more congratulations.

Judith kept her smile in place. Letters often brought good news, but so far none had brought any to her or Emma. Odd that Emma, now the schoolteacher, was the one who'd read the classified ad that had brought them here. Judith had married and Emma remained single. But perhaps that suited Emma, with her sad loss in the war. Only rank necessity had forced them to seek husbands and new homes.

Asa drew near, and she could tell that he wished to leave. But of course, they couldn't without drawing attention to themselves. And rain continued to pour down the windows. She smiled at him, encouraging. "Let's take our turn and get cake."

"Cake. I love cake," Lily said, and then she did something she hadn't before. Already holding Judith's hand, the little girl reached over and took Asa's hand so that she linked them. "Come on, Colton. You like cake."

A warm rush of hope and then a quick slap of reality, and Judith lowered her gaze. Lily was trusting them, but would Judith be able to keep this sweet child who provided so much company in the lonely cabin? Or would someone else claim her?

They let Lily draw them to the table, where a beautiful array of cakes awaited. Soon she and Lily sat on a crowded bench beside the preacher's pretty blonde wife, Sunny, and her little girl, Dawn, who was about the same age as Lily. Dawn immediately began talking to Lily. Nearby, Noah was somehow getting Asa to engage in a conversation. Colton alone did not allow himself to become part of the group. He ate his cake sourly, and no doubt in response to his stiff stance, no one approached him. What could she do to help Colton? Judith did not know.

Sunny glanced at Colton and then back to Judith. "Give him time," she murmured just for Judith's ears. "Time heals. And prayer."

Judith gave a slight nod. She hoped the woman was right. She'd already faced a challenge with Asa, and now she had Colton, too.

The rain continued to slide in a steady sheet down the windows, and people lingered long into the late afternoon, hoping for a letup. The punch and cake finally disappeared except for crumbs. At last the rain lightened. People gathered their belongings, repeated good wishes to the winning spellers and called their farewells.

When Judith and Asa reached the door, Emma hurried forward. "I'll come for a visit soon. The school year ends this week." She hugged Judith and then was called away. Judith wondered what Emma would do now that she was no longer teaching school.

They'd not had a moment alone for Judith to tell Emma about inviting Father. And then she remembered Emma had received a letter from Mason Chandler. What had he written to her sister?

Two days later, through the open door of the cabin, Judith watched as Emma walked up the path. In a rare break in the stormy weather, today had dawned clear and warm. A good sunshine for drying, so Judith had decided to move up laundry day. She was just finishing up her ironing. "Emma!" she cried with a lifting of her mood. How precious—time to sit with her dear twin and talk. What had she heard from the man who'd asked her to be his bride?

Emma hurried the last few feet to the door, stopped to wipe her feet on the rough mat outside and stepped into Judith's welcoming hug. Then she leaned down to greet Lily.

Judith set the heavy flatiron on the hearth and quickly invited her sister to sit in one of the rockers. Her offer of coffee was refused.

"I can stay only a few minutes. I'm helping Mrs. Ashford by making supper tonight. She's working with her husband to sort and set out a new shipment of goods."

Judith glanced at Lily, wishing she could send the girl outside to play, but of course the child would want to sit with them. Judith lowered her tired back into the chair right next to Emma's, and Lily automatically climbed up into her lap. The kittens vied with each other for Emma's attention.

Judith and Emma immediately put their heads together. Emma drew a letter from her pocket. She handed it to Judith and then picked up both kittens.

But Judith refused it. "That's for you. But tell me what you want to share."

Emma smiled, petting one kitten's head. "Judith, you don't know how special you are."

Emma's words eased her fatigue from a day of standing, scrubbing clothing and lifting the iron. She leaned over and pressed her cheek against her sister's. "Now tell me."

"He apologized again for not being here and for not being able to return more quickly. He said his father is on the edge of death but keeps fighting to live."

Judith nodded, feeling solemn.

"He says another matter has come up, and he may be delayed much longer than he anticipated. He says he'll understand if I don't want to wait for him."

Judith put an arm around Emma's shoulders, waiting to hear what Emma's reaction would be.

"Well, you know I really didn't want to marry," Emma murmured.

Judith tightened her hold on her sister, who had suffered such a dreadful time of worrying during the war and then the loss of the fiancé she'd waited years to marry. "I know." Judith shook off the gloom and offered her good news. "Asa said I can invite Father for a visit this summer."

"Wonderful!" Emma clapped her hands, startling the kittens, who leaped down. "Do you think he would come?"

Lily slid off Judith's lap to play with the kittens.

"Well, after Anne's letter, I think he might want to. I have already written him, and Anne, too, so she can persuade him." She hoped he'd come but doubted he would.

Emma sat back. "That's a relief. I must thank Asa."

Judith almost cautioned Emma not to, but it might do Asa good to know his thoughtfulness was appreciated.

Emma stared into the low fire. "I feel so sorry for Mason. But…"

"But?"

"I don't have to recount to you why we came to Wisconsin. But now I don't know if I want to marry." Emma turned to her with sudden eagerness. "And… I'm hoping the school board will ask me to stay on as teacher here." The words rushed out.

"Emma, really? You enjoy teaching?" Judith clasped both Emma's hands in hers.

"Yes. Then I could move into the teacher's quarters, though I could no doubt still take my meals with the Ashfords. And help out in the store this summer. I like working there. The school board may want to hire a man or someone with more experience. But I have let the Ashfords know that I'd be willing to continue."

Judith squeezed Emma's hands once more before releasing them. Emma's expression settled into solemn lines. "If this school board doesn't hire me, I think that I might find a position at a smaller school nearby. I met other school board members from the participating schools at the bee. So perhaps I don't need to marry now."

Judith pressed down words that tried to bubble up, words about starting fresh after the long war and Emma's dreadful loss and sorrow. But if Emma could provide for herself and didn't want to marry, she should follow her own mind. So Judith merely nodded.

God had provided Emma a way forward, and while Judith's marriage was not what she had hoped, she was much better off than in her father's house. She had come to find peace and a place of her own, and she had gained both of those. She should not have expected more, but she was a woman and she did want more. She wanted Asa's love, as unlikely as that was.

* * *

A rainy, stormy ten days later, Asa did not want to go to town, but Judith wished to talk to her sister and he needed to have Levi Comstock, the blacksmith, do some work for him. So in spite of the all-too-common heavy gray clouds overhead, he hitched up his wagon, and the four of them began to board it.

If the sky hadn't threatened more rain, they would have walked. But he didn't want Judith or Lily to get soaked. Would he ever forget waking in the night and hearing Judith outside pumping water? And Lily in her white gown had looked like a white rag lying on the ground. He hurried these thoughts out of his mind, sweeping away other crushing images of suffering children he'd seen during the war. The war… He focused on helping Judith and lifting little Lily up.

When everyone was set on the wagon, he slapped the reins, and they covered the short drive to town. He parked on Main Street. Judith and Lily went into the store while he and Colton headed to the blacksmith. Colton's normal scowl was in place. But Asa could do nothing about that. In fact, he felt the same expression trying to take over his own face. He smoothed out his forehead. "Judith, don't take long!" he warned over his shoulder.

"Yes, Asa!"

Then he noticed that town was crowded with people. He looked around and realized most of the shopkeepers were standing outside their stores. He found Levi out in back of his shop, which was just yards from the Mississippi River.

Make that feet.

A very few feet.

Asa stared at the river nearly out of its banks. The current, flush with snowmelt and almost constant spring rain, rushed southward. "Levi!" Asa hailed his friend, who hadn't heard their approach.

The young blacksmith turned, his face drawn down into deep worry lines. "Asa." He waved toward the river. "One more good rain and it will be in my shop."

The blacksmith was right. Asa briefly thought Levi should have considered that when he set up shop so near to the water, but forbore saying so. "You in business today?"

"I guess." The man heaved a huge sigh and turned toward the shop.

The three of them had just reached the door when a deluge let loose. They yelped and jumped inside. Asa turned and gazed at the swollen, racing river. Dark worry ran through him like cold river water.

As Levi worked, Asa stood in the open back doorway, watching the river rise. As suddenly as the rain had started, it stopped. But the river had risen. Anxiety churned in his midsection. Work forgotten, he and Levi turned and went out onto Main Street. Again all the shopkeepers stood around, gazing at the river and talking.

Asa heard the words from several conversations.

"We should do something."

"What?"

The standing around in the face of approaching disaster irked him.

More people came out of the living quarters above

stores, wives and children. Two wagons rolled into town. More now standing in the street. More talking.

More words that added up to the same.

"We should do something."

"What?"

Why didn't someone take charge?

He looked to Mr. Ashford, who stood on the porch of his store. Asa recalled Smith's assessment of the storekeeper, "old woman in pants." It had been rude, but usually Ashford stepped up, ready to tell people what to do or what he thought they should do. But not today. Maybe because none of them had lived along the Mississippi for long.

Grimly Asa turned toward the river. With Colton beside him, he walked the length of Main Street in each direction. The situation had become critical. One more rain—that's all that was needed for a catastrophe. When would the river crest? He'd seen a flood before. The Mississippi could swamp the town and everything in it. Or worse, it might even sweep everything, sweep people away.

Irritated beyond measure at the men and women standing around doing nothing, Asa turned and strode toward his wagon. Foolish people. Didn't they see what was coming? Well, he did. The image of what could happen goaded him to action. He tried to loosen his jaw. He had to act. No one else appeared willing to take charge. To do what was necessary to avert calamity.

He climbed up to stand by the wagon bench and lifted his rifle from its place under the seat. He took aim so that the bullet would land harmlessly in the river. And fired. One shot.

Outcries. A few startled shrieks. And every face turned to him.

"We can't just stand around talking," he stated in his loudest, most commanding voice. "We have to take action or Pepin will be swept away."

Openmouthed, wide-eyed, everyone stared at him. Still no one moved.

He ground his teeth in his frustration. Very well, then. He'd tell them what to do. "Ashford!"

"Yes?" The man almost snapped to attention.

"You have cloth bags for flour and such?"

"Yes," Ashford repeated.

"We need to load them with sand. It's plentiful here at the riverside—"

"But—" the man tried to interrupt.

"We need to sandbag the shore from there." Asa pointed to the ground that naturally rose in a bluff north of town. "Down to there, south of town." He surveyed the crowd and fixed them with a fierce stare. "One more rain and the river will breach its banks. But we can build a temporary levee, and the water will flood south of town, where nobody lives."

No one disagreed. But no one moved.

Asa stared at them, his chest heaving, his mind saying words he wouldn't voice.

His thin patience burst. "Ashford, get those bags. Now! Men, get shovels to dig sand to fill the bags! Mothers, take your children to higher ground." He motioned to the east road out of town. When no one moved to obey, he lifted his rifle once more and fired. "Now!" he bellowed.

The rush began. Ashford ran into the store. Men ran to their houses for shovels. Women ran, taking the children up the rise.

"I'll go sound the bell. Call for help!" called out Gunther, the young man courting Amanda Ashford. He ran south toward the school.

"Asa! What can we do?" Emma, with Judith beside her, called out. His wife was staring at him as if she'd never seen him before.

He had no time for that. "Get needle and thread!" he replied. "Those sacks of sand will need to be sewn securely or our efforts will fail."

"We'll carry down my sewing machine!" Mrs. Ashford called out and hurried into her store.

Asa looked at Colton. "Go get your sister and head up with the rest of the children. Keep Lily right with you, and if it rains, get her under cover."

Colton jumped from the wagon and raced straight to his sister, dragging her by the hand to higher ground. Asa hated that he'd been forced to act, but he couldn't let helpless people suffer when he knew what to do. Irritation prodded him. He didn't want to be the one giving orders—once again. He swallowed angry words, stuffed them down and strode ahead to see that the effort to save the town began.

Thoughts of Judith's startled expression intruded over the intense hours that followed. But Asa had no time to ponder his wife. More people, those who'd heard the school bell, streamed into town. And stood there, dumbfounded at the rising river.

Asa wondered about the people around him, helpless in this crisis. He had to show them how to fill the sandbags, where to stack them and how to stack them like a brick wall. But once he got them working, they were like a hive of bees. Asa worked alongside them, sweat pouring down his face, his arms aching from digging, filling, lifting.

Mrs. Ashford and Emma took turns sewing the bags closed. Some women with Judith sat on Ashford's porch, hand-sewing bags shut. The wall of sandbags formed and began to grow. But Judith said nothing to him. Whenever he glimpsed her, she looked at him as if she didn't know him, and then her gaze slid away. She never came near but kept her distance. *I can't worry about that now.*

Asa roamed the line, encouraging, working, not letting despair take hold. "We can do this. I've seen it done. But the wall must be strong and near as tall as me." He saw an older man flagging and moved him off the line, telling him to bring water and a dipper for the line of sweating men.

A few older children ran down and began bringing pails of water to the workers. Hours passed. Periodically women brought out food, and in between filling up sandbags, the men shoved morsels into their mouths and went right back to filling and stacking.

Hours later, Asa once again studied the river level, considering. "Women, just in case the worst happens, start carrying everything you can lift up to the second level of each store. I don't think the water will reach that high."

Gasping, the people gawked at him as if collectively asking, "That high? Is it possible?"

"Yes!" he replied with a resounding shout. "It can go that high. We don't know how high the crest will be here. Get your animals to safety, too. Now go!"

And they went.

Thick clouds hovered over them and masked the sun, which lowered, lowered. Finally dusk darkened the sky. The panting, sweat-soaked men looked to Asa, slumping, silently asking for reprieve.

He walked the line of sandbags along the river. "I know we're tired. But we've got to keep working till we can't see to work. That river—" he pointed toward the Mississippi "—has power you can't imagine till you see it rolling toward you, downing full-grown trees, destroying everything and everyone in its path. This wall has got to be higher than the flood. Keep working, men!"

No one argued. The men bent again, digging up more sand and pouring it into bags. Asa stacked bags and stacked more, making certain they were placed right and would hold against the coming flood.

Finally night closed in around them. Scattered lanterns glimmered. Asa dragged the last few bags and saw to their position. A wall of sandbags nearly chest-high to him hemmed in the riverfront north to south. It would have to do.

"I think we should pause to pray," Noah Whitmore, who'd joined the work, said in the faint moonlight. Everyone bowed their heads. "Father, we've done all we can to save our town. Now it is in Your hands. We ask humbly for You to protect not just our buildings but all the people here. Thank You. In Your name we pray, Amen."

Noah looked to Asa. "Is there anything else we should do?"

Asa turned toward the sound of the rushing river, the danger it posed rushing through him. "The river level has been rising all day. I don't know when it will crest, but I think the safest course is to leave no one in town. Our wall is built right and strong, but one never knows with a river. If you've ever seen a flood, you'll know what I mean."

He paused, drawing in a deep draft of air, not wanting to say what he must. "Townspeople, take your precious belongings and go stay with friends above the rise." He pointed to the bluff behind town. "We have room for guests."

"Excellent," Noah agreed. "We have room for another family. Everyone go to a friend's house. You will be taken in. Now let's go while we have some light." He looked up at the veiled moon. "I feel certain more rain is coming tonight."

Sandy, sweaty and weary, the people began to obey. Nearly everyone who passed Asa said a word or touched his arm. He wanted just to go, but he couldn't leave his post till all were safe.

A familiar touch at his wrist. He looked down and saw that Lily was taking his hand. Colton stood beside her. But where was Judith? He recalled her shocked expression when he sounded his warning shots. What did she think of him assuming command, telling people what to do? And what if all this work was for naught? Had he made the right call?

Chapter Eight

The Ashfords and, of course, Emma rode in the Brant wagon home with Judith and her family. Their daughter, Amanda, had elected to go with Gunther to the Langs' cabin ostensibly to help Gunther's aunt.

The day had taken its toll on Judith. When Asa had stood, fired his rifle and began giving orders, she'd recognized him. In that flash, Asa's true identity had stunned her.

Even though she'd done her best to help with the effort to save the town, she could barely follow simple directions. Why hadn't Asa told her who he was? Why didn't he use his first name? The questions she couldn't ask now with the Ashfords listening swirled in her mind. And what if she were wrong? The vague memory of those days in 1861 and 1865 would not come into focus, leaving her some doubt.

The effort to appear normal had further drained her. When she glimpsed their cabin in the moonlight, she wanted to run inside, crawl into bed and pull the covers over her head. But of course she couldn't.

The Ashfords, Emma and the children needed her to provide a meal, provide bedding. With nothing prepared, she merely brought out bread, butter, cheese and milk and made a fresh pot of coffee. As Emma and Mrs. Ashford helped, the latter provided a constant stream of words, which Judith merely nodded at occasionally.

Soon a cold supper had been eaten, and then sleeping arrangements had to be worked out. Over it all, rain drummed on the roof till Judith wanted to scream her frustration and confusion.

After much offering and refusing, the Ashfords were persuaded to take the bedroom, while Emma bedded down, sharing a pallet with Lily and the kittens near Colton's by the fire. That left Judith to climb the ladder and join Asa in the loft. Of course, on no account must anyone find out that Judith and Asa still slept apart. She could only hope that neither Lily nor Colton would innocently let this juicy bit of gossip out.

She struggled up to the last rung, her voluminous nightgown and robe hampering her. There Asa offered her his hand to help her negotiate shifting onto the loft. She stared at her husband's hand in the low firelight. Doubt hovered within her. Why had he shortened his name and never told her who he was? He knew her brother!

Finally she bowed to necessity and let him help her. Then, both on their knees, they stared at each other. Words, questions jammed in her throat. Yet she noted his exhaustion. That and the fact that they had an audience who might hear every word forced her to remain silent.

He motioned toward the pallet he'd unrolled for her. She crept to it and then sat.

"Night," Asa muttered, rolling into a quilt on his own pallet.

Judith didn't reply. Without shedding her voluminous robe, she lay on her back, listening to the insistent rain, and let her mind return to the first time she'd seen Asa Brant over a decade ago in 1861.

Fort Sumter had fallen. President Lincoln's call for volunteers had gone out, and local men had gathered to enlist and form a militia unit to defend the Union. While their wives and sisters had sewn uniforms of blue, the men, mostly farmers, had finished plowing and sowing their fields and each evening practiced marching and firing their rifles. Then the day had come when the local militia marched to the nearest railhead to ride east and end the secessionist uprising. She felt a pang recalling Emma wishing her fiancé farewell.

She turned back to the memory. She, Emma, their father and the other families of the militia had arrived at the rail stop. In the jostling, excited crowd, Judith heard again the jumble of voices of family and friends who'd come to see their brothers, fathers, sons, husbands and fiancés off to war. Her brother, Gil, had looked so proud that day in the new uniform that she and Emma had sewn him. Leading the militia had been Fitzgerald A. Brant, captain of the Rock River Illinois Militia. The man she was now married to.

That first moment they met here at the dock she'd thought he looked familiar, but why hadn't she recognized him in the days since? She had no explanation except that her mind just had not made the connection.

As she lay staring at the roofing planks, that day in 1861 became clearer in her mind, and she recalled it vividly. Asa had mounted a wagon just as he had today. To quiet the milling, excited crowd, he'd fired his rifle and then commanded his men to board the train by rank.

That's it. It's not the face that I recognized. I saw it only from a distance. It's the man taking command—his voice, his actions—that jogged my memory.

The contrast between that proud, happy day and the aftermath of the long, deadly war rolled through her like the low thunder outside. Sudden tears streamed down the sides of her face. But she held the memory of that day like a photograph in a frame, examining it over and over. Was her memory right?

Was Asa Brant really Fitzgerald A. Brant? And if he was, why didn't he use his first name? Had Emma recognized him, too? What had happened to lead him to change his name? The answer came easily—the war. But that didn't make sense. Fitzgerald A. Brant had done nothing to be ashamed of. Or had he?

Lying on his side with his back to Judith, Asa felt his muscles ache with the day of hard digging. But that did not bother him as much as what he'd done today. And worse yet, Judith's reaction to what he'd done.

Why didn't I just keep my mouth shut and go home? I don't own anything in town.

His conscience smacked him. *You'd leave your neighbors to suffer and maybe die?*

No. But what if I was wrong? What if I ordered ev-erybody to do all that work for nothing?

He could not believe that was true. The swollen river had been rising and truly dangerous. And even the temporary levee they'd constructed might not be high enough, strong enough to hold back the tumul-tuous river.

He recalled Judith's expression as, just moments ago, she'd stared at him from the top of the ladder. What had happened for her to look at him as if he were a stranger? Was it the peril to the town? Was it mere worry? He didn't know. But all day she could barely look at him and had spoken no personal word to him since he'd fired the rifle in town this morning. What was she thinking? Did she fear that side of him, a side she had never be-fore seen?

He groaned soundlessly. He could only hope that the town would survive the flood and that Judith would re-turn to normal. He tried to relax his tight muscles and hoped exhaustion would shut down his thoughts and ach-ing pain. Thoughts of what might come tomorrow and what people might say about him clamored to be heard.

And on their heels, as always when he was overtired, came memories of battle scenes, that day at Gettysburg. He shut his eyes and began counting, the only way he'd ever found to block out the past, the present. Why did his sense of duty keep goading him? Why couldn't he ever just leave well enough alone?

The morning after next, the seven of them had barely finished breakfast when they heard the school bell ring-ing. Mr. Ashford headed straight to town. Asa retreated into the barn, as Judith could have predicted.

Soon she heard Mr. Ashford shouting, "The flood has passed! Come! See!"

Judith stepped outside and looked up at the clear sky overhead. She, the other two women and Lily ran toward the voice calling them. They met others on the way to town.

Then they followed the bend in the road that led down to the river flat where the town sat. From the rise, Judith realized that in the distance, the Mississippi River's level had lowered some. Judith, along with the rest of the people who lived north of town, ran the last few feet to the local sheriff, Brennan Merriday, who stood in the middle of Main Street. They all gathered around him.

"Who rang the bell?" Mrs. Ashford asked, breathless.

"I did," said the sheriff, who had a pronounced Southern accent. "When I got back from my rounds a day ago, Rachel told me about the sandbag levee. Wasn't going to leave the town unprotected, so I perched under an oilcloth up yonder on the rise."

People nodded solemnly.

"Anyway, the flood crested early this mornin' at barely light. I heard it. The water rushin' fast."

"Our sandbags held!" Levi shouted, coming up from the wall they'd built.

"It did indeed," the sheriff agreed. "It's good y'all stacked it high enough."

"It was Asa Brant," Levi said. "He knew what to do."

"Our town is saved," Mr. Ashford said, "thanks to Asa Brant."

Everyone began looking around for Asa.

Judith cleared her throat, forced to give an explanation of her husband's absence and stem speculation. "My husband is a very modest man, a private one."

Everyone turned their attention to her.

"He…he won't want anyone to make…a fuss," Judith said, feeling her way, trying to…do what? Protect her husband? She hoped they would listen to her but had no real hope that they would.

Everyone turned as if to head northward. Toward their cabin? Judith began to panic. Asa had taken refuge in his barn. If they hurried there to thank him, what would he do? Say?

"I think," the sheriff said loudly and with emphasis, "that is understandable. Asa seems a very private man, all right. And we've got enough to do here for now."

Everyone turned and, after a moment of silence, began speaking about what needed to be done to move back into town.

Judith sighed with relief and offered to help the Ashfords move back into their quarters by carrying down the items they'd crowded up from the first to the second floor. If only everyone would stay away from Asa. But how long could that last? Then she wondered again at the invisible wall Asa hid behind. Now that she knew who he was, she was no further ahead in understanding him. It must have something to do with the war. But what? He'd returned an honored veteran—that's what everyone said. She could not come up with a reason he'd altered his identity.

* * *

The next day, Judith rejoiced in the dawn's light, which turned all the trees in front of their cabin to gold. Two days in a row without rain. Had the spring rains played out at last? Could planting begin? A year without a crop could render Pepin nearly a ghost town.

While Judith finished washing the breakfast dishes, Colton was gathering eggs for her. Lily was playing with the new little rag doll Judith had sewn for her after her other Clara had finally fallen apart and had been set on the mantel. Of course, as soon as the meal had ended, Asa had headed for the barn. Judith's heart felt as if it were caught in a noose. She'd begun to care for her husband, but she was no closer to understanding him.

She dried the dishes, gazing around the cabin. She'd come here just wanting peace and a home. Well, she had a home. But trying to reconcile who Asa had been in the past in contrast to his present life and his desire to keep everyone, even her, away did not add up to peace.

"Judith!"

At the sound of her sister's voice, Judith set down the plate, pulled at her apron strings and stepped into her open doorway. "Emma!"

Once more Judith argued with herself. Should she ask her sister if she'd recognized Asa? Sometimes Judith was absolutely certain that Asa was Fitzgerald Brant, but then doubt would niggle at her. If he was, why hadn't he just told her so? Her head hurt with thinking.

"I come with definite good news." Emma glanced toward the barn and lowered her voice for Judith only. "And perhaps not so good news."

Lily, of course, followed Emma inside.

Judith offered coffee, and the two sisters sat in the chairs by the fire. For once, Lily decided to take her doll and kittens to play outside in the sunshine, releasing some of Judith's tension and caution. Nonetheless, she decided to let Emma take the lead in this conversation. "Now, what did you mean?"

"I've been offered the position as Pepin's schoolteacher."

Judith's mood shot upward. "Oh, Emma, I'm so glad. I didn't want you to leave town." She claimed her sister's hand. "I like having you near."

"I must agree. And I will move into the teacher's quarters this week."

"You'll be happy to be by yourself," Judith commented diplomatically.

Emma chuckled. "I really do like the Ashfords. They have treated me just like a daughter, but it will be nice to have a bit of quiet." Emma's face crinkled into a grin. Then she sobered. "Now for the less than good news."

"All right." Judith prepared herself. "What is it?"

"At church this Sunday, Asa is going to be thanked publicly for leading the efforts in saving the town from the flood. And I don't understand why, but I know he will not like that."

Judith's stomach did a roll and a lurch. She swallowed down the reaction. Asa's reluctance for the limelight could have been responsible for just a part of this reaction. But the announcement also stirred up her own confusion over his true identity.

"I've noticed," Emma said, glancing down, "that Asa is, as you said, a modest and private man." Then she looked directly into Judith's eyes. "What's wrong between you two?"

"I don't know, sister," Judith confessed at last. Telling the truth released a band inside her. "He holds himself in so tightly. He won't let me in." Is that why he altered his name? So no one would come near the truth? But why try to hide who he was? He'd come home from the war without shame.

Emma reached over and laid her hand over Judith's, which was gripping the arm of her chair.

Judith wanted to pour out all her fears and worries.

But Lily pranced inside with the egg basket. "Here's the eggs, Mrs. Brant."

"Thank you, Lily. Please thank Colton for me," Judith replied.

Lily danced outside again singing "Mary Had a Little Lamb" to her doll. The kittens romped at her heels, trying to catch her trailing apron string.

"So, should you warn Asa of the intended public thanks?" Emma asked.

Judith gazed into the low fire and then raised her shoulders in a shrug of indecision.

Emma kept her hand over Judith's, and the two of them rocked in silence. Judith went over Emma's question in her mind. Should she tell Asa or just let it happen? And should she confront him? Demand the truth? What if he refused to tell her? What would happen to their tenuous relationship then?

* * *

In the evening, Asa sat at his work table, just holding a piece of leather. The quiet of the barn Asa had sought after supper was disturbed when Judith entered. The chickens in their coop must have heard her, too. They ruffled their feathers noisily. Judith walked over and stroked one of the horses that had swung to look at her. Then she came and sat down beside him, something she had never done here before.

Startled and wary, Asa hazarded a glance toward Judith and then focused on his leather work. Her nearness flowed over him as usual. He fought it as usual. He felt like he was drowning in his need to pull her close, bury his face in the crook of her soft neck and feel her silken hair against his cheek.

"Asa, Emma told me that the town is planning to thank you publicly at church for leading the effort to save the town from the flood."

Asa sucked in air so sharply he nearly coughed. *He should have expected something like this.* The past came rushing at him.

His wife did not look at him but pleated her skirt with her fingers. "Asa, what you did was good. I don't know what would have happened if you hadn't stepped forward."

He heard Judith's words as if from a distance. His heart pounded and his ears roared with cannon fire. He tried to push all the past back into its box. It wouldn't go.

Then Judith rested a hand on his arm.

He turned to her. In the low light, her eyes glowed. Amid the mingled smells of horse, cow and leather,

her sweet fragrance slipped into his head. He closed his eyes, savoring her sweetness.

"I know you won't want to go to church or to be thanked," Judith said. "But I've thought it over."

He wanted to disagree, but his reaction to her hand on his arm had caught him around the throat. He couldn't speak.

"If you just go to church and accept the thanks with a few words, it will be over and people will put it in the past. If you don't go, it will just stretch matters out and cause a lot of talk. Bring more attention to you, to us."

With his free hand, he rubbed his furrowed forehead. He let out a gust of irritation. "You're right." He couldn't say more because suddenly he yearned to tell her everything, let it all out.

She gazed at him as if asking something of him. What? He couldn't guess what she wanted. And he couldn't dare to ask.

Wrenching his gaze from her pale face, he painstakingly wrapped up his self-control once more, tucking his words deep inside. He would know better next time. Next time he would just go home and let whatever happened, happen. Or he'd try to.

Sunday morning came, and Asa dressed himself as if preparing for a firing squad. Judith had the right of it. He would just go and get it over and be done with it. If he didn't, it would cause a bigger fuss.

When he'd come home from the war, he'd tried to do the same, just let people talk, but it seemed like the attention would never end. So he'd come here, where nobody knew him. His aggravation with the present situation burned like the low fire they left in the hearth as the four of them set out for church. He had timed their departure to make sure they arrived just as the service would start. Judith had watched him all morning and had uttered no objection to this alteration to their usual Sunday morning routine.

The spring rains had finished with them, and the ground was drying out. Soon he could till and plant. He concentrated on going over his plans for this year's corn and hay crops and harvest, trying to keep his dread at bay.

They entered the schoolroom at the last possible moment and sat in the back in their usual pew. Heads turned, but Lavina Caruthers was starting the first hymn, so everyone rose and began singing.

Asa forced himself to concentrate on the hymns and then the sermon. Noah preached about becoming a new creation. Asa stared at Noah. Really? Asa felt as old as the mountains, and as burdened. His right leg started acting up, jittering. He planted his heel firmly on the wood floor.

The sermon finally ended and Noah looked directly at him. "Before our special recognition, I would like to announce that Miss Emma Jones has accepted the teaching position here in Pepin for this coming school year."

The rest of his words were drowned by loud approval, most notably by the children. Some shouted, "Hooray!"

Then Noah held up his hands for quiet and the congregation settled down again, though many snuck glances toward Asa.

"I don't have to recount to you the events of this past week. And I know that Asa Brant, who led the efforts to keep our town safe from the river, is a modest man who did not do what he did for thanks. But I'm sure all of us want to thank him for showing us how to protect our town. Asa, would you please stand?"

Asa rose, his heart thumping his breastbone.

"Our thanks, Asa," Noah said, and then he began the applause that surrounded Asa.

Asa was unable to move or speak. Finally he reached down and took his wife's hand. She rose to stand beside him.

Asa managed to nod in reply and then sat back down.

The applause waned, and then Noah bowed his head and prayed, "Father, thank You for our town coming through the flood safely. Thank You for prompting Asa to take action so decisively. Thank You for the sunshine this week. And bless the planting of our crops. Amen."

Asa could finally draw breath again. He allowed people to shake his hand on his way out of the school. He nodded and nodded and then he was finally outside again.

Mrs. Ashford planted herself in his escape path. "We want you and your family to come to Sunday dinner."

He stared at the woman.

"That's very kind of you, Mrs. Ashford," Judith said, appearing at his elbow.

"We want to thank you for taking us in—"

"That's not necessary," Judith said. "You took Emma in."

Mrs. Ashford summarily waved the objection away. "Come now. I've a roast simmering over the fire, and potatoes and carrots, and I made rhubarb crisp."

Judith clasped his hand and tugged. "That sounds delicious, doesn't it, Asa?"

He nodded, wanting to run up the road. But he held himself tight together and went along.

Judith kept up a light conversation with the storekeeper's wife. Asa suffered through the visit and meal. He nodded or shook his head whenever a comment was directed to him and tried not to bolt down the food. Or choke on it.

Finally he ate the last bite of his glossy pink rhubarb crisp with whipped cream. Unable to stop himself, he rolled the tart flavors around in his mouth. Then the old tug to shy away from enjoying life and the feeling of guilt over surviving the war reared up, and he set down his spoon.

"You cook good," Lily said, licking her lips.

Mrs. Ashford chuckled and appeared pleased.

Finally Judith was saying their thanks and edging toward the door. Asa trailed her down the stairs and waved goodbye over his head, not looking back.

The four of them walked home. Each step away from town lifted Asa's spirits. They mounted the last rise to their homestead. He couldn't wait to reach his barn, go inside and shut the world out.

When they arrived home, they first went inside and

began to shed their Sunday clothes. The "ladies" went into the bedroom, leaving the "men" by the fire. As Colton undressed beside Asa, he stopped and looked up at him. "You and Mrs. Brant are married, right?"

Asa nodded, his mind already in the barn.

"Then why do you sleep in the loft and she sleeps in the bedroom?"

The question rendered Asa mute.

"My ma and pa always slept in the bed, and Lily and me slept in the loft." Colton studied him with a confused and slightly put-out expression.

Asa scrabbled for an answer. "We haven't been married very long." It was all Asa could come up with.

"Oh." Colton obviously considered this.

Before Colton could ask him how long a husband and wife had to be married before they slept in the same room, Asa said, "As soon as you're changed, I need you to bring in water."

Colton nodded, sliding on his everyday shirt.

And for the first time, the fact that Colton never complained about chores struck Asa as odd. As the boy finished hanging his Sunday best over the back of a kitchen chair and began donning his everyday pants, Asa studied him.

Another thought occurred to Asa. Colton rarely did anything that amounted to real play except when he sat with the kittens. Asa would have to talk to Judith about this. She was a woman. She would know about children.

"Ready?" Judith asked from behind the curtain.

Asa quickly did the last of his shirt buttons. "Yes, ma'am."

Judith came through the curtain with Lily behind her. Colton opened the door. "Lily, come help me get water."

Lily hurried to her brother. "I can't carry much."

"I know, but you gotta help. Children help with the work."

"Okay, Colton."

Asa watched them go, wondering at Colton's readiness to do chores. Was he still uncertain of his place here?

Judith faced him, an odd cast to her face. "Why didn't you tell me that you're Fitzgerald Brant?"

Asa felt his tongue slam back against his throat. Where had that come from? He'd dreaded this since the day he'd first seen her. He turned and hurried out the door, heading straight for the barn.

His wife followed him closely, and then she was in the barn with him.

He stared at her, watching her lips move as she repeated her question, but he found his throat choked. He could only look at her, a roaring in his ears.

She spoke some more, but when he didn't speak, she frowned. She stood on tiptoe and kissed his cheek. And she left.

Slowly Asa's hearing returned to normal along with his heartbeat. How had Judith recognized him?

Colton appeared. "I took in the water. What do you want me to do now?"

Go away. But of course Asa couldn't, wouldn't say that. "It's Sunday. No work on the Sabbath."

Colton cocked one eyebrow at him.

Asa needed to be doing something. Try to keep his

reactions to Judith's words at bay. How had she figured it out? What if she told someone?

"Play outside," Asa said, heading toward the house.

Lily was playing outside the door with the kittens.

Asa passed her and shut the door behind him.

With the water dipper in hand at the counter, Judith turned to him.

"No one must know who I am," he ordered, pinning her with his intent gaze.

She put down the dipper. "Why didn't you tell me who you were? That you were my brother's captain?"

"No one must know who I am," he repeated.

Judith gazed back at him. For a long time.

Finally she nodded.

With relief, he turned away.

"But sometime," she said, "and soon, we will talk this out."

He ignored her comment and walked out the door. *No, we will not, Judith.*

Chapter Nine

Judith stood, quivering, gazing at the staunch oak door, the door Asa had shut against her. Again.

She picked up the tin water dipper. She fingered its long handle. Then hurled it at the door. It hit, bounced back and then rattled a bit on the floor before subsiding.

She had not thrown anything in temper since she was a child. And why had she now? It didn't solve anything or make her feel any better. In fact, the act mimicked her flimsy attempts to break through to Asa. He was the hard oak door. She was the flimsy tin dipper.

She walked over, bent and picked up the poor dipper with sympathy for it. What could a tin dipper do to an oak door? *Did I make a terrible mistake coming here and marrying Asa?*

In the barn, she'd told him when she'd recognized him. She'd wanted to talk about it, know why he'd kept his war record a secret here. But then the look on his face had wrung her heart. So pained, so lost. She hadn't been able to help herself. She'd kissed him. But her kiss had no power with him. She pressed a hand over her heart, which was aching for this good man. *Maybe if I'd been born pretty...*

Lily opened the door. "Can I have a drink of water?"

"Please?" Judith prompted automatically.

"Please?" Lily skipped over to her, dolly on her arm, kittens at her heels.

Soon Judith held the full dipper out.

Lily sipped from it. "Thank you!" And the little one skipped outside, singing to her dolly, kittens scampering after her. Lighthearted, unburdened.

Still holding the dipper, Judith walked to the open door and gazed out. In the yard of coarse, vividly green wild grass, Lily played with the kittens. Colton sat on the ground by the barn door, whittling. A peaceful scene.

And of course, Asa was holed up in his barn. Tears sat just behind Judith's eyes. Frustration had caused her to throw the dipper. Frustration and anger at being left out of the one life that had come to mean the most to her.

On the day of building the sandbag levee, she had finally discovered a clue to why Asa shut her out. Now she'd finally confronted him about his true identity and he'd forbidden her to talk about it.

Forbidden her. *What am I going to do with this stubborn man?*

She glanced over her shoulder at her shiny new Singer sewing machine. Asa had bought it for his bride. He'd brought home kittens. He'd taken in the children. He'd saved the town.

Nevertheless, he never let her get close to him.

Would they continue to live separate lives? He in the barn, she in the house? He in the loft, she in the bedroom? Was that how a marriage was supposed to be?

No, please, no. Asa, you've won my loyalty. You've gained my respect. Why can't you let me in? Why can't you let me love you?

That last question mentally stopped her in her tracks. *I love Asa Brant,* Fitzgerald *Brant, my husband. But he doesn't love me.*

No, Asa did not love her. But her husband could not stop her from loving him.

She blinked away tears that threatened, set down the dipper, stepped outside and sat on the bench beside the door. She called to Lily, and the little girl came to her. Judith drew her up on her lap and began testing her on her alphabet and talking to her of going to school this fall. And she felt the comfort of God flowing over her. *God is a very present help in trouble. Yes, He is. Asa needs to know that.*

The next morning proved to be another one with bright sunshine and cloudless blue sky. After weeks of storms, Judith with Lily at her side walked to the Ashfords' store to help her sister move into the teacher's quarters. Judith longed for a few moments alone with her sister. She wanted desperately to talk to someone about Asa and his secret. However, she must not. But perhaps Emma had also recognized Asa.

At the back of the store, at the foot of her stairs, Gunther Lang, Amanda Ashford's beau, had positioned a two-wheel cart. He helped load Emma's trunk and valises onto it. Mrs. Ashford stood, wiping her eyes. "I'm going to miss you. You've been such a ray of sunshine in this hard spring."

Emma gathered the woman into her arms. "You will not miss me. You will see me every day. I'll be eating at your table and helping in the store. And I can never thank you enough for your kind hospitality. You took me in like a daughter."

Judith watched Emma, who always knew what to say, comfort the woman and move her from tears to laughter.

"I'd come with you, but we have a shipment of fabric to display," the storekeeper's wife said.

"Judith is here to help me. Lily, too. And I don't have that much to do. I'm so grateful the teacher's quarters come furnished. I'll see you for lunch!" Emma waved, and soon she was walking with Judith toward the schoolhouse. Lily skipped along beside them, her dolly over her arm bobbing with each step.

Gunther was waiting for them at the teacher's entrance beside the cart. As soon as Emma unlocked the door, he dragged in her trunk and set it where she wanted. Soon he'd brought in the rest of her belongings, wished Emma well and bid them goodbye.

The two of them efficiently unpacked Emma's dresses and hung them on the pegs along the back wall. The large room had a fireplace, a bed, a table with two chairs, and two rocking chairs. Judith knew that the plain room would soon burst with colorful decorations and Emma's artistic touch.

Lily moved around the room, touching everything.

Then, with permission, she moved through the connecting door to do the same in the schoolhouse.

Now alone with her sister, Judith tried to come up with a way to introduce the topic of Asa. Then, distracting Judith, Emma set out on the mantel a framed photo of their parents taken on their wedding day.

"I didn't know you had that," Judith said.

Emma frowned. "I'll let you have it if you want. But I was afraid that our dear sister-in-law might throw it away."

"Emma! She wouldn't do such a thing."

"I caught her trying to." Emma pressed her lips together for a moment, her lovely face lined with worry. "She and Gil had fought the night before."

Gloom settled over Judith. "I'm glad you saved it, then. You keep it. I brought Mother's Bible and her journal with me. I confess I didn't want to leave them for the same reason."

Emma rearranged the silver framed photo on a starched white doily. "Mabel Joy is one of those people who must have all the attention, all the love in a house or family. And thereby renders herself unlovable."

Judith shook her head. She longed to bring up what she now knew about Asa but could not. Asa did not want anyone to know who he was. She couldn't understand that, but she must obey his wish in this. And certainly if Emma had recognized him, she would have said something by now.

Lily danced back into the room. "Do I get to go to school?"

Emma stooped to eye level with the little girl. "I hope so. How old are you?"

Judith watched her sister charm Lily. A fear tingled around Judith's heart. Would she and Asa be keeping the children? Or would some family member come to claim them?

She shouldn't hope that none of the children's family would come, but how lonely and quiet the cabin would be without them. A silent sob tried to work its way through her. She tightened her self-control, reminding herself of her vow to love, honor and obey Asa Brant. And except for his self-imposed barrier, he was a good husband, a good man.

In his barn, cleaning out a stall, Asa heard a voice call out. "Hello! Anybody home?"

Asa grudgingly stepped to the door.

A slight, white-haired man with a valise in hand stood in the yard.

"Yes?" Asa asked, wanting to hurry the man away.

The man removed his hat. "I'm looking for the Brant house."

"You found it." Asa did not recognize the man.

"Is Judith around?"

The question sent a ripple of caution through Asa. "No."

The man paused, eyeing Asa. "Are you Asa Brant?"

Asa nodded, hoping that he wasn't guessing right. Judith had said that her father probably wouldn't come.

The man then moved forward, his right hand out-stretched. "I'm Dan Jones. Your father-in-law."

Dismay washed through Asa, but he automatically gripped the man's hand. "I..."

The man grinned in a sad way. "I surprised myself. I never planned to take a trip up the river. But..." He shrugged, his face falling. Then he looked at Colton, who was as usual standing in Asa's shadow. "Who's this, then?"

Asa pulled himself together. He couldn't be rude to Judith's father. "This is Colton. He and his sister are staying with us. Boy, shake the man's hand."

Colton obeyed, greeting Jones in his wary way.

"Judith's in town," Asa explained.

"I must have missed her. Is she coming back soon?"

Asa nodded, trying to think of how to handle this. He noticed the man shifting the valise from one hand to the other. Judith had said her father wasn't well. "I'll take that." He did so and led the man into the cabin. "Sit."

His father-in-law settled in Judith's rocker. "You got a nice place here."

"Thanks, Mr. Jones." The worry that this man might recognize who he was, as Judith had, prodded him. Asa wanted to head back to his barn. But civility required that he stay.

"You can call me Dan."

Asa nodded.

"A drink would be welcome."

Asa shook himself mentally and poured the man coffee from the pot still warm over the fire.

The man sighed with obvious pleasure. "Judith's coffee. I've missed it."

Asa hid his surprise. Judith did make good coffee,

but this had been hanging over the fire for a few hours. How bad could the coffee this man had been drinking be? Then Asa recalled his own excuse for a cup of coffee. Another of Judith's skills.

"I'm keeping you from your work," Dan stated. "You don't need to stay with me. I'll just sit a spell. Travel has me tuckered out."

Asa looked at the man, trying to believe he had come. Who would show up next? Gil? "I'll be in the barn."

"I'll call you or come if I need anything."

Confused, irritated and wary, Asa left Dan there. *Why can't everyone just leave us alone?*

As Asa finished cleaning the stall and making the final preparations for planting, he found that he was listening for the sounds of Judith returning. Then he heard Lily singing. He stepped outside and hurried to intercept Judith.

A glance toward the cabin told him he was too late.

Dan must have heard the singing, too. He had also come out the door into the yard.

Judith, with Lily, appeared as she walked the last rise to their clearing in the pines. She looked to Asa and smiled.

Her smile went straight to his heart. *I don't deserve her.*

Then Judith's face expanded into a dazzling smile he'd not seen before. He wished he was the kind of man who warranted such an expression. But he'd told her to keep his secret. But what else could he do?

"Father!" Judith cried out, running forward. "Father! You came!" She threw her arms around Dan, weeping.

Dan looked over his shoulder to Asa. "Women got to cry," he said ruefully.

Asa nodded and then, feeling unnecessary, reentered his barn.

Judith could not stop crying. Seeing her father had released all the tears she had been holding back.

Then she realized that Lily was clinging to her leg and weeping, too, but in fear. The child had misunderstood her tears of joy and relief.

Judith sucked in air and, releasing her father, stooped down. She clasped Lily to her. "I'm sorry, sweetie. This is happy crying. My father has come to visit us."

Lily hiccupped, tears trembling on her lashes. "He's not a bad man?"

"No, he's a very good man," Judith said. "Sometimes when a person—"

"A woman," her father inserted.

She knew he was teasing her, trying to lighten the mood. "Hush," she mock-scolded him. "Sometimes good news is so good it makes me cry."

Lily did not look convinced of this as she wiped away her tears with her fingertips.

Judith rose and took Lily's hand again. "Lily, this is my father, Mr. Jones. Father, this is Lily, who lives with us."

"Is her brother that youngster, Colton?" Dan asked.

"Yes," Lily said and curtseyed. "Pleased to meet you, mister."

Dan bowed to Lily. "Likewise."

Judith's mood lifted. Her father was teasing again.

In the months before she and Emma had left for Pepin, there had been no teasing in their home.

"Come in, Father." She looked up at the sun right overhead. "It's time I set out lunch." She glanced at the barn. Asa had sought his usual refuge. But he must have heard her and her father. She sighed. Her father arriving, another unwelcome development for Asa.

"I met your man," Father said. "He welcomed me, took me inside and gave me coffee."

Surprise tingled up Judith's spine. "He did?"

"Yes. Then I told him to get back to his work. A farmer can't waste a good day like this entertaining."

Judith nodded, leading Father into the cabin.

Lily remained outside, greeting the eager, leaping, purring kittens, who evidently had missed her.

Judith went about preparing lunch, wondering what Asa thought of her father appearing. She doubted he was pleased, but as usual, he had done the right thing and welcomed his father-in-law. *What am I going to do with that man?*

The five of them sat down to lunch, the children and Dan on the bench opposite Judith and Asa. He hid his displeasure at this latest invasion. He'd advertised for a wife, and now he had a wife, two children, two kittens and suddenly a father-in-law. He'd had to force himself into the cabin. He said his usual prayer and began eating, trying not to look sullen.

As usual, Judith had served up a tasty lunch, rabbit stew and dumplings. Asa concentrated on his meal, savoring each creamy bite.

Judith sat, not eating.

One glance told him she was fretting. Wasn't she happy her father had come?

"Mrs. Brant cooks good," Lily commented, swinging her feet and eyeing the new face at the table.

Colton spoke up, something he rarely did. "I caught the rabbits with my snares."

Dan patted Colton's shoulder. "Good for you. I used to catch rabbits for my mom, too."

Asa felt that cinching feeling in his chest. When would they hear from Sterling, Illinois, from the Farrier family? Then he thought of living here without the children. Did he want to hear from their family?

"Father, I'm really happy you've visited," Judith said, smoothing the white oilcloth beneath her fingertips. "I just didn't think you'd come."

"I didn't think so, either, but then Anne...you remember our neighbor?"

Judith nodded and finally picked up her fork to begin eating.

The tightness in Asa's chest loosened.

"She stopped by," Dan continued, "and sat on the porch with me a spell, and pretty soon I told her about your invitation." Father tugged out the tattered letter from his pocket. "I hadn't expected you to invite me. But Anne said, why not go? Good to see your girls."

Judith heard the words, but she heard more than that. Her father's unhappiness came through. She tried to think of something to say but could not speak her mind about Mabel Joy or what their neighbor Anne had revealed to her about Gil's behavior. Not in front of the children, and sometimes things were better left where they lay.

"How long can you stay?" Judith asked and took her first bite of stew.

Her father rubbed his chin. "I don't know."

Judith managed to swallow her mouthful with difficulty. What would Asa think about this?

"Now tell me about our Emma," Dan said. "That Mason Chandler wasn't here to meet her? What was that about?"

Judith was happy to turn the discussion away from Illinois and fill her father in on Emma's delayed fiancé and Emma's new career.

Finally lunch had been eaten. Asa rose and thanked her for the meal as he always did with "Good meal, ma'am."

Judith knew that Asa was vexed. She couldn't blame him, really. She'd asked to invite her father for a visit, but she hadn't expected him to come. It had only been a faint hope.

"I'd offer to come and help," her father told Asa. "But traveling for several days has me beat. I think... I just need to sit a spell."

"Rest," Asa said, and with Colton, his shadow, he left the cabin.

"Your man doesn't string many words together, does he?" her father said, rising and moving toward the rocker by the fire.

"No." Judith bent to kiss her father's forehead, and then she gathered up the dishes. Lily sprang up to help her. Judith tried to keep her worry unseen. Yet things at home must been very bad indeed for her father to come.

Lily interrupted Judith's thoughts. "He's snoring," she whispered, pointing to Dan.

Judith turned, and she heard the familiar whiffling her father often made in his sleep. "Older people get tired more easily, and he's come a long way."

Lily accepted another dish to dry and nodded solemnly. "We had a grandpa in Illinois. I 'member him. He used to rock me."

Would this grandpa come to claim the children? A dreaded thought. Judith observed Lily glance longingly at Dan.

"I had a grandpa, too. They are good rockers." Judith tried to keep the conversation light.

"Can your pa be my grandpa now?" Lily asked.

The innocent question stung Judith's heart. "We'll see. I don't know how long my father will stay." *I don't know how long you and Colton will stay.*

Emma's life had taken form. She had found a place and a job. Judith had a husband who was hiding who he was, pulled back into his shell. Judith rubbed her head and tried not to think of tonight, when her father would take the bedroom and she would have to face her husband up in the loft again. *Lord, help untangle this knot of problems. I can't.*

Evening came, and Asa faced another night with a visitor to contend with. Soon the children and the kittens were tucked into their pallets on the floor, and Judith had persuaded her father to take the bedroom. As she climbed up the ladder to the loft, Asa looked at Judith's worried expression and held out his hand.

She gazed at him and then accepted his help getting safely into the loft. For a moment he wanted to draw her hand till she leaned into him. In the firelight he could see her large eyes, luminous and so serious.

Before he could stop himself, he stroked a few tendrils of hair away from her face. Touching her flashed up his arm like lightning. Her sweet scent enveloped him. Sweet Judith.

"I'm sorry," she whispered. "I wanted him to come, but—"

He stroked her cheek. So soft.

"Asa," she whispered and rested her cheek in his hand.

He thought he might fly apart at the sensations she ignited within him. *This is my wife. My Judith.* But there were children and her father sleeping below, and he had no right to touch this lovely, sweet woman. He had no love to give her. He wished the war had not burned away his heart.

"It's all right," he muttered and moved his hand. "Night." He turned and rolled away into his bedding, his heart thudding like a mallet against his breastbone. He strained within the trap he'd lived in for years, alone and empty. *God, I don't deserve her and don't ever want to hurt her.*

The next morning, Judith and Lily went to pick wild mushrooms, succulent morels, in a clearing east of town. Asa with Colton went to begin tilling his land for planting. Asa had been thinking of putting in a small crop for Mason if he had time. They left Dan sitting on the bench outside their door.

Then, with the sun high overhead, they all returned to eat lunch together. But Dan was not in the cabin or the barn. Asa saw how this worried Judith. Where had the old man gone?

The sound of whistling announced Dan, who came walking up from town. He waved, and Lily ran to tell him all about picking wild mushrooms and how she and Judith were going to fry them so they could eat them with bread and butter.

Soon lunch of breaded and fried mushrooms with thick slices of buttered bread had been eaten, and the children were sent out to play. Lily went willingly, but Colton eyed them and left with slow steps.

Dan looked directly at Asa. "I'm not here just for a visit." He paused. "But don't worry. I'm not moving in with you."

Asa stared at him, his thoughts scattered. "You're family," he objected.

Dan chuckled. "Yes, but you see, I've had enough family for a while."

"Father, don't—" Judith said in a soothing tone.

Dan patted her hand. "As your husband has said, we're family. I'm sure you've told him about Gil and Mabel Joy." Dan looked straight at Asa. "No woman was ever misnamed more exactly."

Asa sipped his coffee, watchful.

Dan shook his head as if exhausted. "But my son is no better. After you girls left, matters got a lot worse.

Gil goes to the saloon and drinks every night. And I mean drinks till he can barely ride his horse home. And then his wife greets him with loud quarreling."

Judith, who had been stacking plates to carry to the dry sink, stopped. "Father, no."

"Judith, yes. I was so happy Gil had survived the war that when he came home, I shut my eyes to what was happening. I should have stood up for you girls. Put a stop to both of their bad manners and fighting right away." After patting her hand, Dan looked directly at Asa. "I meant what I said. I'm not strong enough to farm anymore. My heart gives me trouble. But I'm going to find work here doing something. And—" he emphasized the word "—I'm going to find a room to rent somewhere."

"But, Father, there isn't a boardinghouse here."

"Levi has a lean-to…he rents it out," Asa said. "Stayed there myself when I first arrived."

Judith from her place sent him an unhappy and confused look.

Asa shrugged. It was the truth.

"Levi?" Dan asked.

"Blacksmith," Asa replied.

Dan lifted both brows. "Oh. He's the one who told me where your place was yesterday. Seemed a good young man."

"He's solid," Asa said, thinking of the younger man who always managed to set Asa at ease. "My best man."

"Now, Judith, I'll be right in town. I'll even let you do my laundry," Dan teased.

Judith bowed her head as if acknowledging defeat.

"And I will drop in for meals." Dan grinned. "You cook as good as your mother ever did. And that's saying something."

Asa sensed Judith watching him and checked to make sure his face hadn't given anything away. He'd gained not only Judith but also the children and now Dan. *I just wanted a wife, just a wife.*

Two days later her father moved into the blacksmith's bachelor quarters at the riverfront. Judith, with Lily and Emma, had insisted on coming to see his new home. And Colton, who had taken a liking to her father, tagged along, too. The children went inside with Father while she and Emma stood in the doorway. The room was too small for all of them to fit in comfortably.

"You see, it's just right for me," their father said.

The single bed against the wall of what amounted to a lean-to against the blacksmith's shop did not impress Judith. Levi's hammer continued to clang against the anvil right next door. Lily sat on the edge of the bed, swinging her legs.

"I'll get a good breeze from the river," Father continued.

Judith wondered if the insistent pounding of the hammer on the anvil would get on her father's nerves. It was getting on hers.

"But you can't spend a winter here," Emma objected.

"No, Levi says he has a loft above his shop that stays warm in the winter from the forge that burns low all night. So I'll bunk in the lean-to in summer, get the cool river breeze in the evenings. And I'll move up to

the loft in winter to keep warm and cozy. I'll be fine."
Father patted Emma's arm.

Judith knew that it was probably best for her and
Asa not to have her father living with them. She'd slept
in the loft with or at least near Asa last night. Being
close to him when she didn't know what he was really
thinking had been uncomfortable—more than uncomfortable. They'd been married months and were still
living like friends, not husband and wife. Levi's hammer stopped and she heard the sizzle of red-hot iron
plunged into water. At the thought of her uncertainty,
a similar sensation roiled in her stomach. She inhaled
a steadying breath.

"And I got a job this morning!" Father crowed, interrupting Judith's thoughts.

"What?" she and Emma exclaimed in unison.

"I walked over to the dock when a boat pulled in.
A passenger hailed me and asked if I would run to the
store and buy him some tobacco for his pipe. I agreed.

"And afterward," he continued, "Mr. Ashford said
that he's been wanting someone to take notions, tobacco and such on a tray to each boat to sell to the passengers. Some boats give enough time to run up to the
store and some don't. Says he'll give me ten percent of
every sale." Father beamed at them. "And I can keep
the tips. Got me a dime this morning."

Judith tried not to frown. Her father had been a prosperous and successful farmer, and now he was a peddler living in a lean-to. It wasn't right. But after the
war, her father had not stood up to Gil who had come
home a different man, a man with problems. Perhaps

her father's weak heart and his relief that Gil had been spared accounted for this. So his leaving the farm, letting Gil and his wife have it for now, followed this pattern of avoiding the truth.

"Now, I know what you're thinking," he said soothingly. "But I have my own place. I have my daughters near. And I'll have some peace and quiet and people nearby to talk to. I'll enjoy meeting the boats."

Emma chuckled. "I think you're right."

Judith recalled their neighbor Anne's letter. Yes, this was better than their father having to put up with what was going on at their farm.

Finally she, with Lily and Emma, stepped out onto Main Street. Colton remained inside for a final word with her father.

Then a woman cried out, "There's Lily!"

Judith looked around and saw a thin woman in a sadly faded dress climbing down from a wagon bench, a man on the bench beside her.

Lily cried out, too, in obvious fear. She ducked behind Judith and wrapped her arms around Judith's waist. "Don't let her get me! He'll hurt us!"

Colton bolted from the lean-to. He took one look at the woman and man and raced away up Main Street, toward home.

Judith put it all together. This must be the couple who'd mistreated the children and caused them to run away. Judith burned with outrage.

Chapter Ten

"Mr. Brant!"

Behind the plow, Asa heard Colton's voice. The shrill fear in it washed over him like ice water. He pulled back hard on the reins of his straining team. "Whoa!" He tied off the reins and rushed to the child over the uneven, newly tilled earth.

Colton stopped and bent over, bracing his hands on his knees and gasping.

Asa grabbed his shoulder. "What, boy?"

"Smith...in town... Lily."

Overhead an eagle shrieked, mimicking Asa's reaction within.

Asa lifted the panting boy and threw him over his shoulder. He leaped over and around the furrows he'd just plowed. *I should have expected something like this. Why did I let them go into town alone?*

"Put me down!" Colton demanded, catching his breath and straining against Asa.

Without stopping, Asa let the boy slide down to the

ground, and they were running together. The mile to town rasped his nerves. Would he get there in time? If Smith touched a hair of Judith's...

The two of them burst through the forest and raced down to Main Street. A crowd had gathered near Levi's. Asa could see only the top of Judith's white bonnet.

"Asa! Help!" Judith shrieked.

Asa sped up, his hands fisting. The crowd parted for him.

Smith was standing there, his jaw thrust out. Threatening Judith. Levi and her father stood beside her. Lily cowered behind Judith.

Asa planted himself between his wife and Smith. Dragging in ragged breaths. How to stop this man without violence? Without upsetting the children? Judith?

"You!" Smith roared. "You took our kids!" He dodged around Asa, reaching toward Lily.

Lily screamed.

Asa sidestepped, blocked him again. "Hold up!"

Smith ignored him, pushing past him.

"Hold up!" This time Asa thrust himself against Smith, their two bodies slamming together.

Asa dodged Smith's fist. And landed a hard right to Smith's jaw. His arm vibrated with the impact.

Smith grunted. Cursed. Charged.

Asa's fist shot forward, connecting with Smith's jaw.

The man staggered. But recovered.

Ignoring outcries all around, Asa dodged Smith's fists. Sized up his opponent. Smith was beefy, barrel-chested, so Asa kept his distance. Fending off Smith's blows. Waiting for the chance to end the fight.

"Smith! That's enough!" Levi roared, moving to Asa's side. "You are brawling on Main Street!"

Smith leaped back, his fists raised and panting. Facing two opponents.

"What are you thinking?" Levi shouted. "Accosting a decent woman in broad daylight?"

Asa kept his guard up, panting.

"He took our kids," Smith blustered.

"He did not!" Judith moved into Asa's line of sight. "These children ran away from you! They were living in a cave when we found them!"

Even Smith quailed before Judith's wrath. But only for a moment. "Those two kids are ours," Smith yelled. "Their parents give 'em to us."

"No, they didn't!" Colton shouted from beside Levi. "My pa didn't even like you!"

Smith started toward Colton.

Colton stood his ground, making Asa proud.

But he couldn't let Smith touch the boy. One more time, Asa blocked Smith.

The man growled his frustration and swung at Asa.

The moment Asa had been waiting for had come. A quick feint with his right and a punishing uppercut with his left.

Smith went down like a sack of rocks.

A woman behind Asa shrieked. "Sam!" She hurried over and dropped to her knees beside the inert man. She was the shabby woman he'd seen at the cabin, Smith's wife.

"He'll be all right," Asa said, panting, his knuckles stinging. He moved past her to Judith and heard Lily crying. He picked the girl up. "Are you—" he gasped for breath "—all right, Judith?"

"Yes." His wife pressed against him, her trembling denying her word.

He laid one arm around her shoulders and pulled her closer. His chest heaved not only with exertion and the rush from fighting but also with outrage. Smith had almost attacked Judith. And Lily was shaking and weeping with fright. Asa glanced around for her brother.

Over Judith's shoulder, he glimpsed Levi resting an arm around Colton's shoulders. Asa drew in enough breath to speak. "Boy, don't worry. You're staying with us."

Colton's tight expression relaxed a fraction.

Then Asa realized that most of the town encircled them. He closed his eyes. He hated everyone looking at him, them.

The Ashfords pushed to the front. "Are you all right?" Mrs. Ashford asked him.

He nodded and glanced over the heads around him, toward the rise out of town. How soon could he get his family away, home?

Groaning, Smith shoved his wife away and sat up, rubbing his chin. He glared at the gathering. "The preacher give them to us. Those kids are ours."

"No, they aren't," Ashford snapped.

"Shut up, you old namby-pamby!" Smith snapped in return. "This isn't none of your affair."

Ashford bridled at the insult.

"Smith," Asa said. Lily still quivering against him

added an edge to his voice. "The children are with us now. And that's that."

Smith got to his feet. He glared at everyone. "This isn't over."

"Yes, it is," Asa said with starch in each word. "You stay away from my family." He let his expression say, *Or else.*

"Yes," Judith said. "Anyone can see that the children don't want to be with you."

"He's a bad man," Lily declared. "He hurt us."

The crowd's mood darkened. People moved closer, glaring.

"Spare the rod and spoil the child!" Smith countered.

"There's a difference between loving discipline and harsh treatment." This came from Judith's father.

Asa nodded in agreement. As did most of the gathering.

"This isn't over," Smith repeated. "I'll get the law on you."

"Ha!" Asa responded with scorn.

The Smiths got into their wagon and drove away.

"You all right?" Asa asked Judith again.

Judith pressed her cheek against his shoulder. Her softness touched a tender spot buried deep inside him.

Then she stepped away and bent to stroke Lily's face. "Now, Lily, Mr. Brant protected us. You don't need to be afraid."

Asa reeled in his yearning to hold Judith close, to reassure himself she had not been hurt. His feelings didn't make any sense anyway. He could see she was unscathed.

"That's right, Lily. You don't have to be afraid," Ashford said, sounding more than aggravated. "This town won't let the Smiths bother you again."

Asa hoped that was true, but he wasn't leaving the children and Judith alone at the homestead or in town anytime soon.

"We should talk to the sheriff," Mrs. Ashford said. "And Noah. They will understand the law."

Young Gunther Lang stepped out of the crowd. "When I go home, I will tell Mr. Whitmore what I saw here today. He will know what to do."

At this, the people in the street began to return to their own business. Asa shook Levi's hand, thanking him without words.

Asa longed to pull Judith close once again. Thank God, he'd been able to get here in time. That thought gave him pause. It had been a long time since he'd thanked God for anything. But he did thank God for Judith.

And a glance at Colton, who'd run to him for help, and the sounds of Lily's soft sigh as she relaxed against him at last, caused him to utter the same words again silently. He would make sure his family stayed safe.

That night in her voluminous robe, Judith was waiting in front of the low fire for Asa when he returned from checking on the stock before bed. The windows were open, draped with fine cheesecloth to let the evening breeze in while keeping most of the mosquitoes out. The tree frogs were peeping constantly. Usually their song soothed her, but tonight her frayed nerves caused her to wish for silence, peace.

The children had been too upset to sleep by the fire as usual. Colton was already asleep in the loft, and Lily slept in Judith's bed. Judith felt off-kilter herself. This morning's confrontation had given her much to consider. And witnessing violence had shaken something loose inside her that wouldn't settle down. More than ever she wanted the children to stay with them. But what did Asa think? Then she recalled that he'd called them a family today. Did he realize that?

"Asa, sit with me?" She hoped he wouldn't refuse. She knew he wouldn't want to talk, but she needed to know what he was thinking. She hoped she could tell him her thoughts. And try to make sense out of what she was feeling.

He hung his hat on the peg by the door and came and sat, creaking the rocker by the low fire. "You all right?"

His blunt words did not mask the concern in his voice.

From the corner of her eye, she scanned him. He looked tired and concerned. His thick brown hair was growing and needed cutting again. She resisted the urge to brush it back from his face.

"I think I'm recovering. I was so very shocked... frightened." She drew in a steadying breath.

"I'll keep you safe." The firelight flickered over his profile, a strong one.

"I know you will." The stress of the day had exhausted her. She'd gone about doing her chores and caring for the children but feeling as if she weren't really there. Without strength for delicacy or hinting, she went straight to the point. "What are we going to do about Smith?"

He edged forward, his wrists draped over the chair arms. "You and the children aren't to go anywhere without me till this is settled."

Her terse husband had obviously been thinking about this and had been ready to inform her of his decision.

"I won't go anywhere without you, and I'll keep the children in my sight. I don't trust that man."

Asa snorted in obvious agreement.

"What do you think the law is about orphans?" She couldn't relax against the chair back. Nerves kept her stiff.

"Don't know. I'm going to ask our sheriff. Don't think Smith has any real claim. But we have to be ready if Smith presses the issue."

"Why would he even want them? He didn't seem like the kind to take in orphans." She clapped her hands, flattening a stray mosquito.

"Free labor."

Judith gripped her chair arms. "I see."

Asa let out a sound of disgust. And sat back, again creaking the wooden chair.

Asa's willingness to talk and not shut her out reassured her. He did want to keep the children, or at least, he did want to protect them. A trace of leftover fear shuddered through her. *I don't want to lose them.*

Asa's hand rested gently on her arm. "I'll keep you safe, Judith," he said again.

She pressed her hand over his. "I know you will."

The sight of Asa running down Main Street to her aid once again clutched around her heart. She drew his large, rough hand up to her cheek. "Oh, Asa," she whispered. She wanted to say more, but how could she?

His true identity and the unknown reason why he hid it lay between them. He would keep the children safe. But what if no relative came forward for them? She wanted to ask Asa to promise that they'd keep the children. But again, the fact that he could not open up made her uneasy. Yes, Asa would keep her safe. She could count on that, but would the wall between them remain, never crumbling?

Sunday came again, and Asa walked into the church, Judith beside him, with Colton on his other side. Lily, who usually insisted on holding Judith's hand, gripped his instead. Dan and Emma had met them at the schoolhouse door and entered with them. At their accustomed bench, Asa let Emma and Dan move in and sit, then Judith, and finally him and the children. Due to this week's trouble, Asa noted that their entrance garnered as much notice as he'd dreaded. He let Judith respond to the nods and greetings.

Several times this week, Asa had wanted to walk over to the sheriff's or preacher Noah Whitmore's house and consult them about Smith, but he had been unwilling to leave his family or take them with him because the children would overhear. He would talk to both men after the service.

Finally the wall clock ticked to ten and Noah, looking unusually solemn, moved to the lectern. "Before we start our usual worship service, we need to address what happened just a few days ago right on Main Street."

Asa felt the congregation's concentration on Noah intensify. A few leaned forward. "I don't need to explain the situation. And our sheriff is here. He will address you, also. First, I have received a reply from the postmaster of the Farriers' hometown." He drew a letter from his suit pocket. "I'll read it."

Asa sat, hope rising, and then a blast of sudden loss, a letdown. Did he want to send the children off to strangers? He tightened his hold on Lily, who sat on his lap.

Noah read the brief letter stating that the postmaster had not received the first letter. That the Farriers were well known in the area and there were some cousins in the county. The postmaster would contact them and also try to find out if they knew Colton Farrier Sr.'s brother's whereabouts. He would write with more news when he received any.

Then Brennan Merriday, the sheriff, rose from beside his wife Rachel and son Jacque. "I just returned from rounds. I'd been worryin' about the orphans. So when I found a telegraph office, I telegraphed the county sheriff where the Farrier family used to live. I asked about the Farrier kin. He replied that he would look into it."

Brennan paused, shifting from boot to boot. "I don't know the law about minor children left orphaned. But as the law here, I hereby publicly declare the Brants as the legal foster parents of the Farrier children until their blood kin can be found. If…anyone tries to do or say different, they'll have to deal with the law." His expression promised no quarter would be given. "You children, don't you worry. You're safe." He nodded once decisively and sat down.

Relief went through the congregation like a communal exhalation. It did not touch Asa. He would protect his family.

"Now, Mrs. Caruthers, will you lead us in our opening hymn?" Noah said and moved aside.

Asa and Judith rose with the congregation. His wife joined the singing. Asa still held Lily, who wrapped her arms around his neck. "You're safe," he whispered in the little girl's ear. She gazed into his eyes, trusting.

Cannon fire tried to disrupt his mind, interrupt the words being sung. Lily sighed and relaxed against him, muting the past. Asa glanced at Judith beside him, her sweet soprano voice charming him. An old scripture came to him, something about God setting the solitary man into a family. Then the war, the faces of men who hadn't come home to their families, streamed through his mind.

The old guilt roared through him, and he heard nothing but gunfire. He felt the walls closing in on him. He edged out of the rear pew and walked outside. The sunshine bathed his face, and he dragged in air.

Lily clung to him and then patted the back of his neck. "Don't worry," she murmured. "Don't worry."

He shut his eyes, willing away memories, the rush of battle, the screams of men and horses falling.

Her attention on the leader of the singing, Judith felt Asa leave with Lily. Had she missed something? Was Lily upset? Should she go after them or stay? Others had glanced at Asa as he left. If she went out, too, that would only garner more attention. And her husband hated attention. That much she knew. She began praying as she tried to go on singing. The song ended and another started.

More people were beginning to glance over their shoulders, no doubt wondering where Asa had gone and why. What had just been discussed caused more notice. Usually if a parent escorted a child out, others accepted the child needed discipline or a moment to regain control. But Lily was never a trouble in church.

Judith decided she must go and bring him back in if possible. Otherwise, gossip and speculation would run rampant after the service. But what had caused Asa to leave? Praying with each step, Judith slipped from the pew and left the church as quietly as she could. She glanced around the school yard, bound by the forest on three sides and the river to the west.

At first she couldn't see them. Then movement in the shade of the trees caught her eye. But she had trouble believing what she was seeing.

Asa sat on the rope swing under one of the outstretched branches of an ancient oak. Lily faced him and rested against his chest, her arms wrapped around his neck. Judith watched the swing move gently back and forth, creaking wood and rope. Lily was humming along with the hymn wafting out of the open school windows while Asa gazed into the trees to the river beyond.

The sight of the big man holding the little child halted Judith. Yet drew her like an arrow released from a bow.

The man of few words, her husband, holding and swinging Lily.

She started toward them, loath to disturb the peaceful interlude. But knowing she must. "Asa, Lily, we need to go back inside," she murmured, holding out her hand. "Mr. Whitmore will begin preaching soon."

Lily lifted her head. And sighed. "We got to go in, Mr. Brant. Thanks for swinging me. It's too big for me to be on alone."

Asa rose.

The impulse to hurry to him and throw her arms around his neck, as Lily had, nearly overwhelmed Judith. But this was not the time or place. She kept herself firmly in control.

Asa let Lily cling to his hand as they came abreast of her. Judith then walked on the other side of Lily, holding her hand. Judith led them inside to their pew. People smiled and nodded, obviously assuming that Lily had gone to the necessary or had wanted soothing after her scare this week.

Willing to let them assume whatever they wished, Judith sat down and smiled at Colton. Would she ever forget the sight of her husband gently swinging Lily? No, never. And that triggered another ache. The thought of losing the children even to family twisted around her lungs, tight and painful. *I don't want them to leave us.*

Though Judith tried to give her attention to Noah Whitmore's sermon, her mind wandered. She kept trying to let go and trust that God would do what was best for the children, Asa and her. But trusting God was often the hardest task required of a Christian. And coming to Pepin had not changed that.

But then another scripture came to mind. "I can do all things through Christ who strengthens me." She had decided to love Asa Brant, love her husband, and now to trust God with the children's future. Nothing could stop her loving and trusting. With this, peace filtered through her.

At the end of the service, her father, sitting on the other side of Emma, rose. "Preacher, I'd like to say something."

"Certainly, Mr. Jones. First let me introduce you. For those of you who haven't met him, this is Mr. Dan Jones, the father of our new schoolteacher, Miss Emma Jones, and Asa Brant's wife, Mrs. Judith Brant. Welcome, Mr. Jones."

Dan nodded to Noah. "I just want to thank all of you for welcoming my daughters to your town. As soon as I stepped off the steamboat, I was welcomed. I'm living at Levi's shop. My Judith and her husband wanted me to live with them, of course, but I felt I shouldn't intrude on the newlyweds."

People smiled at this.

"Anyway, thanks for welcoming me, and if I can ever do you a help, just let me know." Dan bowed his head and sat down.

Then Noah led them in a closing prayer, and Lavina Caruthers led them in singing the doxology, "Praise God from whom all blessings flow..."

Asa moved to the aisle and waited for Judith and Emma to precede him as they wended their way out of the school. When they reached the bright, sunny day outside, Judith felt the summer heat enfold them.

Emma claimed her hand and leaned to whisper in her ear, "I received another letter from Mr. Chandler."

Judith turned to her sister. "What did he say?" she whispered in response.

Emma's guarded look told Judith she didn't want to be overheard.

"Come see me tomorrow," was all Emma said.

Judith nodded and then turned to the sheriff's wife, Rachel, the town's baker. The woman had brought a box of cookies for Colton and Lily.

"I know thee bakes, too, but I just had to do something," Rachel said in her Quaker way, her large gray eyes serious. "I hate it when adults don't think of children's feelings." She glanced toward her stepson, Jacque.

Judith accepted the box tied with string. "Thank you."

"That Smith causing a scene right in town." Rachel shook her head.

"I'm just grateful for your husband's assistance in this."

"Don't thee worry." Rachel nodded once decisively, just as the sheriff had. "My husband won't let anybody hurt those children."

Judith thanked her and then let Asa draw her away toward home. The morning had stirred her emotions, but now she could go home, and there would be peace there. She glanced at her silent husband. Sometimes too much peace. But Lily was skipping and singing. And then tomorrow she'd return here to find out if Mason Chandler was ever coming back.

The next day, Judith knocked on her sister's door at the back of the schoolhouse. Asa had walked her and the children to town, but had stopped to visit Dan and Levi.

Emma opened her door and immediately gathered Judith into a welcoming hug. "Sister." They stood a moment, close and warm, together as they had been all their lives.

"I'm so glad you came early," Emma said, drawing her inside. "I am going to help out at the store soon, and Mrs. Ashford is expecting me for lunch."

Judith glanced around, and her prediction of how Emma would soon have the spare room decorated had proved true. Bunches of wild daisies hung upside down high on one wall, drying for future use. An embroidered pillow sat on the rocking chair. A half-crocheted doily with its hook and ball of white thread sat on the table.

Emma lifted a folded letter from the mantel. And offered it to Judith, who waved it away. "What does Mason Chandler write?"

"His father has passed."

Judith expected Emma to announce this news in a more positive tone. Now Mason should return. "And?"

"And now—" Emma grimaced "—he has something else to do before returning."

"I see." Judith folded her hands in her lap.

"I don't think this has anything to do with me," Emma said, setting the letter back on the mantel. "And it's not unreasonable for him to have legal matters, such as property to take care of, after a death."

"That's true." Judith tried to keep her expression and tone bland. Whatever her sister decided to do about her absent prospective husband was none of her business.

Emma chuckled. "You are one in a million, sister. Anybody else would be giving me advice right and left."

Judith lifted her shoulders. "Emma, you always land on your feet."

"Yes." Emma gazed around at her quarters. "I'm happy here."

Judith felt the identical phrase rise in her to be spoken. But was she happy here? Her heart squeezed tight. Would Asa ever let her in, open up to her?

Emma was watching her.

"I'm fine." But Judith knew she'd said the words too fast.

Emma nodded, obviously deciding not to pursue this topic.

Relief relaxed Judith.

Soon the sisters were walking arm in arm into town.

An unexpected sight halted them.

Smith's wife had tied up the wagon and team in front of Ashford's store. She appeared to be waiting for something. Was Smith in the store? The sisters weren't the only ones watching her. Two people were out sweeping their porches, and Mr. Ashford was standing just inside his door, staring at her. Judith couldn't see the woman's face, hidden by her poke bonnet.

Then a steamboat whistle sounded.

The woman leaped from her seat on the wagon and hurried down to the dock, a small satchel in hand.

The boat docked.

Their father walked out of his lean-to and down to the dock, carrying his tray of goods. The Smith woman boarded the boat.

A few passengers bought items from their father. Then the steamboat whistled again and headed out southward into the current, the paddle wheel turning.

"What was that all about?" Emma murmured.

Judith gazed at the team and wagon abandoned at the store. Then stared at the receding steamboat, dumbfounded.

The store door flapped open and closed. "Well, what do you think that was all about?" Mrs. Ashford, still in her apron, appeared on the store porch beside her husband.

"Looks to me like Smith lost a wife," the storekeeper said laconically.

"Serves him right," Mrs. Ashford said.

"Now, Katherine, we're not to judge," Mr. Ashford said the words but did not sound like he meant them.

"Humph." Mrs. Ashford flounced back inside the store.

Judith agreed with both the Ashfords. What they'd witnessed proved difficult to interpret any other way. If it were true, if Smith had lost his wife, she didn't like to think how Smith would react. He'd lost the children and now a wife? And he had a temper, too, a bad one.

Emma sighed. "Poor woman." She kissed Judith's cheek. "I'm due in the store, sister."

Judith pressed her cheek against Emma's and then walked across Main Street to Levi's, where Asa and the children were visiting.

Her father was returning from the dock, carrying his tray back toward the store. As they passed each other, he greeted her with cheer but went straight to Ashford, money in hand.

Judith sighed. Emma was right, as usual. Her father looked happy, more like himself a decade ago. A new place, new people, a new purpose had all enlivened him, and she could only be grateful.

"You ready?" Asa asked, turning toward her.

Though his words were terse, she heard the concern behind them. Of course he'd witnessed Mrs. Smith leaving town, too. And he, too, would worry about Smith's reaction. "Yes, husband, I'm ready to go home."

"We'll be ready tomorrow morning," Levi said to Asa. "I'll spread the word." Levi bowed slightly to Judith. "Asa says it's safe to take down the sandbag levee."

Judith turned to view the wide, flat, sky-blue river. "Yes, the Mississippi appears to have calmed down."

Asa touched her shoulder gently, prompting her to go. With farewells, the four of them turned toward home.

"That was Mrs. Smith," Lily said to Judith. "The woman who got on the boat."

So the children had observed Mrs. Smith leaving. "Yes, I'm afraid it was," Judith agreed and then pointed skyward, changing topic. "Do you see the osprey over the river?" She successfully distracted the girl as they watched the large, light-colored bird hunting for food.

But Colton's face drew down into worried lines, his

forehead creasing. She could imagine that he was still thinking about Smith and perhaps how the man would react to losing a wife, as was she.

As they walked out of town, Asa leaned close to her ear and whispered, "He'll be like a wounded bear."

Judith nodded in reply, but kept up a conversation with Lily about the different wildflowers along the track out of town—white yarrow, daisies and pink-tipped clover humming with bees.

Mr. Smith had been bested by Asa in front of the town, and now his wife had left him for all the town to see. Judith walked closer to Asa, grateful for his protection. Asa was right. *"He'll be like a wounded bear."* A creature no one dared challenge.

Chapter Eleven

The next morning, Asa left Judith and Lily above the store, busy helping Mrs. Ashford make rhubarb pies. Emma was manning the store. Mr. Ashford and Colton followed Asa to Levi's, where the men of the town were gathered. The barkeep was joking and the men were laughing at something he'd said. Turning, the man caught sight of Asa, snapped to attention and saluted crisply.

Before he could stop himself, Asa returned the salute.

"We're ready, captain," the barkeep said, grinning.

Asa burned with irritation at his slip and tried to distract the others with words. "Taking the levee down will be easier than putting it up." It had been decided that they would store the sandbags behind the shops on the high side of the street and cover them with a tarp. One never knew when they might come in handy, and as long as the burlap stayed relatively dry, they would last long enough to be used again before rotting.

A few men had brought carts and wheelbarrows,

and soon the sandbag levee was coming down, bag by bag. Asa organized the men into three groups: one that dismantled the levee, one that carted the bags, and one that helped unload and then stack the sandbags against the rising bluff behind town.

In the midst of this labor, Smith arrived in town. Recognizing him, every man paused as if ordered to.

In turn, Smith obviously did not want to talk to them, but what could he do? He approached them, scowling.

Asa felt a tiny bit sorry for the man.

But Smith soon blotted that out. "I'm looking for ma wife. I sent her in for supplies. You seen her?"

The men fell silent, and all looked to Asa.

He did not want to talk to this man. He glanced at Ashford, hoping he would, but the storekeeper had his mouth clapped shut, glaring at Smith.

"Your wife got on a boat yesterday," Asa said, keeping his tone neutral.

Smith weathered this as if he'd expected it. "Goin' north or south?" Smith demanded.

Asa was not going to say. If the wife left him, she probably had good reason to. He shrugged. "You'd know better than me."

Smith muttered curses under his breath. "Where's my team and wagon?" he snapped.

Levi came forward. "I took care of them last night. Your wagon is back of the saloon, and the horses are hobbled, grazing by the river." He motioned farther south.

Without thanking Levi, Smith swung away and headed toward the riverbank. Soon he passed them, leading his horses up Main Street toward the saloon at the end of town.

The men worked silently now. All watched Smith, looking over their shoulders or with sideways glances. As they continued ferrying the sandbags away from the river, the only sounds were the creaks of carts and wheelbarrows.

Finally Smith had hitched his team and, without a backward glance, drove out of town. Asa and the rest of them could not take their attention from the man's back till he disappeared around the bend into the surrounding forest.

In an unconscious reflex, Asa glanced toward the windows above the store, where Judith was. Sudden fear hitched in his chest. He didn't know what had transpired in the Smiths' marriage to make the wife leave him. But Asa knew that he was not the husband a woman like Judith deserved. Would he suffer the same fate as Smith? Would Judith one day say she'd had enough of his solitary ways?

Then he saw Judith looking down out the upstairs window. She raised a hand tentatively.

He waved, too. No, Judith would never go back on her vow. She would stay with him no matter what. But why couldn't he break through, break free of the invisible ropes that tied him, kept him from reaching for her, letting her know what she was coming to mean to him?

Nearly two weeks passed, and all the crops were planted. Standing at the edge of her garden with Lily, Judith couldn't help herself. She whooped.

From the barn Asa came running, Colton behind him. "What's wrong?" he called out.

"Oh, I'm sorry." She turned to them, pressed a hand to her mouth, embarrassed. "Nothing bad is happening. I was just…excited." She gestured toward her garden. The past weeks had been warm and bright, perfect for growing. "My lettuce is high enough to begin to harvest. We'll have fresh salad today with supper."

"See, Colton?" Lily said, pointing toward the rows of green lettuce.

Asa paused beside Judith. "Sounds good. Real good."

This from Asa was praise indeed.

"I can't wait," Judith continued, trying to prolong this spark of response from Asa, "for the rest of the vegetables to begin to produce. I'm tired of dried and canned vegetables. They are nothing like fresh."

"After the rain stopped, everything dried up fine. I got my crops, and Mason Chandler's, in easy." Asa nodded with satisfaction. "Corn's up to my ankles."

"Knee-high by the Fourth of July," Colton said, cheerful for once. "That's what my dad always said." A shadow passed over the boy's face. And his usual scowl settled back into place.

Lily reached up and gripped Judith's hand as if reacting to her brother's dark mood.

For the millionth time, Judith wished she could do something more than provide food and shelter to help these orphans. But she could not heal their hearts. Only God could.

Then she noticed that Asa was frowning deeply. He turned abruptly and left her side. Practically running to his barn. What had upset him so? They'd merely talked of vegetables and corn.

Colton looked up at her. "Did I make Mr. Brant mad?"

"How could you?" she said. "Everyone knows that saying. It's a true one. And the corn crop is doing well, from what I've seen."

"Then why did he leave us like that?" Lily asked.

So even Lily was noticing Asa's moods. "I don't know, children." She paused, trying to come up with an explanation. She thought of her brother and how he'd changed from a happy, easygoing man to a man she couldn't talk to and who appeared to have forgotten the family they'd once had. Could that be a clue to Asa's shuttered ways? "Mr. Brant was in the war. Sometimes that makes men behave…differently."

The words were completely inadequate, but they were the best she could come up with. Truth to tell, she didn't know if the war was what was causing Asa's silence and efforts to keep her at arm's length. That might stem instead from the fact that he didn't find in her what he wanted in a wife. *If only I were prettier…* It had happened before at home, with Tom Southby, so why not also with Asa? Although there was no real comparison, she mentally sighed, trying not to wish for curly blond hair instead of straight brown and sparkling blue eyes instead of serious brown. Keeping all this to herself, she patted the boy's shoulder. "Go help in the barn."

"Okay." Colton turned away. Lily stayed near Judith, holding her dolly close.

Bending, Judith began twisting off the lettuce, leaving the roots in place so they could grow another leafy crop or two. God had blessed them with good soil. A few seeds, rain and sun and the earth produced food. Every green leaf she lay in her folded apron was a tiny evidence of God's creation and love for them. She prayed for another blessing from God, that Asa would tear down the wall around his heart. And that he could then love her—just a little.

Come Sunday, Asa listened to the last of the notes of the final hymn and bowed his head for Noah's closing prayer. In the room with every window open for any passing breeze, Noah had preached on Christ, the Good Shepherd, whose sheep knew his voice. And for some reason the words had worked their way through Asa's shell into his center. He felt vulnerable and wished they could leave for home right away. And Colton's innocent phrase from a few days ago still plagued him. Fourth of July. The day in 1863 that he couldn't forget. Ever.

He wanted to leave immediately, but of course they couldn't. Today one of the church's summer picnics would be held in the school yard in the cool shade of the oaks and maples. So he let himself be drawn along with the other men. They were hanging their suit coats in the school cloakroom and rolling up their sleeves to set up the tables for the food.

Children were laughing and teasing as the older brothers and sisters spread out worn quilts in the shade. Women were waiting with pressed white tablecloths to cover the tables and set out the fried chicken, biscuits, fresh lettuce salads and all manner of desserts. Helping with the work, Asa tamped down his urge to head home. Doing so would call unwanted attention to him, the last thing he wanted.

The tables were set up and the cloths spread on them. He glanced around and saw Judith chatting with Emma. With Lily's help, she was setting out the large green salad and heaping plate of small fancy triangle sandwiches she'd made. Then the fragrance of fried chicken wafted over to him.

From a hamper, Mrs. Ashford lifted a loaded platter of golden chicken. He salivated. The storekeeper's wife had a way with fried chicken. A good way. He'd also overheard that the sheriff's wife, who was a notable baker, had brought another of her famous three-layer coconut cakes. Just thinking of it made Asa's mouth water.

Maybe today he could just let go of the deep urge to keep separate. Children laughing, a breeze rustling the leaves overhead, all of it eased into him. The resistance to being here weakened bit by bit.

After calling for attention, Gordy Osbourne, a young deacon, was offering grace, and upon "Amen," the bright chatter was unleashed like air from a balloon. Asa let the cheerful sounds roll over him, somehow further soothing his ragged edges within. Then Judith claimed his arm, and they led their family through the buffet line.

Soon they sat in the shade on the old quilt they had brought. Dan and Emma had joined them, and the Ashfords had settled on a quilt next to theirs.

Colton sat beside Asa, as usual, and Asa let himself

enjoy the sight of Judith sitting primly on the quilt with her light blue cotton skirt around her. She had designed this new dress herself, and he marveled at the way she could take a bolt of cloth and make something with such style. His Judith was a talented seamstress. Pride in her swelled within him.

"That new dress is just lovely," Mrs. Ashford said, voicing Asa's sentiments.

"Thank you," Judith said. "My Singer makes sewing a delight. I have to make myself leave it alone some days." She smiled shyly, glancing at him.

"I see Lily has a new dress to match," the woman went on.

Lily hopped up and twirled. "I like it. It's just like Mrs. Brant's."

"Our mother used to sew us identical dresses," Emma added. "Even though we weren't identical. She liked to show people we were twins."

Asa concentrated on eating the food he'd heaped on his plate. Judith was a good cook, but it seemed that their church abounded with such. He glanced once again at the imposing white coconut cake in the center of the dessert table, waiting to be cut.

"Ned and I were talking last night," the storekeeper's wife went on. "We think it's time that our little town held a proper Fourth of July celebration."

"Yes," Mr. Ashford added. "We've always held a special prayer service and picnic here, but I think we should have a parade this year, and speakers."

Asa put down his fork, staring at the man. He held

himself in check, keeping his seat, not revealing how this riled him.

"We were thinking that we'd ask our veterans to address the children about the need to fight to keep our nation free," Mrs. Ashford said in between bites.

Asa forced himself to begin eating again, though tasting nothing. The Ashfords could make all the plans they wanted, but he wasn't talking about the war. And that was final.

Judith doubted anybody else had sensed the alteration in Asa's mood. During the church service, she'd sensed him relaxing, letting go of his recent reaction to Colton's innocent mention of July Fourth. Now he'd tightened up again, and his eyes had taken on a stubborn glint.

"Did you get your flower garden planted, Emma?" Judith asked, changing the subject when Mrs. Ashford paused in outlining plans for the celebration.

"Yes, I've been going around asking for slips of plants—hostas, bluebells and a few lilac shoots—and I think I've come up with a pretty flower bed around the school entrance and my own door. I do love a bit of color."

Unfortunately, this ploy only briefly sidelined the main topic of conversation. The Ashfords and her father returned to the Independence Day celebration plans. Judith tried not to show her own increasing concern over Asa, who'd stopped talking at all.

When Lily finished eating her plate of food, she popped up. "Mr. Brant, will you swing me?"

Judith held her breath. In Asa's present mood, that was a lot to ask.

They were saved by Jacque Merriday and Johan Lang, who came over and drew Colton and Lily into a noisy, gleeful game of tag.

Judith waited till the earliest possible moment that she and Asa could leave without drawing undue attention to themselves. The four of them rode home in silence. The children were tired from the long morning of sitting quietly in church and then eating a big meal followed by over an hour of tag and other games. Judith was exhausted with worry over Asa's mood change. And she hated that. What good did worrying do? But how could she not?

The picnic had finally come to an end, and with deep relief, Asa drove up the final rise to their clearing. The picnic basket contents, now just the plates, cutlery and napkins, rattled in the rear of the wagon. His mind buzzed, but he held the troubled thoughts at bay and stared straight ahead. Soon he would be in his barn, his refuge.

Aware of Judith's concern, he kept his gaze forward. Usually she did not press him, but would she today? He did not want to speak about the war. The track to their place twisted around its last bend, the full leafy green trees and thick pines opening to their clearing.

Shock shot through him. He dragged on the reins. "Whoa!"

His sudden move rocked the wagon. On the bench

beside him, Judith bumped against him. "What?" Looking up, she gasped.

Their door had been smashed from its hinges. Then he glimpsed a few of his hens sitting on tree branches. Shock vibrated within. Concern for Judith and the children's safety washed over him, a hot rush of blood.

Judith tried to start forward.

He swung his arm in front of her, barring her. "Stay!" He slid down from the bench and pulled out his sidearm. He looked to the children, too. "Stay." He first went to check his and Mason Chandler's cows. They were not in the barn. All of his tack and wall pegs and shelves had been pulled down, and some harnesses had been cut. He cursed silently.

Next he raced to the cabin. He halted on the threshold, stunned. Someone had broken everything. Everything. The rockers lay on their sides, their spindles cracked and kicked out. Judith's blue-and-white curtains smoldered on the fire. Broken crockery had been scattered over the floor. Swiftly he moved to the hiding place behind a stone in the fireplace. Relief poured through him. His bag of gold and silver coin had not been discovered.

"Asa, please? What's happened?" Judith called, her voice shrill with worry.

He tore himself from the scene of wanton destruction and went outside. "He wrecked everything." Then words failed him.

Jumping down, Judith ran forward past him. Glancing inside, she cried out. "No!"

The cry cut him in two.

She ran inside and knelt by her Singer sewing machine. "It's just been turned over. It's too strong to be broken."

Nearby little Lily was weeping, clutching her dolly to her. Asa wanted to comfort her, but he stood, pulsing with anger, gulping in air.

"Mrs. Brant!" Colton yelled. "Your garden!"

Judith whirled, started running around the side of the cabin to her garden. "No!" she cried out.

Asa hurried after her, catching up Lily.

"My garden," Judith moaned. His wife stood gazing at what had been her neat garden. Her rows of green sprouts, her fence for the climbing beans and peas had been ripped down. It looked like someone had ridden a horse through the garden, churning and ripping up everything green.

Then beyond, he saw the cows grazing in both his trampled corn and hay fields and he roared with wordless outrage. Anger boiled within him. He set Lily down and swung away. He knew who'd done this. "Smith." And he was going to pay. Now.

Judith saw Asa heading back to the wagon. And she instantly knew what he intended. "Asa!" she called. "Stop! Think!"

Her husband did not pause, perhaps did not even hear her. His silent rage terrified her. "Asa! Wait!" She ran after him. "Asa!" She had to stop him before he did anything rash.

She picked up her skirts and ran faster. "Asa! Please!"

He ignored her. He reached the wagon.

She caught up with him and grabbed his arm.

He shook her off.

She stumbled and fell to the ground. She cried out in surprise.

Asa stopped, swung to her. "Judith!" He bent down and lifted her to her feet. "Did I hurt you? I... Judith... I'm sorry. I was so angry, Judith." Gasping for breath, he held her up and gazed at her. Looking furious with himself.

She settled her nerves with a shake. She gripped Asa's forearms, feeling their sinew and strength. "I'm all right, Asa. I know you didn't mean to push me."

He clasped her to him. "I would never hurt you."

She reveled in this moment of closeness. "I know that, Asa," she murmured, her heart pounding from seeing their homestead ruined, but more from the fear of what Asa might do to Smith. "I know how angry you were. I had to stop you so you could think...consider what best to do."

He held her closer. "He wrecked your garden."

The concern in his voice nearly broke her composure. "He destroyed your crops." She swallowed with difficulty. "Asa, the sheriff is home. We need to bring him here so he can see what's been done. We think it's Smith, but the law must find proof, isn't that right?" She tilted her head back, watched him. Would he go for the law?

He'd let his hat fall back on its leather string and with one hand pushed back his hair that needed cutting. "Judith, you are a smart woman. And as much as I don't want to, I'll do it. First I have to see to those cows.

Then we'll drive over and get the sheriff." He touched her shoulder and turned away.

Judith tried to gather the children, but Colton went after Asa, saying he would help.

As she watched them go, she wanted to head inside and start straightening and righting the damage that had been done, but she knew she had to leave it. Sheriff Merriday must see what Smith or whoever had done to their home. A terrible feeling of violation swept over her. This was their home. And someone had desecrated it.

Lily was weeping. Judith sat down in the grass and drew the little girl onto her lap. Then she glimpsed the two gray-and-white kittens climbing down from an oak tree, where they must have taken refuge.

"See our kitties, Lily. They're all right. And we'll be all right. Mr. Brant and the sheriff will protect us." The kittens scampered to them and climbed into their laps as if frightened, too.

"Mr. Smith is a bad man," Lily whimpered against Judith's bodice.

Judith could not disagree with the child. Judith dreaded all that must follow. Dealing with the law would not be pleasant. An understatement.

Soon Asa and his family on the wagon and the sheriff on his horse returned to the Brant clearing.

While Asa and his family stayed in the wagon, the sheriff on his saddle, scanned the area. He issued a sound of disgust. "Y'all left everything as you found it?"

"Yes." Asa heard the catch in his voice that he couldn't prevent.

"I'm going to look around and take notes about what I see," Merriday said. "You'd be surprised how people will make mistakes when they're mad, leave something behind that will point right to them."

Colton spoke up after not saying a word since he'd helped Asa with the cows. "Smith did this."

"It would appear that is true," Sheriff Merriday agreed. "But in court we'll need proof. The law is the law, son. Isn't that right, Brant?"

Asa did agree, but earlier he had forgotten that. Judith had stopped him from heading straight for Smith in the heat of anger and revenge. Smith could even have counted on that and been lying in wait to ambush him. The burn in the pit of his stomach flared. "We have to let the law handle this, Colton. We're not like Smith."

Colton gazed up at him, looking confused.

"Colton," Judith said, "Mr. Smith did not treat you children as he should have, and he lost you. He evidently has also lost his wife, and instead of seeing that he should change his ways, he took out his anger on us. We are not like Mr. Smith. We abide by the law and try to treat our neighbors as ourselves."

Asa was grateful that Judith was able to say the right words to the children.

"I'll go over everything," the sheriff said, sliding from his saddle, "write down everything I see, and then I'll interview you two about what you saw. I'll do my best." He handed his reins to Asa.

"Of course, you will, Sheriff. How long will it be

before I can go inside and try to set things back to normal?" Judith asked.

"I'll start my investigation there," Merriday said and headed toward their wrecked door.

Lily was sitting with her head in Judith's lap, beside Asa. Both females sat hunched as if beaten down.

Asa slipped an arm around Judith. He had no words. He hoped she still trusted him to take care of her.

She glanced up at him and tried to smile. "We'll be all right," she said.

He nodded. But he could see a bit of his trampled fields stretching behind Judith's garden. They would manage, but days, weeks of work had been swept away. And the growing season here would not permit him to plant a new crop. He would just have to make do with what survived.

Smith. Asa's gut burned with anger. He drew in a deep breath, helped Judith and Lily down and then, with Colton beside him, drove his horses to the shade of the barn. He stepped down to unhitch them, grateful again that Judith had shaken him back to himself before he'd done something rash. But Smith would pay for this.

Chapter Twelve

The next summer morning, another muggy one, Asa rode beside Sheriff Brennan Merriday. Today they'd confront Smith. The forest crowded up to the uneven two-rut track their horses walked, blocking any breeze from reaching them. Perspiration trickled down Asa's back.

He recognized another landmark he'd seen on his last visit to Smith, a charred and broken tree that had been struck by lightning long ago. "We're getting close," he muttered to Merriday, not wanting to disturb the quiet.

"Good." Though the sheriff had searched Asa's property for hours yesterday, he had been unable to find any hard evidence that Smith or anyone else had been the one who had vandalized the Brant cabin and barn and destroyed their garden and crops. So the sheriff proposed this trip to Smith's. Some items had been taken from the cabin, and the sheriff hoped he might find them in plain sight at Smith's.

An invisible ball had formed in Asa's throat. The

shattered expression in Judith's eyes yesterday lingered, even though this morning at breakfast she'd forced smiles and reassuring words for him and the children. He was unable to shake the weight of awful guilt over what had happened beside the wagon yesterday. He'd been rough with his wife. In his fury, he'd knocked Judith down. The shock of that still unnerved him.

He'd hated to leave her this morning, wanting somehow to make it up to her and unwilling to leave her unprotected if Smith anticipated their move and doubled back to harm his family. But the sheriff's wife and son and Levi Comstock had come to protect and keep company with Judith and the children.

"I don't know if this visit to Smith will work or not," Merriday said, his saddle leather creaking in a quiet rhythm with his horse's gait.

Asa turned to him, feeling the hot sun on his back. "I'm pretty sure it will. The man has no control."

Merriday nodded, his mouth twisting at one corner. "I'm always surprised at how stupid thieves and such are. And how often they are ready to tell you everything. Some like to brag, and some just can't control their mouths." Merriday shook his head. "How much of your crops do you think you lost?"

Since yesterday after the picnic, anger had burned low in Asa's stomach without letup. At this question, it spiked, spurting acid into his throat. "I think I lost over half of it." Or, he hoped he could salvage half. Smith had not been thorough, and some corn was already righting itself and straining toward the sun. But for certain, he would have none to sell, and that meant little cash.

As if reading Asa's mind, Merriday said, "Don't you worry. Folk hereabout will help."

Asa wanted to refuse any help, but he had Judith and the children to think of. And it was unwise to spend all his gold and silver. That was there in case of any emergency. "I think I'll be all right," Asa said, putting up a good front. "My leather goods sell pretty well in town and to people on the boats." But the river trade would end when the Mississippi decided to freeze over.

Merriday nodded solemnly.

A doe bounded in front of them across the track. Yes, he could hunt, too. The area abounded in deer. The motion drew Asa from his thoughts. "Smith's place is just ahead around that bend," he cautioned.

"Remember, let me do the talking."

Asa agreed and slowed more. He wanted to fight Smith, not talk, but he reined in his anger. He needed a clear head. "We better do a little reconnaissance."

"Yep." Merriday slowed his horse and slid down. Soon both of them had tied their horses to young saplings off the track. They edged through the pine trees, stepping carefully, making little noise. They communicated with motions.

Soon they found a spot where they could view the Smith property. Except for smoke from the chimney, the homestead did not appear to be occupied. The place was eerily silent.

Merriday leaned close and whispered, "Where would he go?"

Asa shrugged. He'd come ready for a confrontation,

and this atmosphere of emptiness, vacancy disconcerted him. Crows cawed, flying high overhead.

"Does it look to you like smoke's coming out around the door?" Merriday asked, pointing to the cabin.

"Yes." Asa stood up straight, enlightenment shining clear. "He's gone and set a fire in his cabin to burn everything."

Merriday also bolted upright. "It might be a trap."

Asa looked at the forest surrounding them. "The squirrels are quiet. They'd be chattering if anybody was moving around."

Merriday considered this and nodded. "But better safe than sorry. Let's check out the barn first. I'll go around the other way. When you hear an owl call, move in careful-like."

Asa nodded and waited. Finally he heard the owl whistle, and he moved through the trees and brush alongside Smith's clearing, his sidearm in his hand.

Bent over to make himself less of a target, Asa hustled through the tall wild grass and met Merriday. Except for dirt and trash, Smith had left little in the barn. Then, with stealth, they approached the cabin.

When the sheriff moved to open the door, Asa barred him with an arm. "If we open the door wide, we'll feed the fire with more air. The fire will flare up. I know we've had a lot of rain, but better to keep this fire under control. Not spread it to the forest."

"What do you suggest?" Merriday watched him intently.

"We need something to carry water in."

Out back they rummaged around the man's junk pile

and found a chipped pitcher with a broken handle and a rusted bucket that could still hold water. They returned to the door with the leaky vessels full from the well.

"I'll open the door a crack and you throw your bucket of water inside," Asa said.

Merriday moved into place.

Asa opened it and white smoke rushed out. For the next several minutes, the two men drew water and threw water inside till the smoke lessened, and then they opened the door wider and finished putting out the fire on the floor of the cabin. They stepped outside, drawing in clean air and coughing.

"That must have been smoldering for hours," Merriday said at last, wiping his streaming eyes with his sleeve.

Asa nodded grimly, doing the same. "He's left, and he didn't want anybody else to have his cabin."

"And maybe he hoped the fire would spread to the forest and endanger others." Merriday spat into the grass, his spittle black from inhaling smoke.

Asa's throat was raw from the smoke, too. "Well, one good thing. It looks like Smith has packed up and left."

A gray-and-white cat climbed down the rough bark of a tree and waded gracefully through the tall grass. It paused about ten feet from Asa, meowed, then waited to be acknowledged, sitting on its haunches.

"Hello, mama cat, you remember me?" Asa stooped and held out a hand. "I took your kittens home."

As if she understood his words, she hurried to him and rubbed against his bent knee.

He felt a twinge of relief seeing the cat had not been

hurt. Probably too sly to be caught. "Mama cat, I guess you'd better come home with me and see your little ones. Come on." He waved his hand.

The cat let him lift her onto his shoulder, where she rode as the two men walked back to their horses.

"I will still send out a notice to the surrounding jurisdictions about the incident and tell them Sam Smith is wanted for questioning in connection with it."

Asa doubted this would do any good. "At least he's gone." Or he'd better be.

"I think he is. He'd want to put miles between him and the humiliation of the children running away from him, then being beaten in a fight on Main Street and finally having the whole town watch his wife leave him."

That did make sense. Asa and the sheriff untied their grazing horses and rode away, the mama cat curled on the saddle in front of Asa. Smith's destruction at Asa's place still chafed him, but what could he do? He'd come to do battle, and the enemy had retreated.

"That kind of man makes his own bad ending. What a man sows, he reaps," Merriday commented. A red fox at the edge of the forest peered at them. "Someday he'll run into someone who'll get the best of him bad."

Asa couldn't disagree. Now that Smith had disappeared, all he wanted to do was go home, set things to right. Again he recalled Judith's shocked expression looking up at him from the ground where he had pushed her in his anger. How could he set that to right?

"What do you think of this idea of having speeches in town on the Fourth?"

Asa's gut twisted. "I'm not giving one."

Merriday chuckled drily. "Me, neither."

Asa's will hardened. No one was going to make him talk about the war. Period.

The next evening, Asa and Judith sat on the new bench outside their door, exhausted from company. A steady parade of people had dropped by all day, family by family. Every visitor had brought something, like the bench Noah Whitmore had made. And staples like flour and sugar. Baked goods. Peace had finally come when everyone had at last gone home. With all the company, Asa still hadn't been able to apologize to Judith for knocking her to the ground on Sunday. Too much to do, too many interruptions and his lack of knowing what to say.

Now, in the lowering light, with sunset streamers of red and gold above and behind the trees, Colton and Lily ran around in the wild grass, trapping yellow-green glowing fireflies in a jar with a pierced lid and squealing with excitement.

Asa wondered if Judith was as exhausted as he was. It wasn't just riding to and from the Smiths' place. It was the guilt, the anger and the uncertainty. He'd had all the crops planted and everything had been going smoothly. Now this.

"I didn't expect so many neighbors to come," Judith said, patting the bench with appreciation.

Asa nodded.

The children squealed and called back and forth to each other, "I got one!"

"I know people said they had spare items and wanted

to give them to us," Judith said. "But many items looked brand-new. Such kindness."

"I never thought I'd be taking charity," Asa said, bitterness etching his throat.

"Charity means love, Asa." She glanced up at him. A cicada shrieked nearby. "Our neighbors were showing us their friendship, their concern and their sorrow over the wrong done to us. Wouldn't we do the same if it had happened to Levi, for instance?"

Asa gathered the words he had to say. What did he want to tell her? *I'm sorry I'm not a very good husband. You deserve better.*

"We got ten!" Lily called out in shrill excitement, interrupting.

"Wonderful," Judith replied. "See if you can double that!"

"I'm sorry, Judith." Asa finally put into words the burden he'd carried since he'd pushed Judith down.

She glanced at him. "For what?"

Her easy forgiveness only caused the guilt to weigh heavier. "I knocked you down."

"No, you didn't. I bumped against you and stumbled. That's all." She rested a hand on his sleeve. "Asa, you would never hurt me. We were both upset, and it was just an accident."

He clasped her hand. "Judith…"

Then she cupped his cheek with her free hand. "It's all right, Asa. We're going to be all right."

Her soft hand against his face melted a tightness in his chest. He knew he should pull away. He couldn't.

Instead he leaned into her hand, seeking her softness like a starving man seeking bread.

"Asa," she whispered. "Asa." She leaned forward.

And he could not stop the pull toward her. Her lips were less than an inch from his. He didn't deserve this good and kind woman, shouldn't kiss her. But he felt his resistance weakening. He let his mouth dip toward hers.

Lily cried out.

They jerked apart.

"Lily!" Judith called.

"Colton pushed me!"

Asa nearly kissed me. Judith trembled deep inside. No man had ever kissed her, really kissed her. The peck Asa had given her in front of everyone at their wedding did not even come close to a real kiss.

"Colton!" Asa called out. "Don't push your sister!"

"I didn't," Colton snapped back.

At this insolence, Asa moved to rise.

A sudden thought prompted Judith. She gripped Asa's lower arm.

He paused, glancing her way.

"Children, if you can't play nicely together, you'll have to go to bed early," Judith pronounced.

Both children grumbled but separated and began chasing fireflies again.

Asa relaxed where he sat next to her, glancing at her sideways for an explanation for stopping him.

She lowered her voice. "Brothers and sisters fight. Colton and Lily haven't been. They haven't been be-having normally for siblings. They've been through so much heartbreak. This bickering is actually a good sign."

Asa obviously considered her words. He nodded slowly.

She sighed, letting go of his arm. She rested her hand on the bench between them.

And Asa let his hand rest on hers.

This small gesture released something tight inside her. She spent a few moments cherishing this contact with her husband. A new, unusual feeling, and finally she was able to identify it. Hope. At home in the midst of her brother's turbulent marriage and Mabel Joy's meanness, she'd lost hope. Now she was again feeling it. She and Asa might become closer. She just needed to be patient.

Days later Asa, with Colton at his side, was once again standing at the edge of his fields, staring at what was left of his corn and hay. Would he have enough silage to feed his stock over the winter or enough corn to supply his family's need for corn meal? Over three fourths of his corn crop had been destroyed. The hay had been battered, but he judged he could harvest most of it. Would it be enough to weather the winter without depleting his hard money?

He heard the creaking of a wagon and hoofbeats. He turned. Who was coming now? Two conflicting reactions vied within. Though grateful for the way the town had come to their aid, he didn't want anybody's help, didn't want to need anybody's help. This confusion churned inside.

Smith had gotten his revenge, two-fold.

Asa with Colton walked to the house to see who had come.

Noah Whitmore and Martin Steward were climbing down from Whitmore's wagon. Asa swallowed his bruised pride and waved in welcome. These were good men, men he respected.

"Asa!" Whitmore called out. "We've brought back your chairs."

Asa hurried to be the one to help the preacher, a notable woodworker, lift down the repaired rockers.

"The new wood parts don't match exactly, but I was able to get the rockers back into usable shape." Noah removed his driving glove and smoothed his palm over the wood. Asa understood this. He liked the feel of leather, and Noah loved wood the same way.

Asa couldn't quite voice his thanks, so he nodded, gripped Noah's hand and shook it.

Soon the repaired rockers were back in place. Since Judith and Lily were out looking for wild berries and herbs, Asa offered the men cool buttermilk from the springhouse and cookies from the jar. The men and Colton sat on the benches at the table, which Noah had been able to put back together without taking them away for repair.

Asa knew he should make conversation, but he was at a loss for words. He'd heard that saying many times, and now he owned it.

"We're all really sorry about what happened," Martin said.

Asa nodded, chewing the delicious oatmeal cookie

and trying to focus on its sweetness. The kittens sat on the floor by Colton, watching him eat. Mama cat, already at home with them, lay on the threshold, soaking up the sunshine.

"There's not much we can do to make up for—" Martin began.

Asa cut him off. "Not your job."

"We're a community," Noah said, "and everybody needs help sometimes. After all, you planted Mason Chandler's fields because he isn't here."

Asa did not reply. Mason was a friend. Without his suggestion to advertise for brides, Asa wouldn't have Judith.

Noah continued, "But we didn't come to offer you help—"

"—but to make a suggestion," Martin interrupted, "if you'll listen to us."

Asa grimaced at his own lack of grace. "Go ahead."

"Well, a few years ago," Martin said, "I hurt my back and couldn't harvest my crop. The Langs brought in my crop, and Gunther stayed with us to take care of me. I was as weak as a kitten, helpless, couldn't even walk to the necessary alone." Martin's tone still revealed how humiliated he'd felt.

This admission caught Asa's attention. "That's hard."

"Yes, I was very grateful for their help, but it was a humbling experience." The younger man looked directly into Asa's eyes. "And I was thinking that we all got our crops planted late this year. The rain and storms set us back. So we'll be in a rush to get the crops in before hard winter sets in."

Asa stopped chewing and listened. What was the man trying to say?

"I was thinking that since you won't have much to harvest, you could go around and help others get theirs in faster. And they could thank you in corn and other produce for Judith to put up for winter."

Asa tried not to absorb the wave of repugnance that washed over him. He'd never been a hired hand. He'd always worked his own land.

"And Asa," Noah said, "it's just for this season. We could use your help. Every year brings its own challenges."

Asa couldn't argue with that. "I'll think on it."

"You do that," Martin said. "If you decide to help your neighbors, we'll make it be known. Men can ask you then."

Asa nodded, still dealing with his urge to say no. A man with a family couldn't do just what he wanted.

"I almost forgot." Noah pulled a folded letter from his hip pocket. "A letter came from Illinois, and I think it might be about the Farrier family."

Asa received the rumpled letter that had traveled miles up the river. He just stared at it. Then he tucked it into his shirt pocket. "I'll wait till Judith comes home."

"Good idea," Martin said. "Womenfolk like to be in on opening letters."

Noah grinned. "You're learning, Martin." The preacher turned to Asa. "I remember when he was a green newlywed."

Asa tried to look as though he were amused, too. But he was the green newlywed now, and he knew he was doing a poor job as a husband.

Then he heard Judith and Lily singing.

The men rose almost as one to go out and greet Judith and Lily in their matching blue dresses and white bonnets. Asa stood back and weathered all the social chatter that Judith handled so well, asking after each man's family and smiling at Asa for offering them refreshment. Lily and Colton lured the kittens outside to play. Mama cat followed her little ones.

Soon the two men climbed back on the wagon. As Noah drove them away, Martin called over his shoulder, "You think about our suggestion and let us know!"

Judith turned to Asa and lifted an eyebrow.

He wanted to head to his barn and start another leather belt to sell, but he forced himself to repeat what they'd said.

"You don't want to work on other men's fields." She said it as a statement, not a question.

He frowned in reply.

"What's that in your pocket?" she asked, touching the letter.

He pulled it out. Evidently the motion drew the attention of the children, and they came running back to them. In that moment, their presence wrapped around him. He'd been alone for so long—even when among people. How had it happened that he now had a family and Judith? He handed the letter to her. Would the Farrier family be coming to claim the children?

Judith didn't want to open this letter. She didn't want to lose the children, who filled Asa's silence, separating them. Holding the battered paper, she read the return address on the back: Mrs. Edith Waggoner, Sterling, Illinois. Then she realized that Asa and the children were all looking at her, waiting. "Well, I guess we should open it and see who Mrs. Edith Waggoner is."

She slid her finger under the wax seal and spread out the diamond-shaped paper that enclosed the letter and the one-page letter itself.

June 12, 1873
Dear Mr. and Mrs. Brant,
The local postmaster contacted me with news about members of my extended family, the Farriers. I was very sorry to hear of their passing. Such a sweet couple to leave us at a young age. I am Mr. Colton Farrier's aunt, his mother's sister. I understand their children are staying with you. Thank you for taking them in. I will try to contact Colton's brother, Matthew, but that will take time. He's traveling in the West. I will keep in touch with you on this matter. May God bless you for your kindness to my great nephew and niece.
Yours faithfully,
Mrs. Edith Waggoner

Judith had wanted to hear from the children's family and at the same time hadn't wanted to. She wanted the children to stay. They already had been knit into a family, the four of them. Yet she felt shame at the relief this simple letter brought her. *I'm being selfish. God may merely want us to care for them until their blood kin can claim them.* She forced down the feeling of possessiveness.

"So, who is Mrs...?" Lily asked, looking up and then leaning against Judith.

"She is your father's aunt, your great-aunt," Judith said, smoothing back Lily's hair. "She sounds like a nice lady."

"She's not coming for us?" Colton asked sharply from Asa's side.

"No, but she is going to try to locate your father's brother. You remember him, don't you?" Judith replied as Lily wrapped her arms around Judith's waist. No doubt this uncertainty was upsetting the children.

"Yeah, I 'member him," Colton muttered, looking at his feet. Lily appeared confused.

Judith shook herself. This was not about her. These children needed reassurance. "But you are with us now and will stay with us till..." She looked to Asa.

"...till some of your own blood comes," Asa said. "Already promised. I won't give you up till good kin comes. I won't let anybody hurt you."

Judith nodded. "Now I need to get into the kitchen and start cooking. Or there will be no dinner today."

Asa touched her shoulder.

She turned to him.

He looked as if he wanted to say something, but then just shook his head and headed to the barn.

She thought over the little she'd heard about the visit from the two men and wondered about what Mr. Steward and the preacher said. Would Asa seriously consider what they suggested?

But most of all, she reveled in the way he'd touched her shoulder. Hope lifted within her again. Maybe Asa was coming to terms with the fact she wasn't the kind of woman he'd been looking for in a wife. She entered the cabin and went about sorting the wild herbs and berries she'd gathered. And began humming. Her mother used to say, "Where there is life, there's hope." Judith clung to that hope.

In town, Judith and Asa had met Kurt Lang on the general store porch. His wife, the first schoolteacher in Pepin and now the mother of a sweet little baby boy, sat on the shady bench. Judith sat beside her, Lily at her elbow, gazing at the baby, who blinked at them. Judith had written a reply to Mrs. Waggoner, and they had all decided to walk into town to mail it. Judith could tell Asa was champing at the bit to leave town. But she needed a few more moments of woman talk before returning to the quiet cabin.

A steamboat was just docking, and a passenger was coming ashore. Mr. Ashford passed them, politely nodding as he went. "I'm expecting a large shipment, ladies." He hurried toward the boat with Gunther Lang, Kurt's younger brother, in tow.

"The baby's blowing bubbles," Lily said, sounding intrigued. "I didn't know babies blew bubbles."

Ellen Lang chuckled. "Babies are very interesting creatures." Beside her stood the toddler William, the foundling who had been left on the teacher's doorstep.

Judith wished she could talk to Ellen about mothering orphans. But Lily and Colton were within hearing.

"You got two cows plus Chandler's," Kurt Lang was saying. "You got too much milk, *nicht wahr?*"

Asa nodded without enthusiasm, but Judith wondered what Mr. Lang was getting at.

"Well, do you know how to make *Käse*, cheese?"

"No." Asa looked at the man, obviously not wanting to talk about his lack of knowledge on the general store porch.

"I can teach you how to make cheese," Kurt said. "It is *gut* for food. Then you can use the extra milk better."

"That sounds interesting," Judith said. "Is it very difficult to learn?"

"No," Kurt replied eagerly, "it just takes time and care. People here would be happy to buy it."

Judith noted that this had finally caught Asa's interest.

A stranger in a crisp, navy blue suit bustled up toward them. "Good day! The storekeeper tells me that the man I've come to see is here. Which of you is Fitzgerald Asa Brant, Captain Fitzgerald Asa Brant?"

Shock splashed through Judith, followed by a protective fear for Asa. "Who are you?" Judith demanded, not caring that she sounded rude. "And why do you want to speak to him?" She glanced at Asa. This was the last thing he wanted known here. What would Asa do, say?

For once she felt as if it were up to her to protect him.

Chapter Thirteen

Judith watched the blood drain from Asa's face. Her protectiveness surged. She must do something, but what?

The young man looked taken aback. "I'm from the *Rockford Register*. I'm interviewing men who fought in the Battle of Gettysburg to honor them on the ten-year anniversary of that battle."

Judith could think of nothing to say to this.

"I apologize for my haste," the stranger continued. "But I've got only till this boat leaves to do the interview."

Asa turned and broke away. His feet carried him up Main Street. Soon he had turned the bend out of the sight of town. He did not slacken his pace.

Barely aware of the questioning voices raised around her, Judith hurried after Asa. She must stop him from fleeing. He didn't want attention, and his action now would only bring more. She ran, her corset stays jabbing her with each step. The heat of the day wrapped around her. But she pushed on, focused on Asa, on catching him.

"Ma'am!" The newspaperman was pursing with her. "Ma'am! Wait!"

Judith did not pause. Soon she turned the forested bend of the final rise to their clearing. She glimpsed Asa standing by the barn door. Upon seeing them, he turned and bolted toward the forest, fleeing through their ravaged field of corn.

Breathless, Judith could run no farther. Her lungs were bursting. Pressing a hand over a stitch in her side, she limped to the bench outside her door and sat down, panting for breath. She felt a bit faint and closed her eyes.

"Ma'am?" the persistent stranger said.

She opened her eyes and found him standing in front of her. She stated the obvious. "My husband…will not… agree to an interview."

The young man with fair hair and a fresh face did not apologize and leave as he should have. He gazed at her hopefully like a puppy. "Ma'am, I'm sorry, but my job depends on my getting these interviews right and in on time. And I must get back on that boat. Please, ma'am? *My job depends on it.*"

The young man's plea cut through her worry and discomfort. "My husband will not speak to you. He does not talk about the war." *Even to me.*

"Well, could you answer a few questions for me?" he implored. "I need something to write."

Judith drew on her inner strength. This young man hadn't come to cause Asa harm. He was just doing his job. And she didn't want him to lose it. "Very well. What do you want to know?"

"What has the captain done since the end of the

war?" The young man stood, his pencil poised over a notebook.

"He is homesteading here. He works with leather."

"And you two married?"

"Yes, this spring."

The young man nodded. "What does the captain say of his experiences in the war?"

"Nothing. We do not speak of it." *Though its presence makes itself known, always.*

"His quick and daring action in the Battle of Gettysburg helped turn the tide at a crucial juncture. I'm supposed to ask him how he had the courage to take action on the spur of the moment and without consulting his superiors. How did he have the nerve and foresight to order his men to rush into position to stop the Rebels at the Angle?"

Judith marshaled her thoughts, remembering the name, the Angle, a critical action in that horrible three-day battle. Her brother had been with Asa at this point in the pivotal battle that prevented Lee from taking the war north. She had no idea what to say, but words came. "My husband is a man of action. He never hesitates to do what he sees needs to be done. My brother, Gil Jones, was one of his men."

The young man appeared pleased at this and continued to scribble in his notebook. Then he looked up again. "What did your brother have to say about the captain? Nearly half your husband's company were killed in that action."

Horror clutched Judith's throat. She could only stare at the man openmouthed. Now she remembered those hot July days in 1863. Word of Lee sweeping north and another dreadful battle. She remembered standing beside her sister among so many other women crowded around in front of the newspaper office, waiting for the printing of the casualty lists.

Women had snatched the papers—ink still fresh—from the editor's hands. She and Emma had scanned the paper for their brother's name, and when "Jones, Gilbert Private" did not appear, they'd drowned in relief.

But so many of their neighbors had lost sons, fathers, brothers, husbands that day at Gettysburg. Many other women had turned away, weeping, sobbing. The memory brought it all back, the worry, the tension as battle news reached them slowly, the sorrow for neighbors.

Coming back to the present, Judith could only shake her head at the callow youth with his notebook, watching her. So young. He'd been a child during the awful war.

"If your husband hadn't acted decisively," the reporter said, "the Rebels might have succeeded that day. The battle might have been lost."

With effort, Judith shrugged off the painful memories weighing her down. She cleared her throat. "My husband is a decisive man, a very brave man. And now he just wants to live his life in peace."

A whistle sounded—loud and insistent. "I've got to go or miss my boat. I have two more heroes to interview." The man turned and began running toward town.

He called over his shoulder. "Thank you. Your husband isn't the first one to refuse to talk to me! Men who fought don't want to talk about it! It's odd!" Then the stranger who'd upset their peace vanished beyond the trees.

Judith sat staring at the spot where he'd disappeared. Understanding shuddered through her. Now she knew the awful weight her husband carried. Half his men killed and he gave the order, not a general or some other high officer. Captain Brant had made the move. How did a good man face the bloodshed he'd ordered—even if it had been the right decision?

She closed her eyes and began praying for her husband. They'd made progress. He'd held her hand. How might this interruption from the past affect him? Would he withdraw more? Leave her and the children? Her heart clenched. *Asa, come back.*

"Where's Mr. Brant?" Colton asked.

Startled, Judith opened her eyes. "Colton?"

"What happened to make Mr. Brant run out of town like that?" The boy looked both disgruntled and worried.

Judith brought her mind back to the present. "Where's Lily?"

"The Langs made us stay with them." Colton screwed up his face. "Lily's still there. But I finally got away."

Judith stared at the boy. What could she say?

The truth, of course, and then the spirit spoke to her heart, helping her see the truth. She patted the bench beside her. "Come sit here and we'll talk."

Returning, Asa paused at the rear corner of the cabin. He'd come back to face the stranger and send him on his way. What had he been thinking? His bolting like that would only make for more talk in town. He'd never turned tail in battle, and he'd let a pipsqueak newspaperman rout him. He was disgusted with himself. And somehow spent. The strong emotions had exhausted him.

Colton was with Judith, sitting beside her with his chin drooping. Why did the boy always look like he was carrying the world on his back?

Asa's heart slowed, and he nearly started forward.

Then Judith spoke. "Colton, you aren't old enough to remember the war."

"My dad was in the war, but just a few months. It ended."

A fortunate man. Asa didn't want to interrupt since it sounded like Judith was taking time to say something the boy needed to hear. And if the stranger was nowhere to be seen, there was no rush. He leaned against the cabin's rough, notched-log corner, ready to wait, trying to come back from the shock. The whole town knew now, or would.

Judith said, "Well, Mr. Brant was a captain. You know what that means?"

"I know that," the boy said, truculent as usual. "He was an officer. He gave the orders."

The easy reply grated on Asa, but he remained silent.

"Yes, but I want to talk about you first," Judith said.

"Me? Why?" The boy craned his neck toward her.

"You'll see. When your mother and father passed, you went to live with the Smiths."

Asa observed the boy stiffen.

"I don't want to talk about them," Colton grumbled. "They're gone anyway."

"Yes, but when they didn't treat you and Lily as they should have, you decided to act bravely and leave them, didn't you?"

The boy swung his legs and bent over, his arms folded.

Asa didn't expect him to reply.

But then Colton said, "I saw the snow had melted, so he couldn't follow our tracks easy. So in the middle of the night, I woke up Lily, and we snuck out the window with a blanket."

Judith laid a hand on the boy's back. "And you found the cave?"

"Yeah. We were okay till Lily got sick."

Judith stroked the boy's back. "You were really worried when that happened."

The boy grunted, twisting his head away. "I didn't know what to do."

Asa nearly missed this quietly spoken admission.

"And you were responsible for your sister, weren't you? You were trying to take care of her."

"She's the baby." Colton swung back to look at Judith. "I promised Mama I'd take care of her." Colton's voice cracked on *Mama*.

Judith inched closer to the boy and put her arm around him. "Of course you did. And that's how it was with Mr. Brant. He was responsible for the men he commanded. Now I'm going to say something hard." She paused, obviously waiting for his agreement.

Finally Colton nodded.

"How would you have felt if Lily hadn't gotten better?"

Colton jerked up. "She got better!"

Judith laid a gentle hand on his shoulder. "Yes, because when you saw that she was getting sicker, you went for help. And God had already prepared us to help you."

"He did?" Colton didn't sound convinced.

"Yes, He did. Now think of Mr. Brant in a war where he was the one who had to give the orders."

Colton stared at her for several heartbeats. "You mean he was responsible?"

"Yes, he was. So when he gave an order and some men died, how do you think he felt?"

Judith's gentle voice nearly brought Asa to his knees. *Dear Lord in Heaven, she understands. Better than I.* He braced his shoulder against the rough logs, drawing in ragged breaths.

"He probably felt bad," Colton admitted.

"Yes, he did. But it wasn't his fault. He did what he had to do to win the battle. Bad things happen in war. I hope you never have to face one."

Asa could agree with that one hundred percent.

"Now, Colton," Judith said, "please go back into town and bring Lily home."

Asa watched her pat the boy's back, and then Colton hurried down the road.

Asa could not hold himself back. Somehow Judith's words had freed him. He rushed to her, pulled her up from the bench and kissed her. Nothing like the way he'd kissed her on their wedding day. He had never kissed a woman like this, not even the fiancée who had proved false and, while he was at war, had married another man.

He held Judith tight and breathed in her sweet fragrance. He thrust his fingers into her hair, clasping her face to his. Finally, to draw breath, he ended the kisses but pressed her close. "Judith."

She clung to him. "Asa."

He felt her breathing fast and hard. He knew he should say something, but all words had fled. He leaned down and kissed her again, unable to resist the urge to meld himself to this woman who understood, and in some way to draw healing from her.

Judith reveled in her husband's embrace. She was afraid to speak, afraid to disrupt this wonderful event. She returned his kisses, standing on tiptoe to give him more of her to kiss. He rained kisses over her face as if imprinting his mark upon her. *Asa is kissing me.*

A man cleared his throat loudly.

Judith froze, a bit dazed by Asa's kisses. As his hold on her loosened, she turned to see the Langs with all four of the children.

"We're so sorry to interrupt," Mrs. Lang said, her face pink with embarrassment. "But when Colton returned, we had to be sure you wanted the children. Is everything all right?" Mrs. Lang's voice warbled on the final words.

Judith drew herself together, though she still clung to Asa's arm, a bit unsteady on her feet. She glanced up at her husband. "We're fine." Her face flamed and must be bright red.

"Well, then, we'll be on our way," Mrs. Lang said. The woman studied them for a few more moments.

Then she turned and left with her children and husband at her side.

Lily ran forward, her dolly's head bobbing up and down over her arm. "You were kissing."

Judith's face burned brighter.

"Married folk kiss," Asa said gruffly.

"Yes, Ma and Pa kissed, too," Colton agreed with scorn. "Are you all right, Mr. Brant?"

"I'm good. Let's you and me see if we can catch a few fish for the supper pot."

Judith sank onto the bench. Asa was acting as if nothing had happened. Her whole world had been turned upside down and backward. Yet he was going fishing?

Then he surprised her with a kiss on her cheek. "We won't be gone long." He gazed into her eyes.

She saw something had changed in him, too—even if he was going fishing right after their unbelievable kiss—or many kisses, to be truthful. "Very well," she managed to say. "I wish you good fishing."

The two males set off, leaving her and Lily by the cabin door.

"What are we going to do?" Lily asked.

A very good question, Judith thought. What would happen now? Her lips tingled with the memory of Asa's kisses, and she pressed her fingertips to them. She hoped this would prove to be the start of breaking through to a normal married life between husband and wife, but Asa had let his lips speak without words. There were words she needed to hear and he needed to say. *Lord, please help Asa and help me understand him. Let him love me a little.*

* * *

The evening came, and Judith sat in her rocker in front of the low fire. All the rest of the day, Judith had prayed. What should she say to her husband about the newspaperman? The reporter most likely had let out his secret already. More important, what had Asa's kisses meant? *Will he kiss me again?*

Finally the children settled down in their pallets for the night. Yet Asa did not go to his loft, as usual, and leave her alone to go into the bedroom. He lingered in his chair, rocking and staring into the scant fire. Would he tell her what he was thinking?

Judith sat, waiting and rocking. Before long, both children fell soundly asleep. Still Asa did not leave her. Outside, tree frogs peeped along with the other soothing night sounds, which failed to soothe Judith tonight.

Words jumbled in her throat, but she kept her lips pressed together. Asa must speak, must explain.

"You talked to that reporter?" he asked finally.

Instantly cold apprehension flooded her. What if this angered her husband? "He was young and said his job depended on…"

He rested his hand on hers on the arm of her chair. "I'm not scolding."

She eased in air. "I answered his questions…briefly but truthfully." She let her voice become firm on the word *truthfully.*

He squeezed her forearm. "You are an understanding woman, Judith. A wise woman."

She didn't know what to say to these unexpected compliments. Reeling from this, she knew that what she really wanted was to be a pretty, lovable, desirable wife. But she wasn't. A mourning dove *hoo*-ed softly outside, followed by a whip-poor-will singing its name.

"Judith, I'm sorry I ran away today. I can't believe I did that. I've never run away from anything in my life." His sad tone contrasted with the insistent bellowing of a bullfrog at the nearby creek.

"I know you're a brave man, Asa." Suddenly her concern overrode her unease. "I think I can understand why you don't use your first name. I hadn't thought about it, but I remember the big welcome-home event for you and the militia. People couldn't discuss anything but your action in Gettysburg. You are also a modest man, a private man. I can understand that you were tired of people always wanting to talk about what you did in the war."

He cleared his throat. "That's it exactly. But I should have just faced it. And now everyone here knows anyway." He rubbed his face with one hand.

The lonely whip-poor-will sang out again in the last of dusk. In the dim light, Judith needed to know what he expected of her now. "What do you want to do? How do you want me...us to handle this?"

"They've been after us veterans to speak. Maybe I have something I want to say. I can't decide what's best."

Judith wanted to ask what he wanted to say, but the words wouldn't come. Again she wanted to say much, but an inner urging told her to be silent.

The next morning after breakfast, Asa had decided to visit Noah Whitmore. Because he was a veteran, too,

Asa felt he would understand why Asa had overreacted to the newspaperman. Perhaps Noah could help him go forward. But knowing people would want to question him about the reporter and his escape, Asa pulled his hat low and skirted Main Street staying in its shadows. And he'd started out early to avoid discussion.

He'd left Colton at the cabin in spite of the boy's insistence he wanted to come along. Asa must speak to Noah alone. As he hurried toward Noah's, the sun blazed on the crown of his hat. The day would be a warm one, and Asa only wished his decimated corn and hayfields could have been benefiting from it fully. He couldn't dwell on that now. He heard the whistle of an arriving steamboat and was glad. That would distract everyone in town, and he'd slip past to the road toward the Whitmores' place.

Last night, after telling Judith that he was thinking about the town's Independence Day celebration, he'd risen and drawn Judith and into his arms. He could no longer staunch the need to hold her softness close and breathe in her sweet scent. He knew other women would insist he explain everything. And he couldn't. He didn't know yet what he should do, how to leave the past behind once and for all.

Still, he'd allowed himself to hold her. She hadn't pushed him away or spoken. She just let him hold her, a boon. He pressed kisses to her forehead and then released her and headed to the loft, wondering if he would ever be worthy of his lovely, sweet wife.

When he reached the end of Main Street, his father-in-law, Dan, hailed him. "Look who's come for a visit!"

Disgruntled over Dan's calling attention to him, Asa turned. Then he gawked at the man standing next to Dan. Gil Jones? For several moments he couldn't speak. What would bring Gil here? And what had happened to the man? He looked awful. And the expression on his face… He had blood in his eye, aimed right for Asa.

Gil didn't approach him, just stayed at his father's side, glaring at Asa.

"We're going to get Emma, and then we were coming to your place," Dan said, beaming.

Asa came out of his surprise, walked to Gil and offered his hand. "Gil, it's good to see you."

Gil's chin jutted forward, but he shook Asa's outstretched hand. "I didn't know you'd married my sister. You left off using your first name." The words were an indictment.

What was eating Gil? Asa shrugged, not letting on that he noticed Gil's umbrage. "Decided to make a fresh start."

Gil stared at Asa. "And are you?" he growled.

Not reacting to the snide question, Asa wanted to ask about Gil's wife and farm, but the man's belligerent expression stopped him.

"Well, come on!" Dan urged, shooing the men forward. "You two will have plenty of time to bring each other up to date. Let's go get Emma! She's the new schoolteacher here, son."

This brought Gil back. He dropped Asa's hand. "Emma's a schoolteacher? I thought she got married, too." Again the man sounded put-out.

"No, her man was called away. He's coming back,

though." Dan shook his finger in Gil's face. "And don't sound so surprised about her being a teacher," Dan scolded. "Your sister started in the spring, and everybody's delighted that she stayed on."

Gil kind of shook himself. "I'd like to see Emma," he said in an odd tone.

"Come on, then." Dan turned to Asa. "Where were you headed?"

"Nowhere special." Something prompted him that he should stay with Gil and Dan. Gil was not only his wife's brother but also a man he'd gone through war with. And who appeared ready for a fight. If Gil decided that he wanted to argue with Judith, Asa would put a stop to that. "Let's go get your schoolteacher sister."

When they'd reached the teacher's quarters, though welcoming, Emma had been visibly shocked to see her brother and a bit cautious. Now the four of them were walking up the final rise to Asa and Judith's clearing, and Asa wondered what Judith would say to the brother who'd deprived his sisters of a home—even if that hadn't been his intention.

In the midst of kneading bread dough, Judith heard voices and walked to the door of her cabin. Who was coming now? Her heart sank with the possibilities, not all good. And right in the middle of her bread making? The most inconvenient time.

"Judith!" her father called her. "Come out! See who's here! You'll never guess!"

The ridiculous thought that Gil and Mabel Joy had come for a visit during the growing season flitted through her mind. She decided not to wipe off her doughy hands so whoever it was would realize she couldn't leave her half-kneaded bread and would excuse her.

So with gooey hands raised, she walked to the open door and stepped outside. One glance at the track to their clearing rooted her to the spot. Gil? He looked like a rumpled tramp. If his shirt and pants had ever been washed and pressed, it hadn't been this week. His hair needed cutting, and he'd grown a scraggly beard.

Then memories of Gil and Mabel Joy arguing late at night after Gil had come home from the saloon and the particularly unpleasant one of Mabel Joy throwing a bowl of bread dough at him flashed through her mind. "What are you doing here?" She heard the sharp edge to her voice and regretted it. "Is your wife with you?" She hoped not.

Gil halted about fifteen feet in front of her. "No," he snapped. "Mabel Joy didn't come."

Bemused by his coming, she stayed where she was, her doughy hands still held high. "Gil, sorry. I didn't expect to see you here. Welcome, brother." Her final words fell flat.

Gil appeared to get himself under control. "I wanted to see how you all were doing." He glanced darkly at their father.

"We're doing very well," Emma spoke up. "But I can see that we must let Judith get back to her bread dough. Asa, why don't you show Gil around your place while I help my sister with the bread?" Emma came forward, turned Judith toward her cabin and walked with her.

Lily had come out and was standing by the door, a small lump of dough in her hand.

"Hello, Lily. That's our brother, Mr. Gil Jones." Emma waved toward the men who were moving toward the barn door, where Colton stood.

"Oh, is he going to live with Mr. Jones?" the little girl asked.

"I think he's just come for a visit," Emma replied. She reached down and took the girl's dough. "Why don't you go and join the tour?"

Lily looked up at Judith uncertainly. "Mrs. Brant?"

"Yes, Lily, you can go and see what the men are up to and remind Mr. Brant that he promised to make you a swing today."

The little girl brightened. "I will!" She skipped out the door.

"So, what's this mean?" Emma asked when they were alone inside. "And why does Gil look like he chewed nails for breakfast?"

Judith turned to the large quantity of dough on her wooden board. She attacked the dough with both hands.

"Hey!" Emma cautioned, humor in her tone. "Don't take it out on the innocent dough."

Judith glanced over her shoulder. "Emma, why do you think Gil is here?"

"I suppose we'll have to wait and see," Emma replied, since neither of them could further the discussion.

While Emma sat and talked about town news, Judith returned to kneading her dough. If only people were as malleable as bread dough. Would Mabel Joy turn up next?

Judith finished kneading her dough and set it to rise, while outside the three men and Colton managed to build and hang Lily's wood-and-rope swing from an old spreading oak bough. With Emma's help, she managed to rustle up a decent lunch for seven of salt pork, beans, biscuits and a wild dandelion salad with a warm, sweet, pungent vinegar dressing. Everyone finished the meal with canned peaches and whipped cream. Why was Gil here? she again wondered.

"Good eats," Gil said.

Judith had noticed he'd eaten like a starved man. She itched to ask him if Mabel Joy had given up cooking but held the words within. *Not my place.*

A more worrying thought pinched her. Had Gil just up and left his wife, the family farm? She saw the same questions in Emma's and Asa's eyes, or thought she did. Her father, as usual, appeared to accept Gil's appearance with joy and without question. So maybe she and Emma were the only ones wanting to know what was so wrong at home. And why Gil appeared so angry.

And in the end, what could she do? She was just a daughter. She had done the expected. She had married and left home. The farm would go to Gil, and because of her father's failing heart, it had been in Gil's charge. But that was what was expected. No one had expected a Southern wife and fighting and Gil's drinking. No, indeed.

Chapter Fourteen

Asa wondered again why Gil had come. He recollected all he knew of the man from serving with him for four long years and all he'd heard about Gil after the war from Dan and Judith and Emma. Well, it probably wasn't any of his business, but he needed to be ready for whatever came of this visit. From the neighbor's letter and Dan's account, Gil had been trying to wash away the war with liquor.

Asa had briefly tried drowning his nightmares and flashes of memory with alcohol. But had soon stopped. It deadened his mind only for a while. When he sobered, he felt worse than before, not better. Had Gil finally realized this?

Outside a blue jay sounded his raucous call.

This appeared to prompt Dan. "Well, I've got to get into town," he said, pushing to his feet. "Ashford is counting on me, and I'm sure some more boats will be docking this afternoon."

"Is that why you met my boat?" Gil asked. "You

can't be peddling." His voice spoke of embarrassment and aggravation.

Dan smiled, evidently missing Gil's disapproving tone. "I work for the store, meeting the boats to sell tobacco and notions."

Gil looked horrified. "Why would you do that?"

"I love it!" Dan walked to the door and retrieved his hat from the peg. "I meet interesting people every day."

The children begged to walk with him to town and Judith allowed them, telling them to come right home when her father told them it was time to go. Then Judith kissed her father's cheek and began to clear the table.

"I'll walk with you, too, Father," Emma said, rising. "I'm working on lesson plans for the coming school year. And Mrs. Ashford might need me this afternoon."

Asa waved the four off and then turned to Gil. "Come on. I'll take you for a walk around. Introduce you to our neighbors."

Gil ignored this invitation. He leaped to his feet and moved to confront Judith, her arms full of tableware. "What is our father doing living in a shack and peddling?"

Asa saw red. Stepping between Gil and Judith, he shoved Gil back, nearly off his feet. "No one talks to my wife like that. No one."

Gil swung a fist.

Judith cried out.

Asa easily dodged the blow, grabbed Gil by both shoulders and slammed him down on the bench behind him. "That's enough, Private!"

Gil glared, breathing hard. "Still the captain?" he sneered.

"Still the private?" Asa replied in like tone, tamping down his anger.

At this, Gil turned his face away as if suddenly shamed.

Judith set the dishes in the tin dishpan. Without comment, she carried the pan of dishes outside to wash, leaving them alone.

"Gil," Asa began more gently, "Dan was welcome to come live with us or with Emma. He chose to make his own living arrangements and found his own job. We weren't happy about it, but he enjoys being in town, talking to people and living on his own."

"Well, I don't like it."

"Gil, you are welcome here, but why have you come?" Asa asked.

Gil did not respond but rose and faced Asa. "I'm going for a walk." He turned, and Asa let him go. After waiting for Gil to put some distance between them, he walked outside and went straight to Judith.

She looked up, worry in her expression, her hands in the soapy water.

Asa tried to think of words to allay her worry. "I'm sorry," he mumbled for lack of anything else to say.

Then Judith leaned her head into his shoulder.

Her seeking comfort from him robbed him of speech. Her silken hair brushed the sensitive underside of his chin.

"Thank you for defending me," she murmured.

"No one talks to my wife that way," he repeated, letting himself rest a hand on her slender back.

She rubbed her face against his shirt, setting off waves of sensation in him. "I know." Then she looked up, pulling away. "Do you have any idea why my brother has come? Why he's so angry? Is it about Father?"

Bereft of her touch, he lifted both shoulders and spread both palms in a gesture of not knowing.

"He's so angry."

Asa nodded. He remembered Gil's quick-trigger temper, something that he hadn't come into the war with, but that battle after battle had fed. That's why he'd remained a private throughout the war. "Don't worry, Judith. I'll keep close. And if he acts like that again, I'll send him on his way." He wanted to brush her cheek but he kept his hand at his side.

"He should be home," Judith said despairingly. "We're right in the middle of the growing season. I don't understand how he could leave the farm, our livestock... It doesn't make any sense."

Asa permitted himself to pat her shoulder. "No, it doesn't." His brother-in-law's appearance baffled him. And he didn't trust the man to keep from letting his anger get away from him. Asa must stay close to home.

"I'll pray about it," Judith said. "God knows why."

Asa nodded. Judith's faith was strong, but Asa was troubled and would be on his guard. He wished he'd been able to talk to Noah Whitmore today. He couldn't go that far out of town with Gil nearby, as dangerous and unpredictable as an unexploded shell, filled with deadly grapeshot. But the sheriff lived just up the road.

He was a veteran and, recalling their trip to find Smith, Asa realized he could talk to him, too. And seeing Gil like this prompted him even more.

Asa mentioned this to Judith and left, telling her to run there if Gil came back. He couldn't understand how Dan had missed the edge of anger in his son's voice and manner. One thing was certain, however. Gil had not come here for any good reason.

Judith spent the afternoon making her eight loaves of bread and trying to overcome worry with prayer. Fortunately Asa had earlier constructed Lily's swing out in front of the cabin. After returning from town, the child spent the day swinging and singing to her dolly, while Colton had decided to stay in town with Dan to meet the boats.

Judith kept busy piecing together scraps of leftover cloth into the window curtains. Smith had burned her pretty blue-and-white gingham ones. Trying to make the scraps into something that didn't look like a mish-mash meant intricate sewing and ironing. She tried to keep her mind on her task, the steam rising from the damp cotton as she pressed it. But she also wondered why Asa had gone to talk to the sheriff. Did it have something to do with the reporter's visit yesterday? Or was it about Gil?

And what was she to make of her husband's kissing her yesterday but still keeping her at a distance? They'd been married for nearly three months and they still lived together like friends, not husband and wife. The gulf between them yawned like a canyon.

Judith was just finishing the ironing and almost ready to hang the curtains again when she heard a familiar voice greeting Lily. Mrs. Ashford. Judith's heart slipped a bit downward.

She set the hot flatiron on the hearth to cool safely and walked to the open door. "Mrs. Ashford," Judith kept her tone light and welcoming, "what brings you to my door?"

The storekeeper's wife in her white bonnet bustled up to her. "We need to talk."

Judith for once welcomed a chance to talk. So much had happened yesterday and today. Also, it occurred to Judith that Emma had not stayed so they could talk matters over in private together. Judith should have thought that odd. But she'd been so distracted, that she hadn't—then.

"I saw that your brother from Illinois has come for a visit. And there's so much talk in town about that reporter yesterday." Mrs. Ashford untied her bonnet and gazed pointedly at Judith as if saying she would not be put off.

Judith sighed silently. What the woman said was probably very true. "Why don't we sit out here?" She motioned to the bench. "It's such a lovely day. And we'll get the breeze here."

The woman sat down, and Judith joined her on the bench. She let the summer green leaves fluttering on the surrounding maples and oaks among the thick pines soothe her. Lily's singing blended with the chittering black-and-white chickadees that had flown down and were vying with the chickens for seed in the yard.

"Well, I'm not one to gossip," Mrs. Ashford began, "but I thought you should know that your brother has spent the day in the saloon."

Ignoring a further sinking feeling, Judith knew that Mrs. Ashford liked to talk, but she'd noted that the woman did not, in fact, gossip. Whatever she thought, she said to people's faces. So Judith responded in kind. "I'm sorry to hear that."

"Well, it has upset your father. He even went into the saloon and tried to draw your brother out. Gil refused."

Judith sighed and bowed her head. "Poor Father," she murmured, listening to the soothing, steady creak of the wood and rope of Lily's swing.

"I know that your father is not that kind of man. Many men will drop by the saloon and have an ale in an evening and then go home to their wives. Even Ned does so at times. Men like to have a place to talk like we have our quilting circle. But your brother…" Mrs. Ashford fell silent.

"Is Emma working at the store?"

"Your sister wasn't needed today and fortunately doesn't know this. I didn't like to expose a maiden lady to such…" Mrs. Ashford's voice trailed off.

"Well, thank you for coming to me and letting me know." Judith leaned against the rough log wall behind her for support and sighed. Again.

The woman nodded with pursed lips. "I wanted you to know so you can handle whatever comes of it." The woman leaned forward. "Now, what happened with that reporter fella yesterday? He called your husband Captain Fitzgerald Asa Brant. I think I've heard that name somewhere."

Judith let her eyes shut for just a moment. "Mrs. Ashford, I know you will keep this in confidence until my husband is ready to speak of it. But yes, he was a militia captain in the Union Army."

"That's nothing to be ashamed of."

"No, it isn't. But Asa doesn't like talking about it, so he left off his first name. You see, he was widely known in Illinois and southern Wisconsin, I expect, and people kept pestering him to talk about the battles and such."

Mrs. Ashford considered this. "Yes, Ned and I came up from southern Illinois, so we hadn't really heard of him. But people can be so insensitive." She shook her head in disapproval.

Judith swallowed her amusement over the irony of this comment. "I know," she replied with a straight face. "So if people ask, just tell them what I said. It's a fact."

The storekeeper's wife looked solemn. "We didn't lose a son in the war, but I don't think anybody was untouched by it. And the South just won't settle down and accept that slavery is over and the Union is one."

Judith nodded. Reconstruction, as they called it, had not gone smoothly.

The woman rose. "I must get back to the store."

"Thank you for the warning." Judith rose, too. "And for caring about us."

"Well, you've had it rough lately," Mrs. Ashford replied, "coming here to marry a man you barely knew, taking in the children, hosting us during the flood, having Smith wreck everything here and dealing with that reporter." The woman straightened and smoothed her skirt, shook her head sadly, and started off for town.

Judith sat again, weighed down by the woman's list of all the trials she'd faced the past few months. But the greatest trial of all was getting close to her husband. Breaking down the wall around Asa.

After Asa came home from visiting the sheriff, he had a lot rolling around in his mind from their conversation. He could see by Judith's expression that she hoped he'd tell her why he'd gone. But the matters he and Merriday had talked about were still percolating in his mind. He wasn't ready to speak, not yet. He sent her a half smile, hoping that would be enough for now, till the children were asleep, and then perhaps he could tell her something.

She had bowed her head in acceptance and gone about preparing a supper of fresh-baked bread with butter and leftover beans, enough to feed her father and Gil, too. But by the time supper was on the table, neither had appeared.

Colton came in with Lily, who danced around the table, unaware of the tension surrounding her. The four of them sat down. Asa said grace and the meal began.

"You put different curtains up," Lily said. "I like them. You used some of the same cloth that you made my Sunday dress out of."

Asa glanced at the windows. He noted how carefully Judith had constructed them, a patchwork of leftover fabric. He hadn't protected his family and with the damaged fields, they couldn't spend cash as easily as before. Asa looked down and realized that they were again eating off his old bent tin plates, which even Smith couldn't destroy. Unable to provide for his family, Asa burned with shame.

Judith's soft hand pressed his, resting on the tabletop. "It's fine. We have each other. We're fine," she repeated.

He turned his hand over and gripped hers. His throat thick, he nodded. The four of them ate. Lily's happy chatter about her dolly and her new swing filled the silence.

"Am I too late?" Dan stood at the door, his hat in hand.

"Of course not, Father." Judith jumped to her feet. "Come right in."

"I'll wash up first." He ducked sideways to the outdoor basin.

Soon Dan sat beside Asa, staring at his plate.

Judith said, "Children, if you're done, you may be excused."

The children bounced up and, collecting their firefly jar, headed outside in the golden gloaming. Judith and Asa sipped their coffee while Dan nibbled at his bread and butter.

Finally Dan rested his head in his hand, staring down at his barely eaten supper.

"Father, Mrs. Ashford visited me today. I know what's bothering you." She turned to Asa. "She thought I should know that Gil had gone directly to the saloon this afternoon."

Asa digested this.

Dan groaned. "He's shaming me in front of the whole

town, just like he did at home. I could barely show my face there. Why did he come? Just to embarrass us? I can't figure it out."

Asa was sorry that Gil was causing Dan, a good man, pain, but he could do little to ease it.

Judith looked to him, pleading in her eyes.

"If he's been drinking all day," Asa said drily, "he's past reason. I'm sorry, Judith. Going now and trying to get him out would just cause a nasty scene right in the middle of town."

His wife nodded slowly, solemnly.

Dan groaned again. "Why did he come?" he repeated.

Asa had no answer, but after speaking to Brennan Merriday he felt more confident about what Gil needed to hear. He hoped it would be enough.

Once again Asa and Judith sat side by side in front of the hearth with its low cook fire smoldering under ash, banked for the night. The children were snuggled onto their pallets with light cotton summer quilts over them that Judith had carefully mended.

Judith hoped that Asa would tell her about his visit to the sheriff and discuss what they might do about Gil. From outside she heard what must be raccoons fighting over something, screeching high and angry. This brought to mind Gil and Mabel Joy's frequent squabbles. Why did they act like that?

"I know you're worried about your brother," Asa said quietly when the children had both fallen into deep sleep.

"I can't even imagine a reason for his coming. Not one that makes sense. A farmer just doesn't leave his crop in the field and go off for a visit."

Asa patted her hand. "I will talk to him tomorrow. When he's had a chance to sober up."

Grateful for Asa's consoling touch, Judith slipped a hankie from her apron pocket and wiped her eyes. "I'm not so much ashamed of his behavior as confused. Gil was such a good farmer, a good man, easygoing and easy to laugh. I don't recognize the man he is now."

Asa patted her hand again. "I'll do what I can."

"I know you will. You always do." She glanced at him then. The only light was the last of the sun's rays filtering through the windows. "I know I can count on you, husband."

Her words were balm to Asa's ragged spirit. He might never be able to win Judith's heart, but he had won her confidence. That was something to build on. "I know the same about you." He forced out the words and felt her clasp his hand.

How he longed to pull her into his embrace as he had just yesterday. Then she made it easy for him. She rose and held out her arms. He did also and tugged her into his arms gently and respectfully.

Dan knocked on the door very early next morning. In the cool, fresh air, Asa was just coming back from the barn after milking the cows and letting out the chickens. "What is it, Mr. Jones?" Asa called out, carrying a full milk bucket in each hand.

Dan turned.

The older man wrung his hands. "Asa, son-in-law, I need your help."

With a foot, Asa pushed open the door. "Come in. Have a cup of coffee."

Judith turned from the hearth. "Father?"

"Asa, you've got to come with me and bring your wagon." The older man stopped to collect himself. "Gil never came back from the saloon last night. I finally fell asleep. When I woke this morning, I went looking for him." Dan stopped, appearing ready to break down. "He's passed out on the saloon porch…like a common drunkard." The man slumped to the bench, covering his face with his hands.

Judith appeared horrified. Her gaze flew to Asa, an urgent appeal.

"See to your father." Asa set down the buckets. "I'll go get him." He ran outside and hitched his team in record time. He knew why Dan had come to them. He didn't want the whole town to wake and see Gil sprawled in front of the saloon door, bringing shame on the whole family.

He rolled into town, just as the residents were stirring. Doors were opening and he could hear voices. Seagulls were squawking over the nearby river. He pulled up in front of the saloon and there lay Gil, sprawled where he'd probably landed when the barkeep turned him out at closing.

Asa didn't waste a moment. He set his brake, climbed down, and threw a limp Gil over his shoulder and then into the wagon bed none too gently. Within minutes he was driving back out of town, listening to Gil groaning and moaning in the back.

When he reached his place, he again swung Gil over his shoulder and then deposited him under the pump, which he began to work vigorously. Cold water poured down, splashing on Gil's face.

He reared up, snorting and gasping like a drowning man.

Asa eased back from the pump. "Don't say a word," he ordered. He dragged the man to his unsteady feet and with Gil's arm over his shoulders, walked him into the house.

Judith, the children and Dan all turned to gawk as he half dragged Gil inside.

"Judith, coffee please." Asa lowered his brother-in-law into a rocker.

Judith poured two cups of coffee.

Asa accepted one and pushed the other into Gil's trembling hands. "Drink it."

Gil clung to the cup, shakily drew the rim up to his lips and sipped.

"Drink it all. Sober up," Asa ordered him.

Judith held herself together for her father's and the children's sakes. But she longed to retreat to the bedroom and shut the problem out. This home was a place of peace and harmony, or that's what she tried to make it. Now this. Her own brother.

"Children, come to the table. It's time for breakfast." Judith waved them away from where they stood close together, looking uncertain.

"Is he sick?" Lily asked.

"No, he's drunk," Colton said with audible disgust. "You 'member Mr. Smith used to get this way some nights."

Judith drew in a shuddering breath. "Children, please."

The two skirted around Gil and took their places on the bench at the table.

"Asa?" Judith looked to him.

Asa nodded and also took his seat at the table across from Dan, who, looking crushed, sat beside the children. After grace, the children began to eat their oatmeal and drink their mugs of fresh milk. Her father nursed a cup of coffee and a slice of toast. Judith didn't feel like eating but forced herself to. She didn't know what would happen next. And she did not like to expose the children to this.

Needing a connection to Asa, she rested a hand on his knee under the table.

He turned to her.

She didn't know what to say. How could he make this better?

He squeezed her hand and then released it. He ate with a kind of grim determination.

Soon the meal ended and the children went outside to feed the chickens and gather eggs. Judith rose and began her morning routine, though her gaze strayed to her brother.

Gil sat, slumped in the rocker, staring at the cook fire.

"You finished that coffee yet?" Asa asked in a distinctly no-nonsense tone.

"Yeah," Gil muttered. Then the man leaped up, staggered out the door and was sick.

"More coffee," Asa told Judith.

"I think, Asa, that a soothing tea might be better," she said, looking at him.

"You're probably right. Brew some, please." Asa rose and went out to help Gil.

Soon the two came back in. Gil sat at the table and was able to drink a cup of peppermint tea and nibble some dry toast.

Finally Gil raised his head and looked at them, his gaze scorching them.

"What did you come here for?" Dan demanded. "Just to shame your family? Again?"

Obviously startled by his father's words, Gil looked like a cornered animal, an angry one.

Judith moved to the rocker, wishing she were miles away. She turned it to face the three men at the table. "Why did you come, Gil? I insist you explain yourself. You had a reason for coming this far. What is it?"

"I came to bring our father home, where he belongs." Gil's face twisted with irritation. "Why did you leave the farm? There was no need."

"No need?" Dan said, incredulous. "You shame our family by becoming a drunk. You and your wife fight day and night. Is that what I want to hear?"

Gil looked shocked.

"What are you thinking?" Dan demanded. "Or do you think at all? You come here right in the middle of growing season? What farmer does that?" He rose, agitated.

"Father." Gil reached out and grabbed Dan's sleeve. "Come home. I've lost all my family."

Except your wife. Sympathy stirred in Judith, and she decided the time for her to speak had come. "Gil, we love you, but you've been going down the wrong path ever since you came home from the war. I do not know how bad the war was. You and Asa do. But you cannot let it rob you of the rest of your life. You say you lost your family, but you really forced us to leave."

Her words appeared to hit him. He looked ready to argue. Instead he slumped and held his head in his hands. Long moments of heavy silence passed. Then he gazed at them, head still hung low. "How did everything go so wrong?"

"I don't know," Dan said, "but you'll have to figure it out. I'm going to town. I've got a job to do." He walked out.

Judith rose, also. "Gil, perhaps Emma and I should have confronted you over…how your wife treated us. But we didn't want to argue or cause a family rift." Tears tried to come when she thought of all the misery she and her sister had suffered in silence and finally left behind.

"Everyone blamed Mabel Joy for you leaving," Gil said, sounding aggrieved.

"Mabel Joy did not want us in her house," Judith said, unable to keep the ire from her voice. "She made it quite plain."

"That's not right—"

"Gil, you've been sunk in your own well of misery. You didn't take any notice of what Mabel Joy was saying or doing to us. I've never met a more contentious woman in my life." Judith felt a mix of relief at being able to say this out loud to her brother and sadness that the truth was so painful.

"Gil," Asa spoke up, "you need to choose whether you want to keep on the way you are or change course." Asa motioned toward the walls. "I lived in this cabin for two long years before deciding that I needed to begin living again. So I wrote to Judith and gained a wife."

Judith turned, blinking away tears.

"You don't understand," Gil muttered.

"I do understand." Asa rose. "Gil, we spent four horrible years fighting to stay alive. We did it because it had to be done. But think—do you call what you're doing now living?"

Asa's forthright challenge took Judith's breath away. And made her very proud. Then she wondered if Asa was aware of the irony of him telling Gil to break with the past. The reporter's coming and Asa's reaction had indicated that the war indeed still bound up her husband. But perhaps she was wrong. Certainly she was no man's dream wife. Yet could her brother and her husband leave the war behind and find peace? And perhaps love?

Chapter Fifteen

The next day Gil sat at the table, wearing an old faded and patched outfit of Asa's while Judith pressed Gil's freshly laundered clothing on the board set up near the dry sink. As she worked, Judith wished she knew why Asa had gone to the sheriff's a few days ago. Did it have to do with the newspaperman?

Last night she'd been happy when Gil had gone to spend the evening with Emma because Judith had wanted so much to sit and talk to Asa in front of the fire about Gil. But her obviously preoccupied husband had wished her good-night and gone straight to his loft.

Now Judith concentrated on the hot flatiron, not wanting another one of those little iron burns on her hands. They mimicked the nicks and burns she suffered from Asa always holding her at arm's length.

"I feel like death warmed over," Gil muttered.

Judith gazed at him. Had the drink "got" her brother? Would he return to the bottle? "I'm sorry."

He gazed at her mournfully. "I want a drink in the worst way."

Judith held her breath.

"But I'm not going to go to the saloon." He rested his head in his hand as if it weighed a ton.

"I'm sorry," she murmured again.

Gil leaned forward and rested his head on the table. "I remember the man I used to be before 1861. I don't know if I can go back to that, be like that again."

"I don't think you can," Judith replied, finishing the points of the shirt collar.

He looked up, dismayed.

"But you can make peace within yourself. And with Mabel Joy. Gil, we were raised right. Our parents showed us how to live in favor with God and man. The war made you forget that. You can't let that evil time destroy you. You are stronger than you know."

Gil gazed at her glumly. "I hope so."

She set the iron on the hearth and shook out the warm shirt. "Here. Everything is clean and pressed. You can go in the bedroom and dress. Just leave Asa's clothes on the bed."

Asa appeared at the door. "I'm going to visit Noah Whitmore, Judith. Would you like to ride along?"

Taken by surprise, Judith stammered, "Yes." He'd said he was going, but she didn't expect him to take her.

"You can visit with Mrs. Whitmore," Asa said.

I'd rather visit with you. Judith folded up the wooden ironing board and Asa propped it in the corner of the kitchen for her.

Gil walked out of the bedroom.

"Now you look more like yourself, Gil," Asa said. "You going into town to spend time with your father?"

Gil inhaled deeply. "Yes."

"I'm driving through town. We can drop you off."

Soon the five of them arrived in town. Gil slipped down and, with thanks, headed to Dan, who was walking up to meet them. "Leave Colton!" Dan called. "He can help me meet the boats."

So with only Lily riding in the back, they drove up the rise eastward out of town toward the Whitmores' place.

Judith wanted to speak to her husband, but Lily's presence forced her to remain quiet. *What are you thinking, Asa? Why are we going to visit the Whitmores?*

Before long they jerked to a stop at the Whitmores' cabin. Sunny Whitmore, with her son on her hip, hurried outside. "Hello! Welcome!"

Asa helped Judith descend and then swung Lily down by her waist, then swirled her around in a circle, making the child giggle with pleasure.

"Now, be good, Lily," he said.

"I will!" Lily ran toward Dawn, the Whitmores' daughter who was playing with long-eared brown pups near their mother in the wild grass.

"Would you like tea or coffee?" Sunny asked, letting her son down onto the grass. He toddled off toward the pups, too.

"How about some of that good spring water I've heard about?" Judith smiled, but from the corner of her eye, she watched Asa head toward Noah, who was planing a board stretched between sawhorses.

Judith watched as Sunny filled two mugs with icy

spring water. Then she followed Sunny to the shady bench outside the door, where they could watch the children play.

"Tell me what's the news from town," Sunny said innocently.

Judith could hear the rumble of both husbands' voices, but they were too far away for her to make out words. Judith decided to tell Sunny about her brother so she would hear the truth, not what the town gossips came up with.

After listening silently, Sunny gripped Judith's wrist. "I'm so sorry for your brother." She glanced over her shoulder at their husbands. "I don't think any man came through the war without trouble."

"Did your husband serve?"

"Yes," was all Sunny said.

Judith wondered about this. She turned again, trying to see, to hear what Noah and Asa were discussing. She had a hard time believing her silent husband was talking to the preacher.

Finally Asa and Noah joined the women. "Are you ready to go home, Judith?" Asa asked.

"If you are," she replied, rising. She thanked Sunny for her hospitality, and the Whitmores walked them to their wagon. Asa swung Lily up onto the bench and then helped Judith up.

"So we'll expect you at the Fourth of July Celebration Meeting on Sunday evening, just after supper," Noah said.

"I'll be there." Asa climbed onto the wagon bench and maneuvered the team to head back to town.

They all exchanged goodbyes, and Judith held her peace till they were far enough from the Whitmores not to be overheard. "So you're going to the meeting to plan the celebration of the Fourth?" She kept her voice low and neutral.

"I am."

She wanted to ask more but hesitated. The two of them had moved to a better place, and she didn't want to say anything to upset that. "May I come, too?" she asked tentatively.

"I think you should."

Judith breathed in and out slowly. That was a good sign, wasn't it? But what had brought her husband to volunteer for a committee about a celebration he didn't want anything to do with? Only God knew, and she'd have to trust Him.

A few days later, Judith and Emma stood with their father, Asa and the children, all facing Gil. A steamboat heading south had docked, and Gil was going home today. Days of sobriety and good meals had helped Gil look more like himself than he had for a long time.

"You'll come for a visit, then?" Gil asked Dan.

"Yes, I'll come down before the river freezes for the winter—if Mabel Joy writes me a letter of invitation."

Gil pressed his lips together and bowed his head in agreement.

Then Gil kissed Emma's and Judith's cheeks.

When he was close, Judith whispered into his ear, "Remember what Mama always said. The only person you can change is yourself."

Gil paused and then hugged her close. "Yes."

Releasing her, he offered his hand to Asa, who clasped it. "Perhaps next year before planting, you and your wife will take a boat up and come visit us."

"I'd like that," Gil said, shaking Asa's hand.

The boat whistle sounded.

Gil bent down and gave Colton and Lily each a penny. "For candy."

"Thank you!" the children chorused in unison.

Gil walked down the dock and onto the boat. He moved to the railing, and as the boat maneuvered out into the current, he waved to them.

They waved back till the boat disappeared around the bend, gulls circling overhead and squawking.

"Can we go buy our candy?" Lily asked, dancing on tiptoe. "Please?"

"Go ahead," Asa granted. "Then come right home."

The two raced toward Ashford's store. Dan wiped his eyes with a handkerchief. "I hope he keeps to the narrow path."

"Father, we can pray. Only God can change a life," Emma said. "I've received another letter from Mason Chandler. He will return sometime later this summer. The business he must take care of is taking longer than he anticipated."

Judith could not tell whether Emma was as disinterested as she sounded or not.

"Mason's a good man," Asa said.

Emma did not reply to this. "Well, I promised Mrs. Ashford that I would fix lunch today. Father, you're invited if you'd like."

"Thanks, Emma," Dan replied. "I'll be over when I see the storekeeper shut down for midday meal."

Emma left them, and Dan headed toward his lean-to.

Judith looked up at Asa.

"I guess we'd better go home," Asa said. He offered her his arm.

She suddenly felt proud. This wonderful man had married her. He didn't love her, might never love her. But he respected her and would always protect her. She must be patient with him. The advice she'd given her brother played in her mind. *"The only person you can change is yourself."* Now, if she just knew why he was going to that meeting. Well, she would attend and find out.

Sunday evening came. Leaving the children to play outside, Judith and Asa entered the schoolhouse. By now Judith could have predicted who the committee would be, and she was nearly right. Near the door open to the breeze, Noah, Martin Steward and the Ashfords had arranged the front school benches to face each other. In addition, Mrs. Ellen Lang, the first schoolteacher, had come. Everyone greeted them as Asa ushered Judith toward the nearest empty bench. While the children played outside in the school yard, Sunny Whitmore tended the toddlers and babies off in the schoolteacher's quarters.

Judith watched the proceedings with some misgivings. She recalled how angry Asa had been when the reporter had brought up his full name and military service that day in town, and all because of the part he played at the Gettysburg battle, early July 1863. Evidently neither the Ashfords nor the Langs, who had witnessed this, had spread the news. No one else had brought it up to her. Judith was grateful. Yet why was Asa, who wanted no mention of the war, here at this meeting? Her right leg jittered with nerves. She forced her heel flat on the floor.

Then the sheriff and his wife, Rachel, walked in and sat down beside her and Asa.

"Now that we're all here," Noah said, "I'll open the meeting with prayer."

The meeting began. Martin took notes. The efficiency of the discussion impressed Judith.

"I think we should have someone, some veteran, speak," the sheriff said.

All heads turned toward Noah, which made sense to Judith. He was the unofficial leader, the preacher, the one who spoke to them every week.

"Just so," Noah replied. "Asa, how about you?"

Judith felt her lips part in surprise.

"If you think I'm the one for the job," Asa said with a nod of his head.

"Yes, I think you're the one to speak," the sheriff said.

Was this the same man who had refused to talk to the newspaper reporter? Most everyone in the room looked surprised, and Judith realized that her jaw had dropped. She closed it quickly.

Then the meeting ended with prayer for the coming celebration, and the gathering dispersed. Asa led her and the children home in the gathering dusk. Like a real mother and father, Asa and she prayed with the children and settled them into their pallets. Asa walked her to the bedroom curtain, kissed her forehead and headed to the loft. His chaste kiss surprised and thrilled her. And confused her.

She wanted to call him back, ask him what he was thinking, planning for his speech at the celebration, but the words shriveled in her throat. She must be patient. "Good night, Asa."

"Good night, Judith."

She held in a sigh and went into the bedroom alone again. Why, oh, why couldn't she have been born pretty? Why couldn't she and Emma have been identical twins?

The Fourth of July dawned bright and hot. In the late afternoon, the whole community gathered in the school yard for a grand picnic to start everything off. Judith pressed her hankie to the perspiration around her face at the edge of her hat. She'd dressed for the occasion in her best light blue summer dress and hat. Asa wore his Sunday best, and the children were spit-shined and starched. Lily sported new pink ribbons on her braids. If only Judith could calm the quivering in her stomach. What was Asa going to say in his speech today?

The children ate quickly and were engaged in a boisterous game of tag. The adults sat in groups at the few tables and on quilts in the shade, the hum of voices cheerful and lively. Judith's nervous stomach had not allowed her to eat very much at all.

Emma leaned close to her ear. "You're awfully quiet today."

Judith smiled as much as her tight lips allowed.

"What's bothering you?"

Before Judith could think how to reply, Noah Whitmore called to the children to stop playing and come to the schoolhouse.

"Time for our program to commemorate the signing of the Declaration of Independence!"

The ladies finished putting away the empty plates and bowls into hampers, and the husbands set them into wagon beds. Then the families gathered and solemnly entered the schoolhouse as if it were a Sunday morning. Though she smiled at everyone, Judith felt her heart trying to hop into her throat.

At the front, Noah waited till everyone had settled down, and then he opened with prayer. Lavina Caruthers rose to lead them all in singing "My Country, 'tis of Thee." Judith could not stop watching Asa from the corner of her eye. As he sang, he looked so calm. Why?

Asa rose and walked out of the schoolhouse quietly.

Judith nearly followed but realized that she shouldn't call attention to his leaving. Had he changed his mind? Gone home? Dread pooled in her stomach.

Three schoolchildren—Jacque, Johan and Dorcas—rose and moved to the front of the schoolroom. Emma asked them questions about who wrote the Declaration of Independence, where and when the writing took place, why it was important.

The sheriff slipped from the room, then Noah and a few other men. What was going on? Judith fanned herself and worried her lower lip. Emma tried to get her notice, but Judith ignored her.

Finally the children recited the beginning of the doc-

ument that had begun their nation: "we hold these truths
to be self-evident, that all men are created equal, that
they are endowed by their Creator with certain unalien-
able Rights, that among these are Life, Liberty and the
pursuit of Happiness…" Afterward the three bowed and
Emma curtseyed. The gathering sitting on the benches
applauded them enthusiastically.

Then a pause came. Everyone looked around. What
was next?

Judith fanned herself more rapidly. Oh, dear.

The door between the classroom and the teacher's
quarters flapped open with a bang against the wall.
Asa, in a uniform she had never seen since coming here,
marched into the room, followed by the sheriff who'd
served for the Union, Noah and a few other men she
didn't know well. Some wore uniforms like Asa, others
merely a military hat or insignia pinned on their coats.

"At ease," Asa ordered.

The men stood behind him in a line and in military order. Asa approached the teacher's lectern that
Noah used as a pulpit on Sundays. He stood for a moment looking into the audience. "Good evening. I am,
or was, Captain Fitzgerald Asa Brant of the Rock River
Illinois Militia. I served all four years of the war." He
turned to the men behind him and in turn, each one
stepped forward and recited the same kind of information about himself.

Then Asa stepped to the lectern again and faced the
crowd. "I left off my rank and first name when I came
to Pepin. I was tired of talking about the war. I'd lived

it for four long, dreadful years, and I did not want to talk about it anymore." He paused, gazing at Judith.

She was aware of tension in the room. Everyone was alert and listening intently.

"But we've—" he waved to include the men who continued to stand behind him "—decided it is time to speak of the war." He gripped the sides of the lectern and gazed straight into Judith's eyes. "We had to fight the war. The South was never going to give up slavery on their own. The friction between the North and South had already reached a dangerous level. It shouldn't have surprised us when the South seceded."

He drew in a deep breath. "I heard captured Rebel soldiers complain that we should have let the South go. But that wouldn't have worked. We would have had a constant border war along the Ohio River and elsewhere. Slaves would not have stopped fleeing to freedom. We could not continue as a house divided against itself." He shrugged. "So the war came just as it did when the British government wouldn't let America go from English governance."

He looked around the room. The silent, watching room. Even the babies seemed serious and silent. "I fought at Gettysburg, the three-day battle that prevented Lee from carrying the war into the North. I was merely a captain, under orders from higher officers. But at one point in the battle…"

He paused. "I knew that I was seeing movements on the part of the enemy that the higher officers could not see from their posts. And no courier could carry the information to them in time."

He stared into the audience, his jaw firm. "I made the decision. I gave the order…on my own without consulting my commanding officer. My unit rushed into a breach that had opened at a critical moment. For this, some called me a hero."

He glanced toward the ceiling and then toward the audience again. "If it had not succeeded, if it had been the wrong decision, I would have been court-martialed. That's the way war is. Men make decisions. And in war men live or die because of them." He halted as if struggling with emotion.

Noah came up beside him and gripped his shoulder.

"Half of my men," Asa said, his voice low and grinding, "died that day upon my orders."

A muted gasp rippled through the schoolhouse.

The sheriff came up and stood on Asa's other side. Asa straightened. "But it was the right decision. It helped defeat Lee. Still I am troubled by the men who died that awful day. I often wonder how General Grant and our late President Lincoln carried the weight of their decisions. I'm sure—" he nodded toward Noah and Brennan "—that each man here could tell you about a similar day. But they asked me to speak for them. We had to fight the war. But we'd just as soon not talk about it. We thank you for your understanding." Asa stepped back.

Noah moved to take his place. "Before we begin celebrating again, I'd like everyone who lost a loved one in the war to rise and say the name of the fallen."

Over half the room rose and, one by one, said names, often with tears. When the last one spoke, Noah motioned for all to rise. "We are going to smile again now and continue celebrating our nation's birth. Our country was worth fighting for and abolition of slavery was worth fighting for. Men died. Yet this is a happy occasion."

The congregation appeared to shake themselves and straighten up as if the cloud over them had passed.

Noah beamed at them. "Folks, there are games set up, and later we will have fireworks." He raised his hands to urge them on. "The old has gone away. Behold, all things are new! Go and celebrate!" He waved them out.

The Ashfords led the procession of veterans out the door. Judith rose and went with the children outside.

Soon Asa found her. He'd taken off his uniform and his suit coat. He rolled up his sleeves. And he joined a thrilled Colton to compete in the three-legged race.

As Judith stood with Lily cheering their "men" on, she turned over all that Asa had said. She'd known about his action at Gettysburg, of course, but she had sensed something new today in Asa's voice and expression. What had happened here? And what would it mean for her and her husband?

Night was nearly on them. The summer sky at sunset still glowed low on the horizon. But the gathering had moved to Main Street, away from the forest, to set off Roman candles against the darkening sky over the Mississippi. Even the men from the saloon came out to watch the fireworks that burst over the dark water and reflected on its surface.

Asa kept Judith near, and in the midst of the loud *boom*s, and *ooh*s and *aah*s from the townspeople, he put his arm around her shoulders and drew her close. This public demonstration of affection set off fireworks within her. She held herself still and didn't give in to the desire to turn toward Asa and rest against his chest. But this took a lot of self-control. She felt herself softening toward her husband.

Finally the last blue-and-white shimmering Roman candle sparks fell, and the new night came back into its own with bullfrogs bellowing at the river's edge, cicadas shrieking in rapid unison, and tree frogs peeping.

People began to load their families into wagons. Asa drew Judith nearer to the general store, and Judith wondered why. Colton leaned against Asa, and Lily wrapped her arms around Judith's waist.

"Do we got to go home?" Lily asked, her eyes drooping.

"I think you children should come visit us for the night," Mrs. Ashford said from the porch. "You can sleep in the room Emma stayed in. Tomorrow morning, I'll make waffles with my iron, and we'll have honey and maple syrup on them."

Lily brightened and moved toward Mrs. Ashford's outstretched hand.

Colton held back, glancing up at Asa.

"Go on," Asa said. "It'll be a treat."

Colton didn't move.

"Maybe he'd like to spend the night in my lean-to," Dan spoke up. "I get lonely. It'd be a blessing to have Colton spend time with me."

"Could I?" Colton asked Asa.

"If that's what you want," Asa replied.

Colton turned eagerly to Dan.

"And then, Dan," Mrs. Ashford said, "you bring Colton for breakfast, and you're invited, too."

Dan beamed. "Thank you, ma'am. It'd be my pleasure."

So Colton and Dan headed toward the riverside lean-to. And Lily let Mrs. Ashford lead her into the store. At the last moment, Mrs. Ashford turned, and Judith thought the woman winked at them.

What was this sudden change in routine about? Judith wondered.

Asa drew her arm through his and escorted her up Main Street, waving to people they knew who were also walking home. Soon they were alone on the last bit of road to their place.

Judith longed to rest her head on Asa's arm but didn't want to be forward. Something was happening, had happened. But what?

Finally, in their clearing, Asa paused near their door.

She waited for him to excuse himself and go to check on the cattle. She was surprised not to hear the cows lowing, needing to be milked. It was late for them.

"Gunther Lang took care of our cows," Asa murmured. "And Mrs. Ashford was the one who decided you and I should have a night without the children. She said newlyweds need time alone." He grinned. "So let's not think about anything…"

She waited.

"…but us."

A thrill rippled through her. *Us?*

He led her to the door and, without a word, swept

her up into his arms. He pushed the door open with a boot and carried her inside.

"Asa?" she gasped.

"A bride should be carried over the threshold. I didn't have enough sense to do that on our wedding day. I'm sorry, Judith."

His face had drifted to mere inches from hers.

She was afraid to breathe. "I understood, Asa."

"Well, I was bewildered that day. And I haven't treated you the way you deserve, Judith. I'm sorry."

She circled her arms around his neck. She was having trouble breathing and she didn't think it had anything to do with corset stays.

He let her down.

She nearly protested, but before she could speak...

He dipped down onto one knee. "A lady like you also deserves to hear a proposal in person, not through a letter from a stranger. Judith, I know this is a bit tardy, but will you do me the honor, the very great honor of being my wife?"

"Asa," was all she could think to murmur.

"Will you?"

"Yes, of course." She nearly blurted out, *I love you.* But held herself in check. He must speak of love first. The man must make the first move. Asa wouldn't make it, though. She knew that from her previous humiliation. If only she were the kind of woman a man would fall in love with, a pretty woman. Pain twined around her heart.

He rose and took her hand in his. "Judith, I wrote to you and offered marriage because I could not bear to endure one more winter alone in this cabin with my thoughts and guilt. I needed a wife."

She nodded. She knew that only need would have caused a man to propose to her.

"And when you came, I didn't know how it would affect me. I found I wanted you here with me so much, but I felt so unworthy that a lovely and full-hearted woman like you would be my wife, I froze up inside."

"I'm not lovely," she blurted out.

"Judith! You're a beautiful woman, the most beautiful I've ever known—not just your sweet face and beautiful hair, but your heart is beautiful. You have humbled me."

Judith could not breathe at all now. She stared at her husband openmouthed. *He called me beautiful.*

Then he drew her close and she knew, oh, she knew he was going to kiss her. She stood on tiptoe to receive his kiss, the first almost reverent, but the next melted her knees. She sagged against him. "Asa." She breathed out the word. "Do you really think I'm…pretty?"

"No, you're beautiful and…" He lifted her chin with both hands, looking down at her so tenderly. "Judith, I love you."

Tears sprang to her eyes. The words she'd kept inside flowed out freely. "Oh, Asa, I love you, too." She pressed her face into his shoulder, hiding her tears of joy. How could it be that her husband thought her pretty…beautiful and lovely? Then she recalled the scripture, "He hath made everything beautiful in His time." She looked up then and smiled. This was her time, and all because Asa loved her.

* * *

Days passed and weeks. Some of their crops of corn and hay revived and grew. Asa, with Colton at his side, drove over to Ellen Lang's place to pick up his wife and Lily. Judith had spent the afternoon with a few other women canning ketchup while the children played. The hours spent without her had stretched out like days. When he finally glimpsed her expression, he saw that she had missed him, too.

Wonder of wonders. Judith, his beautiful and caring wife, loved him. He helped her up onto the bench with tender care and then swung Lily around twice before depositing her in the wagon bed with Colton and the mama cat who'd come along for the ride.

Asa wanted to kiss his wife in the worst—no, the best—way. Yet he contented himself with listening to her tell him about the day and the bottles of ketchup that would be coming to them. Just listening to her happy voice calmed again the wound he carried inside. He was healing. He was himself again, and all due to God's blessing.

He thanked God that he had finally found the words to say to Judith. The guilt still rose in him sometimes. So many had died and he had lived. But the guilt melted away each time Judith said his name.

He was not alone. He was not the same. He was loved by Judith and by God. He heard Noah's words again: *"the old has gone away. Behold, all things are new!"*

Epilogue

The first day of school had arrived, a bright, sunny day near the start of September. Asa insisted on walking with Judith and the children to school. This made her so proud, she felt her face rosy with pleasure. They greeted other children and parents on their way to school. Older children walked alone, but the littler ones clung to their mothers' or fathers' hands, just as Colton walked beside Asa and Lily held Judith's hand.

They reached the path through the trees to the school. "I wish..." Colton said and then fell silent.

"What?" Judith coaxed.

"I wish my mom and dad hadn't...you know."

Died? Judith's heart clenched. "I also wish that. But you're here with us."

"You're safe," Asa spoke up. "I'm not going to let anyone take you."

"That woman, that aunt, my dad's aunt, wrote us," Colton replied, looking down at his feet moving over the worn path to the schoolhouse.

"If family comes," Asa said, "I won't let you go away with them unless I'm convinced they would be good for you and you want to go with them. You're part of our family forever, whether you live with us or not."

Colton thought about this.

Johan Lang, already in line at the school door, waved and called Colton's name.

The boy's face brightened. "Okay. Can I go?"

"Go ahead and join your friend in line," Asa granted.

Colton bolted ahead.

"Will I like school?" Lily asked once again.

"You will love school, especially since Aunt Emma is your teacher," Judith replied, squeezing Lily's hand. "But remember in school to call her Miss Jones."

At this Lily smiled and began to skip. Soon all Pepin's children were lined up by age, and Judith and Asa watched the children parade into school.

Then, turning, Asa took Judith's hand and led her back through town. Judith sometimes couldn't believe that it had happened. A man, her husband, Captain Fitzgerald Asa Brant, had fallen in love with her.

She'd come to Pepin to find a refuge, a place of her own, and most of all, peace. She hadn't expected to find joy and love. Her dream of being loved had come true. She'd doubted it ever would. God had answered all her prayers and rewarded her patience with blessings she'd thought impossible. Her heart sang silently, praising God, the giver of all good gifts and the rewarder of all those who diligently sought Him.

* * * * *

Dear Reader,

I hope you've enjoyed returning to Pepin, Wisconsin, for another Wilderness Brides book. (Or coming for the first time—welcome!)

Judith, to me, shows how a loving woman can win a man's heart and change him for the better. However, you notice she didn't *try* to change him. Her acceptance, faithfulness, patience and love changed her husband's heart with God's help. As her mother had taught her, "The only person you can change is yourself."

Now, what about Emma and Mason Chandler? Will he return? What has kept him so long? And will Emma marry him or not? (BTW, I've never met a Southerner like Mabel Joy, definitely an anomaly!)

If you've enjoyed this story, you might want to read the first three books in my Wilderness Brides series—*Their Frontier Family* (Pastor Noah Whitmore and Sunny's story), *The Baby Bequest* (Ellen and Kurt Lang's story), and *Heartland Courtship* (Sheriff Brennan Merriday and Rachel's story).

Fifteen Love Inspired Historical authors contributed recipes and family stories to the "Old Family Recipes" collection. If you'd like to receive a free digital copy of this, please drop by my website www.LynCote.com and subscribe to my newsletter and you will automatically receive your free copy.

Blessings,
Lyn Cote

*Maggie Fillmore's late husband had one final wish—
that their unborn son would inherit their ranch. But when a
greedy relative threatens to take the ranch, there's only one
way Maggie can keep it: a marriage of convenience to the
new Pony Express manager, Clayton Young.*

Read on for a sneak preview of
PONY EXPRESS SPECIAL DELIVERY
by *Rhonda Gibson,*
available September 2017 from Love Inspired!

"Have you come up with a name for the little tyke?"
Clayton Young asked.

Her gaze moved to the infant. He needed a name, but
Maggie didn't know what to call him.

Dinah looked to Maggie. "I like the name James."

Maggie looked down on her newborn's sweet face. "What
do you think of the name James, baby?" His eyes opened and
he yawned.

Her little sister, Dinah, clapped her hands. "He likes it."

Maggie looked up with a grin that quickly faded. Mr.
Young looked as if he'd swallowed a bug. "What's the matter, Mr. Young? Do you not like the name James?" She
didn't know why it mattered to her if he liked the name or
not, but it did.

"I like it just fine. It's just that my full name is Clayton
James Young."

Maggie didn't know what to think when the baby kicked
his legs and made what to every new mother sounded like a

happy noise. "If you don't want me to name him…"

"No, it seems the little man likes his new name. If you want to call him James, that's all right with me." He stood and collected his and Dinah's plates. "Now, if you ladies will excuse me, I have a kitchen to clean up and a stew to get on the stove. Then I'm going into town to get the doctor so he can look over baby James." He nodded once and then left the room.

Maggie looked to Dinah, who stood by the door watching him leave. "Dinah, I'm curious. You seem to like Mr. Young."

Dinah nodded. "He's a nice man."

"What makes you say that?"

"He saved baby James and rocked me to sleep last night."

"He did?"

"Uh-huh. I was scared and Mr. Young picked me up and rocked me while I cried. I went to sleep and he put me in bed with you." Dinah smiled. "He told me everything was going to be all right. And it is."

Maggie rocked the baby. Not only had Mr. Young saved James, but he'd also soothed Dinah's fears. He'd made them all breakfast and was already planning a trip to town to bring back the doctor. What kind of man was Clayton James Young? Unfamiliar words whispered through her heart: the kind who took care of the people around him.

Don't miss
PONY EXPRESS SPECIAL DELIVERY by Rhonda Gibson,
available September 2017 wherever
Love Inspired® Historical books and ebooks are sold.

www.LoveInspired.com

LIHEXP0817